Priyanka Sharma Kaintura – A perpetual observer and explorer, but mostly a mythology-activist who endeavors to separate myth from mythology.

After having worked in corporate for over two decades in the areas of Brand and Communication, across the industries of media, research consulting, offshoring and online jobs, Priyanka decided to write full-time. She believes accurate and opportune communication is the plinth for most of what goes right in this world. And precise storytelling is a pressing priority.

mahadevi

mahadevi
The Unseen Truth Behind Existence

Priyanka S Kaintura

Anecdote
Publishing House
For the love of quality reading!

Anecdote Publishing House
2nd Floor 2/15 Lane no. 2 Ansari Road,
Daryaganj-110002

Published by Anecdote Publishing House
Copyright © Priyanka Sharma Kaintura

First Edition 2024

ISBN 978-81-973806-2-4

MRP ₹ 350

All Rights Reserved.
No part of this publication may be reproduced, stored in a retrieval system, or transmitted in any form, or by any means—electronic, mechanical, photocopying, recording or otherwise—without the prior permission of the publisher. Opinions expressed in it are the author's own. The publisher is in no way responsible for these.

Book Promoted and Marketed by Champ Readers Pvt. Ltd.

Cover design by Vijaylakshmi
Layout by Graphic Tailor
Printed by Thomson Press (India) Ltd, New Delhi

To the one who sowed this idea in my soil. The one who is the seed, the earth, the water, and the sunshine within me. The one who breathes in me. The one who speaks through me. To Mahadevi!

PRAISE FOR THE BOOK

We grow up hearing stories. Along the way, even as we hear newer ones, we also start telling some of our own.

But one story, the mother of all the stories, about how it all started, remains by far the most compelling one. And it was first told here, in Bharat.

Later, in course of time, many seers, civilisations, philosophers, scientists, poets, even the gods through their prophets from across the world, have tried to tell a story, their own version of the very first story, at different times, in different ways, to different fascinating affects.

Here's an audacious attempt to retell the story that the humanity first heard from Bharat, in a refreshingly engaging way.

It is a must-read for even those who may have already read it elsewhere, in bits and pieces, scattered as it is in the voluminous primary sources like the Puranas. But, it is an essential reading for those who grew-up disconnected from their own lore. Read it if only to discover what an incredibly illuminating perspective we have been deprived of, in the name of modern secular education. Priyanka Sharma Kaintura must be congratulated for giving the wealth of her profound understanding of our texts such a contemporary breezy narration.

By Sushil Pandit
Activist and Founder Member, Roots in Kashmir

CONTENTS

Acknowledgments	*xv*
The Wakening	*xvii*

Part 1: DURGA: The Beginning of the Beginning   **1-135**

Chapter 1: KUSHMANDA; The Mother Goddess of
Cosmic Egg   3

Chapter 2: BHUVNESHWARI; The Empress of all Gods   17

Chapter 3: SARASWATI; The Goddess of
Wisdom and Dispassion   29

Chapter 4: SHIVAANGI; The Goddess of
Marital Felicity   42

Chapter 5: MAHAMAYA; The Goddess of Wealth,
Wellness and Liberation   55

Chapter 6: SATI; The Goddess of Love and Renunciation   70

Chapter 7: BHAGWATI; The Goddess of
Feminine Prowess and Justice   90

Chapter 8: UMA; The Goddess of Penance and
Marital Permanence   105

Chapter 9: AMBIKA; The Warrior Goddess   119

The Age of Time   127

Glossary I   128

Part II: The Eye For Durga   **137-266**

Chapter 1: KUSHMANDA; The Mother   140

Chapter 2: BHUVNESHWARI; The Empress   149

Chapter 3: SARASWATI; Wisdom and Dispassion   170

Chapter 4: SHIVAANGI; Marital Felicity   183

Chapter 5: MAYA; Wealth, Wellness and Liberation   198

Chapter 6: SATI; Love and Renunciation   214

Chapter 7: BHAGWATI; Feminine Prowess and Justice   226

Chapter 8: UMA; Penance and Marital Permanence   239

Chapter 9: AMBIKA; The Warrior   254

Glossary II   *265*

Yaa Devi Sarva- Bhuteshu Vishnumaayeti Shabditaa |
To that Devi who in all beings is called Vishnumaya,

Yaa Devi Sarva- Bhuteshu Chetanety-Abhidhiiyate |
To that Devi who in all beings abides as Consciousness,

Yaa Devi Sarva- Bhuteshu Buddhi-Roopenna Samsthitaa |
To that Devi who in all beings abides as Intelligence,

Yaa Devi Sarva- Bhuteshu Nidra-Roopenna Samsthitaa |
To that Devi who in all beings abides as Sleep,

Yaa Devi Sarva- Bhuteshu Kshudhaa-Roopenna Samsthitaa |
To that Devi who in all beings abides as Desire,

Yaa Devi Sarva-Bhuteshu Chaayaa-Roopenna Samsthitaa |
To that Devi who in all beings abides as Reflection,

Yaa Devi Sarva-Bhuteshu Shakti-Roopenna Samsthitaa |
To that Devi who in all beings abides as Power,

Yaa Devi Sarva-Bhuteshu Trshnnaa-Roopenna Samsthitaa |
To that Devi who in all beings abides as Thirst,

Yaa Devi Sarva-Bhuteshu Kshaanti-Roopenna Samsthitaa |
To that Devi who in all beings abides as Forbearance,

Yaa Devi Sarva-Bhuteshu Lajjaa-Roopenna Samsthitaa |
To that Devi who in all beings abides as Modesty,

Yaa Devi Sarva-Bhuteshu Shaanti-Roopenna Samsthitaa |
To that Devi who in all beings abides as Peace,

Yaa Devi Sarva-Bhuteshu Shraddhaa-Roopenna Samsthitaa |
To that Devi who in all beings abides as Faith,

Yaa Devii Sarva-Bhuteshu Kaanti-Roopenna Samsthitaa |
To that Devi who in all beings abides as Loveliness and Beauty,

Yaa Devi Sarva-Bhuteshu Lakshmi-Roopenna Samsthitaa |
To that Devi who in all beings abides as Good Fortune,

Yaa Devi Sarva-Bhuteshu Vritti-Roopenna Samsthitaa |
To that Devi who in all beings abides as Vacillation,

Yaa Devi Sarva-Bhuteshu Smriti-Roopenna Samsthitaa |
To that Devi who in all beings abides as Memory,

Yaa Devi Sarva-Bhuteshu Dayaa-Roopenna Samsthitaa |
To that Devi who in all beings abides as Compassion,

Yaa Devi Sarva-Bhuteshu Tushtti-Roopenna Samsthitaa |
To that Devi who in all beings abides as Contentment,

Yaa Devi Sarva-Bhuteshu Maatri-Roopenna Samsthitaa |
To that Devi who in all beings abides as Mother,

Yaa Devi Sarva-Bhuteshu Bhraanti-Roopenna Samsthitaa |
To that Devi who in all beings abides as Delusion,

Namas-Tasyai Namas-Tasyai Namas-Tasyai Namo Namah ||
Salutations to Her, Salutations to Her, Salutations to Her,
Salutations again and again.

Indriyaannaam-Adhisstthaatrii Bhutaanaam Ca-Akhilessu |
Yaa Bhuuteshu Satatam Tasyai Vyaapti-Devyai Namo Namah ||

To that Devi who governs the faculty of senses of beings of all the worlds, Salutations to Her who is the Devi who always pervades all beings.

Citi-Roopenna Yaa Krtsnam-Etad-Vyaapya Sthitaa Jagat |
Who in the form of consciousness pervades this universe and abides in it,

Namas-Tasyai Namas-Tasyai Namas-Tasyai Namo Namah ||
Salutations to Her, Salutations to Her, Salutations to Her,
Salutations again and again.

ACKNOWLEDGMENTS

With Mahadevi getting into the second print run, my foremost vote of thanks must go to my manager and dear friend Ankit Gupta, for resolving all my apprehensions by making my book his own.

Bakul Pant, my schoolmate and valued friend, for introducing me to scriptures that aided my research and storytelling. Dr. Manish Singhal, Senior Consultant Medical Oncology, Apollo Hospitals, for certifying Ambika Part II as medically accurate. Besides, his text, "I was effortlessly able to imagine the scenes unfolding in front of me," felt positively rewarding.

Bhawna Kak and Manisha Parmar Dubey, my close friends and beta readers, who spent many a day poring over chapter after chapter, consistently offering honest reviews when it wasn't the easy choice.

Acclaimed artist Vijaylakshmi, for painting the cover so captivating. Deepti Aurora for devotedly bringing the interiors of the book alive by her illustrations.

Sukriit Naidu, my 16-year-old nephew, for his Gen Z standpoint and giving me my subtitle - The Unseen Truth Behind Existence.

Pramod Singh Kaintura, my husband, the love of my life, the steel in my spine, the spark in my soul and my walking-talking encyclopedia, for taking me under his wings so I could envisage a life beyond the corporate world, and write.

Bhagwati-Bhagwati!

THE WAKENING

Oftentimes during moments of thoughtfulness, we question the existence of our Creator. We conjecture if this planet that we call home came about simply from a series of coincidences, or if there was a justification to it all. The centrality of the sun. The accurate distance between the sun and earth, enabling the germination of life. Not too close to burn the planet to cinders or distant to leave it cold and lifeless. The gravity just enough to keep the solar system unified, rotating and revolving incessantly. A lone moon keeping the order of day and night. The flawless constituents of air and water on the planet and the timeliness of the seasons across the world. The beginning of life and its gradual, unfaltering progression. The variety of humans, flora and fauna. And so much more. We might wonder if all this is a series of fortunate accidents which led to life on earth. Or is there an unseen force behind the scenes!

We might question Creator's existence, especially during harrowing times, when inexplicable events take place, when we do not understand life or when we bump into a failure. There could be junctures when we try to redefine the word God in our own convenient ways. We might quest after the signs that conform to the image programmed in our mind. Or dismiss it altogether.

And I was no exception until a few years back. Operating from my own philosophies, I had my true and false defined, which were largely governed by favorable and unfavorable situations in my life. As also from what I had known from my environment. I then realized my truth and the whole truth, were non-identical. But what was the actual truth was the question that reeled in my mind. So, I backpedaled to the folklores and bedtime stories narrated to me by my grandmother. I skimmed through several scriptures and visited numerous places of spiritual significance, learning about the whys and wherefores. And what I corroborated and discovered was not only startling but also something that is timeless for this creation. Therefore, I decided to share the utmost revelation through this book.

Mahadevi- The Unseen Truth Behind Existence, is my attempt to draw closer to the ageless essence of the Divine and shatter the several myths we might be dwelling on. This is my endeavor to separate myth from mythology.

Mahadevi is an account of some enthralling events through the multiverse, inhabited by numerous celestial beings, in the backdrop of the genesis of this universe. Recounted by Aadi[1] Shakti[2] Durga, the mother Goddess of all creation, it is a chronicle of Gods and Goddesses, their struggles, the devious web of right and wrong, love in its complete glory, its absence, ecstasies, miseries, and the wars of the worlds.

This book is branched into two parts. Part I is Mahadevi's narration of the stories from ancient Hindu texts for the rational mind. It is divided into nine chapters,

---

[1] Aadi – The first one
[2] Shakti – Energy. Another name for Mahadevi

named after nine forms of Devi. Part II is an assortment of another nine gripping stories that depict the same nine forms of Mahadevi in today's times. The urban legends are based on both her explicit and tacit attributes amongst the everyday women of *Kala Yuga*[3]. These stories ask a silent yet germane question to all those who worship Her - if they can identify their Durga when they see one. Do they have the Eye for Durga!

---

[3] Kala Yuga – The last and fourth yuga of the Chatur-yuga that lasts for 432,000 years

PART I

DURGA: THE BEGINNING OF THE BEGINNING

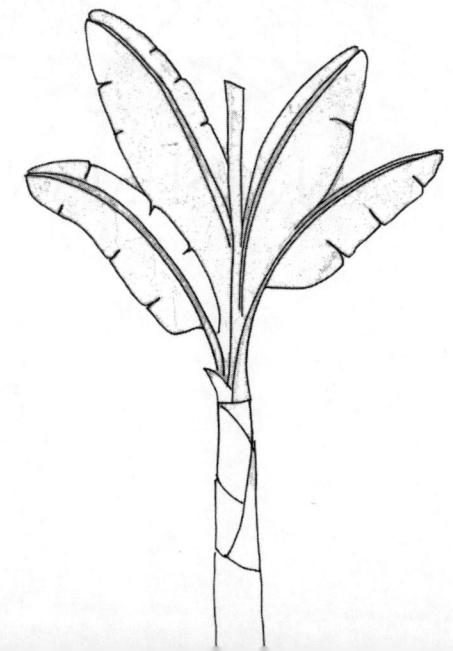

CHAPTER 1

KUSHMANDA
The Mother Goddess of Cosmic Egg

Ku-ushma-anda – The word Ku translates to a little, Ushma[1] to energy, and Anda to egg. Kushmanda[2] is a form of Mahadevi, the mother supreme who birthed the universe with merely a fragment of her energy. Also called Prakriti[3], Aadi Shakti, Parashakti[4], Durga, all worlds are a part of her being and the entire cosmos is her body. All existence is her presence.

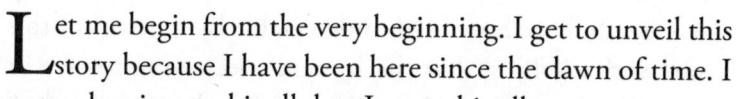

L et me begin from the very beginning. I get to unveil this story because I have been here since the dawn of time. I not only witnessed it all, but I caused it all.

This universe of yours was not formed accidentally, for nothing gets created by coincidence. Especially something as intricately elaborate and gigantic as the

---

[1] Ushma – Energy. Another name for Mahadevi
[2] Kushmanda – The mother goddess. Another name for Mahadevi
[3] Prakriti – Nature. Another name for Mahadevi
[4] Parashakti – The all-pervasive Shakti. Another name for Mahadevi

universe. You do not see the creator, just as you do not see me. But be assured that someone somewhere imagined, designed, and raised the whole creation from the state of nothingness.

You live on the *Bhu Loka*[5], planet earth, which whirls within a planetary arrangement that you know as your Solar System, at the center of which is your star, the sun. Everything within it, including the planets, hundreds of moons, asteroids, comets, and meteoroids, is bound to this sun by gravity. Your solar system is located in an outer spiral arm of your galaxy, *Ksheer Sagar*[6], the ocean of milk, that can be loosely understood as your Milky Way. The big blue marble that is home to you is like a microscopic atom on the canvas of space. Beyond your solar system, there are thousands of other planetary systems orbiting other stars, refuging many other universes. Now, these are the realities you may know already. But how much do you know about interstellar space or intergalactic space? What lies in that vast darkness? Or who!

When your scientists explicate space as dark energy, dark fluid, and dark matter, they are essentially describing me. I, Kaali, have remained undetectable by humans of this time. And anything that the human species cannot see or comprehend appears dark to them. The dark energy or dark *shakti* at the wheel of the big expansion of the universe, as for the creation of the universe with a bang, was me. The immense light that emerged when the universe started to develop, was also me. The subatomic particles which

---
[5] Bhu Loka – Planet earth
[6] Ksheer Sagar – Ocean of Milk, broadly understood as Milky Way

extended to the current size of your universe within a fraction of a second were no other force but me. This universe had no planets, no stars, no moons, no solar system and no gravity at the beginning of time. Literally at the beginning of time, because there was a singularity. Singularity, which is a location in spacetime, a high-density state where both space and time lose their meaning. I am the arrival of time, Kaal's[7] feminine form, Kaali[8].

The collapse of the giant molecular clouds, the countless collisions, and blasts, was me delivering the universe. This led to the birth of your star, the sun, and then to other planets and bodies amidst the lap of gravity, precisely as strong as it needed to be to hold your universe together. I hold not just your planetary system but the entire galaxy in the most primitive ocean of dark, infinite, and unseen waters, which is all me. I am the most primeval, unborn, and undying energy, *aadi* and *anant*[9] Parashakti, the darkest of all, Kaali. So dark that I am entirely invisible to you. The dark matter that I am, makes for over one-fourth (27%) of your universe. That dark matter that I am, does not interact with electromagnetic radiations, which means I do not absorb, emit, or reflect light. This absence of light makes it impossible for the human eye to see me. Clearly, the absence of light is darkness. But more importantly, I am a ginormous amount of energy, *ushma*. Parashakti, the size,

---

[7] Kaal – Time. Another name of Shiva
[8] Kaali – The feminine form of Kaal. Another name for Mahadevi
[9] Anant – The one with no end

and kind of *shakti* you cannot envisage. My dark invisible *ushma*, makes for over 68% of your universe. Therefore, in all, 95% of your universe is just me.

All the other matter, which you classify as normal matter only because you can see and understand it, makes for less than 5% of your universe. Essentially, all that you have seen, known, observed, or measured adds up to less than 5% of this creation. Did you think the intergalactic space is empty? No, it is not nothing. Nothing cannot expand constantly. In fact, expanding now at an accelerated speed notwithstanding the gravity. More space is coming into existence with more dark energy or dark fluid filling it up as it expands. That space is me. That expansion is me, Kaali.

So now you know that even at the beginning, when your universe did not exist, there was me, the vast and infinite darkness, with no beginning and no end. I the supreme cradle of life, come forth as Ku-ushma-anda, the cosmic egg of energy, and from me progresses everything else. As Kushmanda, I birth all creation. As Durga, I nurture, direct, and protect it. And as Chamunda[10], I terminate it all when comes the time. Make no mistake, I am the cause of causes, the reason for the Big Bang and the harbinger of the doom.

I am Kaali. I am Kushmanda. I am Aadi Shakti[11], Parashakti. I am Durga. I am Chamunda. I am the feminine zero energy, endless and unborn. You can simply understand

---

[10] Chamunda – The fearsome form of Mahadevi, responsible for bringing the end of the universe
[11] Aadi Shakti – The first Shakti

me as the Mula Prakriti[12], the cause of all nature. The *prakriti* that you can touch, feel, and see around you. Or the *prakriti* that you can only visualize outside your sight and reach, beyond your planet. I am the mother of all existences there are.

It is not that mankind never detected or recognized me. They did, but as time went by, *manvantaras*[13] after *manvantaras*, humans driven by fear and ridden with doubts, lost their connection with me. Humans are now conditioned to recognize the darkness as malevolence, or the absence of beauty. And arose an entire population of short-sighted, regressed, unwise humans who are relatively ignorant and out of sync with the methods of this universe. But then, that is the nature of *Kala Yuga*.

Towards the end of every *Maha Yuga*[14], when humans diminish culturally and spiritually, it becomes the onset of *Kala Yuga*. Thereafter, mankind plummets to a lower level of progression, much reduced in stature and strength of both body and mind. Humans believe they have progressed since the beginning of their collective memory, but the truth is that they have regressed when seen in a wider time frame. Humans of *Bhu Loka* today have not even touched the first level of evolution when compared to the civilizations of the other universes. Humans are draining the energy supplies their creator endowed them with, dismissing the wisdom

---

[12] Mula Prakriti – The cause of all nature
[13] Manvantara – One age of Manu. A total of 71 Maha Yugas
[14] Maha Yuga – a cycle of four yugas i.e., a Chatur Yuga, which lasts 4,320,000 solar years (12,000 divine years)

of *yugas*[15] of yore, questioning the existence of knowledge before their time and gaining arrogance from their naivety. A direct aftermath of the corrosion of culture and spirituality!

Humans of the earth have barely begun to think of clean energy and have been building massifs of radioactive and non-biodegradable waste. Today, they have sucked the lands and oceans dry mining fuel for something as basic as making fire in their kitchens, to meet aspirations such as flying *vimanas*[16] across their solar system. Despite all that, the Homo sapiens have not found the source or technology to travel freely within their own galaxy, leave alone the awareness of the existence beyond that. They have not been able to get close to their own sun yet, keeping them ages away from leveraging its ginormous power. The power which will be the bringer of the solution to some of their fundamental complications, including human health.

I see everything. But I will not correct you. I will not help you. Or reward you for anything right. I will not even punish you for any wrongs. I will do nothing. You will make your own choices and, from that, your own Karma. That is what all civilizations have done and will do. I will see everything but keep mum. I am everywhere. In everything. I am all around you and I am inside you. I am formless. Colorless. Pure energy. Sheer consciousness. I do not take a body, its limitations, and its pains. Though I can take any form if there is such a requirement. Across galaxies. Across

---

[15] Yuga – a period of time, an age
[16] Vimana – Aircraft

dimensions of time. My purpose is to create and seed, govern, set up processes and destroy when comes the time to move on to the next galaxy and the next universe. Each of which is at a different level of evolution. Some can see me, some cannot. But I see everything. I am omniscient, omnipresent, and omnipotent.

To contain the harm humans of today are capable of inflicting on me, their Mula Prakriti, their ultimate creator, they will be short-lived and so is the *Kala Yuga* when compared to other yugas. But still, the harm will be enough to wipe out the progress of all the yugas that have pre-existed. So, at the beginning of every *Kala Yuga*, the universe is sealed from Bhu Loka. No other races would make themselves apparent to the humans of *Kala Yuga*, nor would humans know of their existence. Human eyes would not have the capability to see greatly, and human ears would be unable to hear the range of sounds the universe will generate. None of their five senses would either have the aptitude or the ability to tune into the universe beyond their own planet.

Even the creator Gods would step down to Bhu Loka on the rarest of rare occasions. Humans will conjecture, study the texts from the past yugas, explore, question, and argue, which they must, to behold the life force of humanity as configured by Brahma[17], the lord of creation. And when this life force would be spent, as Kaali to my Kaal, I would

---

[17]   Brahma – The creator God responsible for the creation of the universe

start the cycle from the beginning to keep the wheels of time rolling.

After the birth of the universe, I kept burning for numerous ages. Earth went through a series of small and big collisions with other parts of the newly born universe before it found its axis and started to cool down. After yugas and yugas of darkness, the stars started to birth and die. There were supernova explosions and unsurmountable amounts of energy generated from them. Amidst the elemental sound of *Aum*[18], upon the blue waters of the ocean planet, which did not make many waves because of the absence of Som Deva, under the immense skies, there was a leaf of *Vata*[19] floating with time. The same primordial ocean Ekarnava[20] which will dissolve every bit of life on earth at the end of each *kalpa*[21] carried guardedly something blue and precious on a leaf of the great Banyan tree, symbolic of immortality and longevity.

It was Sri Hari[22] Narayana[23], the sapphire infant, gliding, playing with his toes, wondering where he was and what his purpose was in a place with only water. After some wandering, he could hear my voice, the voice of the universe echoing within him. I said to him, "Listen Sri Hari, the enormous blue, you are here to create the creator," as he

---

[18] Aum – Or Om, the sound of the universe
[19] Vata – Banyan, the tree
[20] Ekarnava – The primordial ocean
[21] Kalpa – 1 day of Brahma or 14 Manvantara and 15 Sandhi Kaals
[22] Sri Hari – Another name for Vishnu
[23] Narayana – Another name for Vishnu

would in every *manvantara*. His little *Aparajita*[24] like body reverberated with the sound of *Aum* I had seeded in him. Gently, very gently I sent him into a slumber that shall last for some yugas inside the pre-natal chamber of the universe, or my womb. During this deep sleep in the amniotic fluids of Ekarnava, Mahavishnu[25] acquired his complete form, as did his inseparable Anant-Shesha[26]. His serpent bed Shesha drifted on those waters protecting, nurturing, and connecting baby Vishnu[27] uncompromisingly, with the wholesome Ekarnava. In time, the beautiful God grew a bud, all asexually, with an interminable umbilical stalk sprouting out of his navel, outside not inside his body and within it was born Brahma, the creator to be.

Brahma took yugas of arduous *tapa*[28], amassing *gyana*[29] while finding his way out of the stalk, holding to his bosom the luminous Vedas[30]. It was long enough for him to not remember where he started his journey and who he was born from. Once he was birthed, he was bemused to find a gorgeous four-armed sapphire-colored form laying on a coiled serpent, who did not seem bothered by Brahma's presence. It appeared the enormously hooded serpent

---

[24] Aparajita – A flower blue in color
[25] Mahavishnu – Another name for Vishnu
[26] Anant-Shesha – Endless Shesha, the serpent Vishnu sleeps on
[27] Vishnu – The creator God who birthed Brahma, responsible for the preservation of the universe
[28] Tapa – Or Tapasya. Deep meditation with extreme self-discipline
[29] Gyana – Also written as Gnana, but pronounced as Gyana, meaning knowledge
[30] Vedas – A body of scriptures, comprising Rig, Sama, Yajur and Atharva Veda codifying the ideas and practices of dharma

knew Brahma, while Brahma knew nothing. The blue one was wearing a yellow garment and sleeping so deeply that Brahma recognized it was Yog Maya's[31] work, one of my manifestations. Brahma looked around and found no one else. No sign of life. It was just him and Sri Hari on Shesha. Brahma could deduce that the blue God was from someplace else and was sent for something that was to unfold on the planet deluged in water as of now. His personified body and the discus, mace, and conch signified he was a warrior. But Brahma was frustrated, for he did not know who he himself was, and where he had come from. I smiled, for is this not how all prodigious journeys begin.

Brahma watched Sri Hari as he slept serenely with a smile floating on his lips so lovely, yet unruly, that it seeded envy in his heart. Narayana's eyes were closed but Brahma could foreshadow that once they would open, the world will dance on his fingers. He also noted that while Sri Hari's body was pale blue, the sole of his foot was soft pink, quite like the lotus Brahma floated on. And so were his palms. His body was luminous and tranquil but strong enough to inundate the multiverse, quite like the sound of *Aum*. Brahma was wonderstruck and almost resentful of Narayana's presence, but more than that, he was confused about his own existence and the purpose of his life. He was embroiled in numerous thoughts when suddenly he saw two giant *asuras*[32] as big as

---

[31] Yog Maya – The creation enabling form of Mahadevi
[32] Asura – Asura – A class of beings. A race later fathered by Kashyap with Diti and Danu

mountains appear from nowhere. They whooshed in and snatched Brahma's Vedas from him. The giants sniggered and took the tomes deep into the bed of Ekarnava. Brahma was both aghast and petrified. Who were they and what did they want from him? He attempted to wake Mahavishnu up, but to no avail. Brahma even apologized with folded hands for his unfounded malice towards him and pleaded him for help. But Sri Hari was in a *nidra*[33] that survived many a supernova explosion.

In less than no time, Brahma was reminded of the power that had put Vishnu to sleep. He meditated on Yog Maya and beckoned her to help. He looked towards the light that I was, and said, "Oh all powerful Devi, I may know nothing about myself, but I do know that it is you out there. This profound bright light is you. Oh Kushmanda, Devi Bhagwati, Maha Maya, wake up the blue one, else these creatures will kill me even before I learn the purpose of my life. I am no warrior, Mother Divine. Help me!" I gradually lifted my Maya from Vishnu. I first left his body, then his conscience and then his eyes. Sri Hari opened his lotus eyes and found Brahma looking at him in anticipation.

The two *asuras* were Madhu and Kaitabh. Just like Brahma was born from Vishnu, the creator of creators, so were these beings. They were spawned from Vishnu's ear wax that had tumbled into the copious Ekarnava at some point through these yugas while he was in that deep

---

[33] Nidra – sleep

meditative state. Narayana himself, who had consciously birthed Brahma, could not have imagined what he was capable of birthing unconsciously from his grime. So much so that he had to wake up abruptly to neuter it and protect what he had created on purpose. It was a long battle that lasted thousands of years, as Brahma watched the monotony of the fight. One has to rumble with the subconscious manifestations and Brahma was learning the philosophies of creation. It took longer than expected for the reason that Madhu and Kaitabh had been frolicking in the quiet of the potent primeval ocean Ekarnava for ages. *Asuras* had grown strong and gigantic. In the utter stillness of the universe, and the absence of any doctrines whatsoever, they could identify my presence.

The *asuras* were curious beings who looked for me, chanting incessantly a name they gave me, long enough for me to hear it. As beings approach me, I reveal myself to them. So did they, and asked me for *icchit mrityu*[34], a death of their choosing. Although it never ceases to amaze me how even the first life on the planet, with no exemplifications of what life or death truly means, fears death. Everyone born strives to live forever. No seed wants to die unless there is no option other than dying. Competition and incessant grappling to live is part of the genetic code of all things alive. As for me, every effort must be answered. That is the fundamental rule of *prakriti*, no matter who makes the effort. Consequently, I granted them the boon. I gave *asuras* the names Madhu and

---

[34] Icchit Mrityu – The death of choice

Kaitabh, honey, and its bee. Together, they were quite like the insects who work all their lives to collect honey and more honey, without relishing or appreciating its sweetness. The very difference between knowledge and wisdom. I granted them health and environment for life to its maximum potential, which meant a nearly impossible death. Yet death is inevitable.

BHUVNESHWARI

CHAPTER 2

BHUVNESHWARI
The Empress of all Gods

Bhuvneshwari – The word Bhuvana translates to worlds, and Ishwari to governor or the empress. The creator Goddess, a form of Mahadevi, is the sustainer of the brahmaand[1] and the guardian of all realms in the universe. Also called Rajeshwari[2], Parashakti, Durga, she is the silent and unseen queen of the cosmos, who reveals herself only when approached.

Sri Hari being Sri Hari was quick to gather that Madhu and Kaitabh were emboldened by a protection from elsewhere. He meditated his thought on me, communicated with me through his sub-conscience and requested for my intervention. Once beseeched, I always concede, so I told him the way to outwit the *asuras*. After all, I had been watching the brothers. They had developed bodily strength,

---

[1] Brahmaand – Universe
[2] Rajeshwari – Goddess of kings. Empress. Another name for Mahadevi

persistence, and hearts full of desires, but could not mature spiritually because of the lack of any fellowship or guidance.

Narayana called the *asuras* for talks and expressed, "Clearly, you both have earned some formidable powers. This is no small feat, and I am mighty impressed. I wish to bless you with more, let us put an end to this struggle. Tell me what is it that you wish." Arrogant Madhu and Kaitabh befuddled by their victories over Vishnu turned down the offer and mocked him by saying, "Oh blue one, look at yourself, you are toothless! What on this planet can you give us that we do not already possess? It is us who will grant you a boon, go ahead and ask." Narayana did not spare a moment and pronounced," Let me then kill the both of you." This is how, driven by sheer conceit, the *asura* brothers undid what they had collected. They tried to outsmart Narayana but were ultimately slain on his lap above the waters of the ocean. Misguided by spiritual immaturity they took good fortune for their métier. Mahavishnu tore them into pieces, which eventually became the twelve original seismic plates on Bhu Loka. After all, these creatures were not birthed so unintentionally one could tell, for they will rest forever as the plinth of the planet. Every event, agreeable or not, serves a purpose in the chronology of time.

I smiled to myself, for this was the beginning of an epic voyage for Bhu Loka, for the universe, and for me. Over the upcoming *manvantaras*, the blue God would take the *dasaavatars*[3], ten different *avatars*[4], to set the cosmic order.

---

3   Dasaavatars – ten primary incarnations of Vishnu
4   Avatar – incarnations, manifestations

Each avatar would be coherent with the evolution of the earth. Starting with his very first and most elementary form, Matsya, a fish to save Manu from the floods. To Kurma, a giant tortoise for the churning of Ksheer Sagar. To Varaha, a giant boar to save Bhumi from a deluge. To Narasimha, a half-man half-lion for restoring faith. To Vamana, a dwarf to settle the false egos of humans. To Parashurama, a Brahmin warrior who readjusted the power equilibrium on the planet. To Purushottam Rama, the ideal king, son, brother, friend, and personification of sacrifice. To Balarama, Krishna's brother and Krishna, a lover, philosopher, and policymaker, who gave the handbook of life called Bhagwat Geeta. And Kalki, mankind is yet to see.

After Madhu and Kaitabh were slayed, I spoke to Hari, "This struggle was ordained. Like any other in the past, and many others looming in the future." "It was indeed Devi Bhuvneshwari! You may know already that I met Devi Lakshmi; Mahamaya[5], during my *Yog Nidra*[6]. So said she. And that she will enable all that I embark upon until she joins me bodily when the time is right," narrated Sri Hari.

There is a significance and implication of the seats held by respective Gods and Goddesses. It imputes a deeper connotation than what is apparent. The association between God and Goddess is that of the doer and enabler. God is the doer or the one who acts on things and Goddess is the enabler, the life-force, the material strength moored

---

[5] Mahamaya – The conjurer of illusion. Another name for Lakshmi, a form of Mahadevi
[6] Yog Nidra – Yogic sleep

to a God. One cannot do without the other and no one is mightier than the other. But the enabler elects her doer. The doer can propose or try to win his enabler, but it is the enabler with whom rests the final choice. Having said that, the relationship is largely symbiotic by configuration and so will be the relationship between a man and woman, regardless of their kind and type.

Saraswati, the goddess of invincible wisdom, knew her place was with Brahma. I, Durga cannot, for I will be born as Sati, Brahma's granddaughter, but even if I didn't, the process of creation supported by me, so much Shakti, pure and enormous, would be a non-starter. It was not the influence or the force of any kind that Brahma needed to bring about the existence of life on the planet. He sought imagination, knowledge of the discipline, insight and astuteness to know when and how to employ it. My partial form, Saraswati, a personification of that power of the mind, was designed for it.

Lakshmi, another partial form of me. If she did not reside with Mahavishnu, and in her place I or Saraswati did, the process of sustenance would not have been enabled by wealth but by unsolicited wisdom or wasted influence. No amount of intellect or power would get the work done unless there is appropriate involvement of production, consumption, and transfer of wealth.

In the same way, if I did not espouse Shiva[7], and

---

7   Shiva – The creator God responsible for the destruction of the universe

Lakshmi did, the process of cleansing the world would then have been enabled by capital. Whereas an exit of any kind is almost always influenced or affected without notices, without entertaining any preferences. If left to people, they would never know when to leave. Saraswati inspires that wisdom, but then she would not force an exit. When it comes to death, anyone would choose against it, or would like to dictate when and how to die. That exercise of choice with the muscle of commerce would effectually result in catastrophe. The world would lose its balance. The rich would send the poor to die, and the poor would sell their death for obscene prices. There would be a rate list for death that would lead to crimes beyond imagination. Consequently, Lakshmi sits with Hari and I Shakti, sit with Hara[8].

All three of us, Narayani[9], Brahmi[10] and Shivaa[11] in our manifestations as Lakshmi, Saraswati and Sati or Uma, come with unique qualifications but also some disqualifications or lack of entitlement to keep the equilibrium in place. That is how one lives once one takes a form and ceases to renounce one's body. The consciousness has no boundaries unlike the mind and body. Besides, no power once born on this planet must be absolute. Even Gods and Goddesses.

Saraswati would always be a pure stream of imagination with wisdom, intellect, and consciousness. By virtue of that,

---

[8] Hara – Another name for Shiva
[9] Narayani – Another name for Lakshmi, a form of Mahadevi
[10] Brahmi – Another name for Saraswati, a form of Mahadevi
[11] Shivaa – Female form of Shiva. Another name for Mahadevi

she will also be low on patience about the lack of it and have unnecessary attachments to luxury, beauty, and glory. She would be driven by her duty, led by truth enough to separate milk from water, yet uninvolved by the power of ultimate reality. Lakshmi, on the other hand, would always be the provider of joy, splendor, beauty, wellness, sensuality, and sovereignty that only abundance can bring. Abundance from outside and within. She would enable the near impossible and calm the minds and hearts with her presence. However, she will be fickle about where and when to appear and disappear. She would be rebellious, restless, and fiercely independent, which would bring fortunes or misfortunes for no rational reason most of the time. For the same virtues, she will not be easily domesticated. Yet concealed behind this worldly labyrinth, Maya another name for Lakshmi would be liberation, which only a few will find.

Brahmi will imagine creations, for everything that humanity knows was once imagined and seeded. Narayani will bring those imaginations to reality with her sovereign power of wealth. I, for that matter, will always be the supreme force in the universe, pouring out the mightiest motivator of all. A stimulus greater than wealth, an inducement greater than knowledge. The opposite of fear, love. I will be the extinguisher of fear and the very earth for love. No matter what I gain or lose, I will delightedly become nothing in love. No matter how hostile it becomes, I will always be my Shiva's Shivaa. For the power that I am, only Shiva would keep me mellow and transmute Rudra

Kaali[12] to Uma Gauri[13]. Or else blood will color the lands, waters and skies crimson and I will do the dance of Kaal till the oceans of time swallow everything. One needs to be a Shiva to know a Shakti, just like one needs to be a Shakti to know a Shiva.

Back at Ekarnava, I said, "O Brahma, the enlightened one, you have earned your Vedas! You are born from Mahavishnu, the enormous blue one. And you are born to create. The most learned Brahman, the one with the sight in all four directions, you will be called *Pitamah*[14], the father of the universe. You will produce lives from your mind, *manas-putras* and *putris*[15]. Begin creating! You can hear me and see my profound light today. Once you are centered and have found your purpose, you will get to see me in my form." Upon hearing these words, Brahma threw himself on his knees and said with folded hands, "O Kaali, O Bhuvneshwari, of knowledge and of ignorance, of *rajas*[16], of *sattva*[17] and of *tamas*[18], I look forward to the day I get to see you, and I don't seek anything more than this Mahadevi."

As the ultimate controller of the entire material universe with its fourteen planetary systems, I, Kaali, stimulated plans for each of the planets, with a Brahma being the chief executor. Some yugas thereafter was this solar system

---

[12] Rudra Kaali – Furious form of Mahadevi
[13] Uma Gauri – Harmonious form of Mahadevi
[14] Pitamah – The grandfather. Name for Brahma the great grandfather of the universe
[15] Manas-Putras and Putris – Sons and daughters born from the mind
[16] Rajas – Qualities of passion, activity and movement
[17] Sattva – Quality of goodness, calmness and harmony
[18] Tamas – Qualities of ignorance, inertia, laziness

born as were millions of other stars, but Surya was at the center of this one and the *grahas*[19] looped perfectly around it. Mangala, the son of the earth, was born later after an encounter *Bhu Loka* had with an external force.

Then was born Mount Meru[20], the central fulcrum of the multiverse, of which emerged the initial continents, peaks, and rivers. Above the mountain was built Amaravati and the abodes of *devas*[21]. Flora was seeded, as was fauna, beginning with microbes to the higher forms of animal life. Brahma made the first *munis*[22] from his mind – Marichi, Narada, Atri, Pulastya, Pulaha, Angiras, Kratu, Daksha, Bhrigu, and Vashishta. He also birthed from his mind Kardama, Dharma[23], followed by Kaama. Marichi had a son who was called Kashyapa. Daksha, an accomplished Prajapati[24], birthed many daughters from his mind. From the union of these daughters with Kashyapa were born the Devas, Asuras, Danavas, Daityas[25], Kinnaras[26], Gandharvas[27], Nagas[28] and Manushya. They were all given different realms as homes or *lokas*, 7 above the earth and 7 below. This multiverse had 7 Urdhva Lokas including Satya Loka, the abode of the creator

---

[19] Graha – Planet
[20] Mount Meru – Also called Sumeru, the center of the material, metaphysical and spiritual worlds
[21] Devas – Also called as Suras or Adityas. A class of beings birthed by Kashyap and Aditi
[22] Muni – Thinker or sage
[23] Dharma – Cosmic principles and laws which govern the universe
[24] Prajapati – Creator
[25] Daitya – A race of Asuras
[26] Kinnaras – Part human and part bird. Classical lovers
[27] Gandharvas – Celestial musicians and singers
[28] Nagas – Half-human half-serpent

Brahma, Tapa Loka, the realm of indestructible, immortal, and bodiless beings and deities. Jana Loka, home for some of Brahma's spiritual sons. Mahar Loka, a place above Dhruva[29] for enlightened beings such as rishi[30]s and munis. Swarga Loka, a realm between Dhruva and Surya, the abode of Indra where people from Bhu Loka go after death to relish the returns of their good deeds for a period. Bhuvar Loka or Pitra Loka, a realm where spirits live temporarily before they move forward. Bhu Loka, the Earth where entire life is a total of 12 hours of a day of the creator or Brahma's 1 day, excluding the night. These 12 hours are 14 Human *manvantaras*, each of which is a total of 71 yuga cycles, which is four yugas – *Sata or Krita Yuga*[31], *Treta Yuga*[32], *Dwapara Yuga*[33] and *Kala Yuga*. A one thousand cycle of 4 yugas.

The 7 realms below the earth are Patala Lokas. Some of these were designated to select civilizations, and some got designated as the worlds and their orders progressed through wars, politics, and power games between asuras and devas. While a lot was settled, or some would say plotted by Narayana. Atala Loka, the abode of Asura Bala, son of Maya. Vitala Loka, the land of ganas[34], bhootas and pretas who are the masters of gold mines. Sutala Loka, the kingdom of the devout demon king Bali. Talatala Loka, the realm of Maya, the demon architect. Mahatala Loka, the dominion

---

[29] Dhruva – Polar Star
[30] Rishi – Sage
[31] Sata or Krita Yuga – The first yuga of the Chatur Yuga that lasts for 1,728,000 years
[32] Treta Yuga – The second yuga of the Chatur Yuga that lasts for 1,296,000 years
[33] Dwapara Yuga – The third yuga of the Chatur Yuga that lasts for 864,000 years
[34] Ganas – Shiva's companions

of nagas, sons of Kadru, headed by the irascible group of Kuhaka, Taksshaka, Kaliya and Sushena. Rasatala Loka, home of *danavas* and *daityas*. Patala Loka, the lowest realm, also called the Naga Loka, ruled by Vasuki, the serpent king.

Prasuti was Daksha's first wife who birthed 89 daughters. Another 116 were born from his second wife Virini, who he married after a blessing from Mahavishnu when he struggled to bring more species to life. Daksha married 13 of his daughters to Dharma. They were named Shraddha, Srilakshmi, Dhriti, Tushti, Pushti, Medha, Kriya, Budhhi, Lajja, Vapu, Shanti, Siddhi and Keerti. Take a good look at the names and you will again be reminded of the roles of enabler and doer. The names were more like ideas. Another 11 Khyati were married to Bhrigu, Sambhuti to Marichi, Smriti to Angiras, Priti to Pulastya, Kshama to Pulaha, Sannati to Kratu, Anasuya to Atri, Uurja to Vashishtha, Swaha to Agni. And Sati was married to Rudra. To expand the species of humans, the daughters from Daksha's second wife Virini, 10 of them were married to Dharma, 27 to Chandra and 27 to Chandra's Nakshatras.

Prajapatis made or birthed all different kinds of human races and populated different parts of the planet, the brown ones, red ones, black ones, yellow ones, white ones and more. He followed it up by making female forms of all that he had already created so that there could be reproduction. Manu and Shatrupa[35], the *manasputra* and

---

[35] Shatrupa – Manu's partner, created by Brahma, as was Manu. Sometimes used as another name for Saraswati

putri of Brahma, the carriers of life, were also birthed later and given the title and task to populate the various parts of *Bhu Loka*, one *manvantara* after another. The first Manu was Brahma's child from his mind and so was Shatrupa, but there on will be a Manu nominated with his family to seed the next *manvantara*.

Vishnu, meanwhile, created *Vaikuntha*[36] outside the material worlds. Besides, there were many other celestial gifts of unheard divine impact, manifested and concealed in the Milky Way of Ksheer Sagar. Now when so much was being created and more creation was anticipated in yugas to come, there had to be the leveling of destruction as well. How else will there be equipoise? Consequently, it was time to wake up Kaal. And subsequently, it will be time for my Shiva to be by my side. What is Kaali without Kaal, anyway.

---

[36] Vaikuntha – The abode of Vishnu and Lakshmi

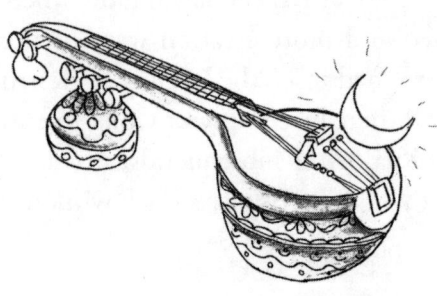

SARASWATI

CHAPTER 3

SARASWATI

The Goddess of Wisdom and Dispassion

Saraswati – Also known as Gayatri, Shatrupa or Brahmi, she is a sliver of Mahadevi and a moniker for wisdom. Her dazzling and profound presence unfailingly fonts disruption, and in due course leads to dispassion and quietude. The goddess of the art of speech, Vac, reigns the dominion of words and their absence. Usually seen unaccompanied, she is averse to unnecessary attachments and driven by her duty and strength of ultimate reality.

The task with Brahma was to bring about life forms and work along with Vishnu and Rudra to provide for this universe. Vishnu, who had created Brahma the creator, was tasked to preserve this universe and take various incarnations to set the principles of life. And Shiva, the unborn and infinite, was given the task to destroy and regenerate the universe as Rudra.

All was going smoothly for Brahma until Saraswati came to life. He had created male humans, gods, and other evolved spirits, but had not yet fashioned a woman. Saraswati, also called Sandhya[1], or his Shatrupa, was the first female form Brahma's mind had conceived. And after she came to life, Brahma's own life changed. He was awkward and perplexed, since his mind played trickeries with him, and his brain did not listen to logic. He desperately wanted Saraswati! Surely some would say it was a case of bad timing because Kama, the God of love, another creation of Brahma, came to life around the same time. Kama's effect, along with Saraswati's presence, made it more complex. I, on the other hand, had already thought of Saraswati to be Brahma's consort in the time to come. But then, this was not something he would have known without going through the journey of pain and pleasure himself. Why just him, no one would.

Saraswati was crafted to be a spectacular beauty with knowledge like none other, wisdom to put that knowledge to dispassionate use and the art of *vac* (speech) to influence and aid Brahma's process of imagination and creation. She turned out so eclectically radiant that her creator could not help being hopelessly in love with his own creation. Brahma did not want to take his eyes off her and wanted her all to himself. He did not know how to feel about it or express these feelings to anyone, for so far, he had felt a different kind of affection for his creations. The fatherly

---

[1] Sandhya – Another name for Saraswati, a form of Mahadevi

kind. Although he never wanted any of his creations to leave him. It was mostly Narada, again his son, who used to send them off to various parts of the universe under the pretext of gathering knowledge and exposure to what the universe contained in its folds. Brahma knew Narada did that on Vishnu's instructions to execute his plan to set up the civilization. But the love he felt for Saraswati, or was it lust, was unlike anything he had felt before. This emotion was arresting his thoughts. She was born out of Brahma's mind, which meant he manifested a woman of his own proclivity, so was not it expected of him to desire her? But who was I to meddle with the sequence of events! And how could Saraswati be ordinary for she was a fragment of me, my silver side, my mellow piece, my white light!

Brahma could not help himself but give in to his desires. Dharma, another son of Brahma, witnessed what was happening as did others. But Dharma being dharma had to report this. He meditated on Rudra, and Rudra appeared. That is how communication works with evolved beings. They are networked on a collective consciousness that does not need an external device, because Yog and technology are consorts in those realms. So, Rudra saw Brahma with Saraswati, and Brahma felt exposed. Sometimes the lines are blurry. Not just for humans. Even the advanced beings and creators sometimes do not know if what is seemingly wrong is merely a manifestation of our belief system or truly justly wrong.

Brahma was not Saraswati's biological father, yet he was certainly a father-figure. He felt humiliated and belittled as Rudra gave him a side glance. His own mind, which was guilt-ridden, made it seem like a mocking gaze

and found it difficult to meet his eyes with Rudra. Yet he still urgently wanted Saraswati, even if that meant giving up all that he had achieved through extreme penance over yugas. Brahma's mind was now a great muddle of frustration, desire, anguish, and embarrassment. When Rudra left, a sore Brahma hurled a curse at Kama for bringing this upon him. With inflamed eyes, Brahma said to his son Kama, "There shall be a day when you, Kama, will shoot one of your love arrows at Rudra, no less! And Rudra will open his third eye at you and turn you to ashes." At the same moment, Brahma promised to himself that he will do all that it takes to bring a day when he will witness Aadi Yogi[2] miserably love-struck, pining, and desirous of a woman as much as Brahma was. He knew in that moment, for his ambition to fructify, there had to be a woman with peerless and unprecedented qualities. Rudra, the ascetic who had never felt the need for a woman before, would not abandon his original love for Yog so simply.

Right from the genesis of the universe, only love has been the most potent driver of all and the persuader like none other. Love is that superlative authority that gets germinated within a person and then no amount of effort can uproot it. Truth is that the effort makes it worse. It is fatal. Sometimes terminal. This authority fuels every great endeavor this universe has ever embarked upon. And I made sure no one was spared. Not even creator Gods, the one who built the universe, who nurtures it and the one who renews it.

---

[2] Yogi – A practitioner of yog

Now Brahma had spoken, and words were not merely words, but promises to be kept recorded in the journals of time. Once spoken, for better or worse, words would take a life. This perhaps was one of the reasons for bestowing voice to the civilizations across the universe. So that everyone who has been given it, exchanges it as if it was a currency that has value as well as cost. Everything spoken would always cause a reaction and then the giver and the taker must live with it. However, a small part of this responsibility will always be with the receiver too, for not causing anything toxic for themselves or others.

Kama fell on his father's feet, "I was only doing what I was born for, which is making people feel love." Kama had found Rati, who was born only for him. While he was born to make others heady, he wanted to stay lost in her arms. He pleaded, "*Pitamah*, it was you who said I had the freedom to shoot my honeyed arrows at anyone. To seed love in any heart. Hari, Hara, or you. Wasn't this then pre-ordained? Why punish me for the purpose of my birth?" This got Brahma's attention, calmer than before, he nodded to Kama. His angst came from the fact that he ached for Saraswati, but could not adjust to the version of truth, that he may have committed incest. Or perhaps could not make peace with the part that he did what he did, but Rudra did not appreciate his delicate state. It is amusing how the most potent power of the material world, love, can be often perceived as a weakness. Especially when it becomes the cause of anguish for someone other than yourself. Brahma then said to Kama, "I cannot take my words back Kama. No one can. So, you will be sure consumed by the fire from

Rudra's eyes. However, whenever that happens the world will not stick together, and humanity will not grow deprived of the love you inspire. For that purpose, you will remain alive in spirit to carry on the affairs of the world. But not in your body to be with Rati. However, I assure you that once Shiva takes a wife, he will restore your body. The same gorgeous body I promise." Kama sobbed. "But first, you will have to turn into ashes. Such is the course of love, even for you Kama," Brahma sighed.

Brahma talked to his son Daksha, about the memory of his insult. He told him how mortifying it was and that he will not find peace till he equalizes it. He justified it to Daksha by adding, "Besides, what I want is nothing malevolent. Aadi Yogi deserves to know love as much as we all do. Rudra will win a lover, or at least a companion." Daksha and Brahma together considered many possibilities but could not think of a woman to match up to Rudra's persistence. Daksha concluded, "*Pitamah*, this plot needs a woman as absolute, as certain as Bhoomi[3]. A warrior goddess with the might to sweep away an entire battlefield all by herself. But sagacious enough to perceive the triumph in standing down. She needs to be a divine alchemy of *Maya* and *Vairagya*[4]. Astute enough to express in her silence. Lovely enough to pierce through Aadi Yogi's armor of Yog. The one who can glide into his heart that has no untaken space or passion for anything but Yog." The two creators of the worlds, Brahma, and Daksha deliberated

---

[3] Bhoomi – Earth
[4] Vairagya – Dispassion and detachment

and discussed. Brahma let out a sigh of despondence, which birthed *Vasanta*[5], the springtime.

The air turned fragrant, and the breeze was heady. The trees and the rolling hills started to burst with blooms. The lakes turned pink with lotus blossoms. The skies wore colors like never before. Brahma now asked *Vasanta* to support Kama to seduce Rudra. They went to Kailasa and followed him to Meru and then to Naagkesara, drowning every soul on the way into an undeniable craving. The entire creation, including the men, devas, kinnaras, yakshas[6], gandharvas and asuras were reeling under mad love. Rishis with grave celibacy gave in. The entire world swooned tranced by it. But not Rudra. He remained untouched in his *dhyana*[7]. And I could not help laughing, which caused some lightning and showers for some days.

Kama came back defeated. "Rudra remains in eternal *samadhi*[8], *Pitamah*. Even when he walks and talks, it is like he is still in a *samadhi*. He is Yog personified. My arrows drop limply around him and turn into ash as they touch his aura. I shudder to think what may happen when he emerges from his *samadhi* and opens his eyes to the world. In which moment will I turn to dust, who knows? I cannot tempt Rudra. Not Rudra!" Brahma despaired. He was now surer than before that no amount of unbridled beauty and stimulus can make Rudra flinch, unless there is a woman for whom he is compelled to open his eyes and, later, his heart, body, and mind.

---

5   Vasanta – Springtime
6   Yakshas – Spirits of trees, lakes, mountains, oceans et al
7   Dhyana – Meditation
8   Samadhi – A state achieved in meditation

Brahma started to correct his conceit and planned to seek help from the blue one, though Brahma always found it grim to accept that he was born from Vishnu. What made it more complex was that Brahma was told stories of how he was lost in Vishnu's umbilical cord for yugas and by the time he came out of it, neither he knew who he was, nor could he recognize his creator. But that is how everyone is born - renewed and uncharted. If left unaided, no one would know where they came from.

Now that Brahma needed Vishnu's astute mind, his mind vacillated between the reality of his origin, which he did not wish to accept, and his dire need for superiority. After all, he was the one raising an entire universe. Furthermore, he was not oblivious to the truth. He knew he would not be Vishnu's first choice if he were made to elect between him and Rudra. But then again, one thing he was completely sure about, that Vishnu would not mock him. Mahavishnu was supple and closer to real-world situations and their fault lines. He was far more accepting of the imbecility on *Bhu Loka*.

Brahma flew to *Vaikuntha*. Vishnu was surprised to see him, "To what do I owe the pleasure? What brought the immeasurable intellect to visit me!" And he was not sarcastic. While sarcasm was one of the most ingenious stealth weapons Mahavishnu wielded, he simply believed in Brahma's brainpower. And deep-down Brahma treasured that. He smiled, sat next to Vishnu, and explained the whole situation to him. He requested for help with folded hands, as also for confidentiality. He narrated to Vishnu how the God of love, Kama, Rati, the mistress of sixty-four fine arts of desire and Vasanta the season of love together, had failed

to make Rudra take any interest in the material world.

Vishnu smiled. Only I, Kaali, knew what that smile meant, and Brahma did not attempt to decipher it. He was listening intently when Vishnu said, "This is Rudra we are talking about, Brahma. You are the *Gyaneshawar*[9], knower of the Vedas, wisdom embodied. Kama, Rati, and Vasanta can only water what is already seeded. Love cannot be forced, for this is a matter of *Chitta*[10], which is the sub-conscious mind. I think there is only one power in existence who can help you, and that is Devi Bhagwati, Aadi Shakti[11]." When Narayan named me, I heard it like a boom in each pore of the endless ocean of my being. Was it Mahavishnu or through Vishnu my other half, my Aadi Yogi, the cosmic dweller Mahadeva[12], my minimalist Shiva calling out for me!

Vishnu piped, "If Devi Durga herself is born in flesh and blood, only she owns both the might and the right to make Rudra open his eyes and desire a woman." He added, stealthily, in his very own style, "You must tell Daksha to go to Ksheer Sagar and perform penance." "Why Daksha? Why not me?" asked Brahma. "Because your son Daksha has a wife. You do not. He can worship Aadi Shakti for a daughter." Brahma saw the point and was now optimistic.

He bowed to Narayana unstintingly and left Vaikuntha. The entire way back, Brahma wondered that the meeting went more like Mahavishnu himself wanted this more than

---

[9] Gyaneshwar – God of knowledge
[10] Chitta – Also written as Citta. Mind, which is not brain but consciousness
[11] Aadi Shakti – The first Shakti
[12] Mahadeva – God of devas. Another name for Shiva

him. He conjectured if there was something he missed to see but found nothing.

Brahma asked Daksha to go for a penance who gladly agreed, but Brahma decided to do his own penance too. He did not want to leave anything to chance. He began unequaled worship to reach his goal.

I, Kaali, had to appear in front of Brahma to fulfill the destiny I had already written for the creation. Brahma was awakened from his meditation by a blinding flash of light that flooded his existence from within. He opened his eyes and was overwhelmed by what his eyes beheld. Brahma was looking at me for the first time. Dumbfounded, he watched me, blinking his eyes incessantly. Then he folded his hands, got to his knees, and said, "O Devi Durga, Maha Kaali, forgive me, for I am entranced! You look as mesmeric and enigmatic as the moonless night." He was referring to my kohl dark skin, which shone in his eyes. Brahma observed my eight arms as I raised one of the right hands to bless him and he gaped at my roaring ride, my lion. He then said, "Maha Chandika, you have three eyes just like Rudra and you wear a crescent moon on your tousled long black tresses, again just like Aadi Yogi. O Kushmanda, Aadi Shakti, Parashakti Durga, the owner of the universe, the absolute reality, the one that contains all the powers of all the gods within her, the goddess of knowledge and ignorance, the goddess of all three qualities – *Sattva, Rajas,* or *Tamas,* the one who is dynamic in feminine form and static in masculine form. You are indescribable," with eyes brimming with pure joy. I smiled.

"O Bhuvneshwari, I do not know what I see Devi. Are you fierce? Or gentle?" said an overawed Brahma. "I

am both Brahma. I become what one invokes," I answered. Gazing at me, he then said, "I don't know what to think Devi, your voice is an intense mix of power and love at the same time," Brahma gathered himself and prostrated to me lying flat on his face.

I asked, "tell me Brahma, what do you want? Must be something extraordinary, something difficult to achieve even for someone as scholarly as you, that you meditated on me with such atonement. Tell me what is it." Brahma mustered all the courage he could, and spoke, "Devi Aadi Shakti, Aadi Yogi Shiva who lives on Kailasa as Rudra cannot be seduced. Be born as a woman and become his wife. My son Daksha is meditating on you, be born as his and Prasuti's daughter, Mahadevi." I knew what was coming, but upon hearing the demand in words, I broke into laughter. Not at Brahma, I laughed at the despondency of love. Even a Brahma was not spared by the melancholies it was capable of bringing. I chuckled at the extent to which one can reach when in love. Of all the things he could ask for, he sought something which was inevitable. Only he did not know it yet and had to cause it. This is why Mahavishnu was cooperative. He was only helping him do what was foreseeable.

Brahma looked nervous. I smiled, raised my hand in blessing and said, "So be it! Brahma, Devi Saraswati is your consort. She will be with you every step of the way as you create the universe." Brahma was pleasantly surprised with this bonus, for the agony from the disapproved love was the genesis of the penance after all. These words from me were all the approval, what he had been looking for. The decisive approval.

Then I affirmed, "Sri Hari is formless, but he took a form as Mahavishnu to preserve the universe. Mahamaya, Devi Lakshmi will be with him as his consort. And I, Kaali, will be born as your granddaughter and Daksha *Prajapati's* daughter. In that human form, I will meet Rudra and be his consort. And while Saraswati and Lakshmi will be my partial forms, Sati will be my full form."

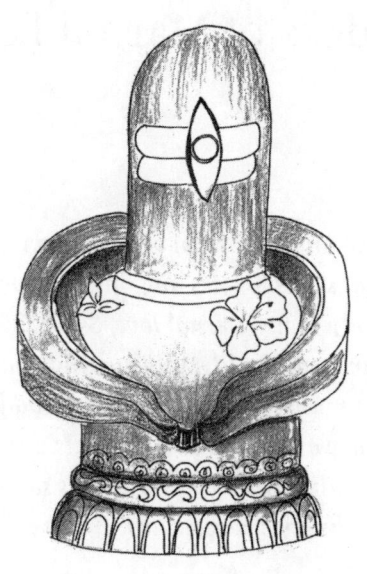

SHIVAANGI

CHAPTER 4

SHIVAANGI
The Goddess of Marital Felicity

Shivaangi[1] – Shiva-Angi, the form of Mahadevi whose entire introduction is that she is Shiva's ang, his body part. The one who shares the body of her eternal love, Shiva. The one who is fused in him, unconditionally, unwaveringly until the end of time. She is the muscle, nerves and blood wadded around the skeletal framework that Shiva is to this universe. The feminine in the masculine, the Goddess who is so immensely all-prevailing yet consecrated in Shiva.

Before Sati was born to Prasuti, I had visited Daksha in his dreams and gave him the news. He felt entirely blessed, but once I was born as his daughter and took my little form in his arms, his joy and his hopes knew no bounds. I was his favorite child, and, like any father, he

---

[1] Shivaangi – The one who is a physical part of Shiva

wanted only the unsurpassed for me. Sometimes parents fail to see that their child's happiness has little to do with what they believe is the failproof definition of happiness. Daksha Prajapati, the second creator of the world, knew so much about the creation, but so little as my father. He pursued the finest, the grandest and the noblest for his precious daughter while she was born with a single desire sown deep inside her heart. To wed the minimalist Rudra.

Daksha, who had once worshipped Mahadevi to ask for Sati as his daughter for a certain reason, now did not hope to accomplish that. What can be said about the capricious human heart! He never encouraged Sati's burning want for a yogi who lived in the wilderness with no wealth, no family, and no desire for anything in the entire creation. He could not conceive the possibility of marrying his beautiful and astute daughter to a self-denying ascetic who compelled the God of desire Kama, to wish in despair that he begins to desire a woman. "What would that Aadi Yogi know of women, love and matrimony!" Daksha suspected.

He did not want for his daughter an unborn *swayambhuva*[2] with no ancestry, no pedigree. The one who did not even concern himself with covering his body for the civilized world and dusted ash on his nine feet large frame. Who owned only one garment fashioned from a tiger or elephant hide, which he unconcernedly draped around his waist revealing his lofty sculpted built. Whose matted hair was hastily tossed into a bun barely secured with *kusha*[3]

---

[2] Swayambhuva – Self-existent. Not born from parents. Asexually born offspring
[3] Kusha – A long, pointed grass considered very pure

strands. Remote connection with civilized ways, cave-dweller, morgue-lover, cosmic-sage, who gallantly wore his own drops of tears, Rudra-aksha around his masculine neck and immense biceps. Rudra, the most convulsed form of the feminine in masculine and masculine in the feminine. Icy Mansarovar, one of the sons of the great ocean, made for his mirror, bath and home. No godly carriages, just a beloved friend Nandi who never left his side and served as his ride quietly and eternally. No celestial weaponry, just a Trident and a bow called Pinaka[4] that could bring the skies to a roar in terror when he electrified it with his touch. No aspirations to build anything, not even a shelter. No love interests or relationships except with the unloved. The likes of noxious serpents; ganas the uncouth, demented, distorted, intercosmic beings; and terrifying bhootas and pretas. Pipes, chillums, and fervent dancing on reasonless joys with the *damaru*[5] in his hand as the universe expand and perish to its beats. A crescent moon sat on his head for only a celibate yogi could know how to tame Som Deva's vacillating disposition and remain blissful timelessly without a consort. And the third eye on his *Ajna*[6] just like me, which the learned Daksha could not appreciate with his two material eyes. Daksha was inept to see Rudra's completeness in his minimalism for he was too occupied with giving Sati what she did not need.

---

[4] Pinaka – Shiva's bow
[5] Damaru – A two headed drum
[6] Ajna - Pronounced as Agya. The third eye chakra

Sati grew up into a resplendently dark and dewy-skinned young woman and her love for Rudra grew stronger with her. She embarked upon the supreme penance. After a point, she decided to move to the middle of the forest to continue her *tapa*, away from the family and comforts of her home. Daksha was not happy about her decision and tried in every way to dissuade her. However, it did not take him long to learn that he could well be the only man who loved her from the day she opened her eyes and gave her all that she did not even get the chance to ask for. Yet Sati's pursuit did not give her the break to appreciate that or reciprocate his fatherly affection in the measures he expected. But that is what makes love so incredible. It overwhelms your wits and incapacitates you to think of anyone else. No one remains of any significance except that one person of your interest.

Daksha could not believe that Sati was the beginning and end of his love in this material world, but the same was not true for her. She had always loved a certain man so interminably that she was incapable of seeing anyone else's contribution or the intensity of love. Most significantly, Sati was unable to see how a love of that magnitude, when not reciprocated, turns upside down. Such topsy-turvy love is like a poisoned dagger that hangs too close to both the giver and the taker. Even if it misses to kill them, it makes no error to scrape them at every abrupt movement. It leaves them rubbed raw, torn, bleeding and laced by toxicity either toward themselves or others.

With time Sati had forgotten everything she ever knew and could not breathe a single breath without Rudra's thoughts on it. She loved Rudra without knowing if he even

knew about her existence in the same world. Sati invoked him in every way she knew. Sometimes worshipped him with flowers, other times with rice and threads. Sometimes under the moonlight and other times under the sun. Sometimes she fasted waterless for weeks and other times she went sleepless in *dhyana* for months. Sati was so centered on Mahadeva that she soon slipped into deep and unwavering meditation. She walked, chanted, and prayed in the state of *dhyana* and performed her rituals in the same state.

Seasons changed, when the sun turned on the heat, she sat with the fire all around her and when the cold winds blew; she sat in the water with her hands folded skywards. Sati sat in dhyana through the rain, hail, and storms. The creepers wrapped themselves around her lap, and the blooms seemed a shade warmer around her body, inviting butterflies of unearthly colors and patterns. The spiders wove intricate sheets of webs from her head and shoulders, snakes slithered a bit more elegantly within her energy circle and ants silently built hills as tall as her. Sati was experiencing bliss already. Her lovely youthful body was illumined. It was difficult to tell for an onlooker if it was the light of veneration by a devotee towards her God or simply the love radiating from one eternal and cosmic lover to another. But then, isn't love in its true form another name for veneration, which takes every ounce of your energy, mind and time, and makes you radiant?

The word had spread already. Rishis and devas watched her in admiration. This is what Brahma sought and Parashakti blessed him with, but the sight of it was something else. He marveled at Sati's single-minded love

and immaculate *tapasya*⁷. Brahma had not seen anything like this since Kama's birth and was reminded of the words I had said to him, "Sati would be my full form!"

Now that all was falling in place and Brahma had settled in with Saraswati, he decided to go to Kailasa to meet Rudra and talk about Sati. He requested Narayana to join him, just to escape any uncomfortable situation, if at all. He was well aware of Rudra's reverence for Sri Hari and Sri Hari's for him lest there was a need to convince Rudra. Mahadeva was sitting leisurely, stroking his hand over Nandi's neck and an enraptured Nandi had his head raised, making soft jingles from the bell around his neck. It seemed they were talking about something delightful. Narayana and Brahma landed close to them, debarked their *vimanas* and walked towards Rudra, "Obeisance O Pashupati Nath⁸, hope we aren't interrupting you both," said a pleased Vishnu. Rudra looked in their direction with an unusual gleam in his eyes somewhat knowingly, "What an auspicious sight to see you both together walking up to me." "Obeisance Mahadeva, a thousand obeisance!" said Brahma as Sri Hari folded his hands in *namaskara*⁹ and bowed to Rudra. They joined Rudra on seats made of rocks and tiger hide.

"Mahadeva, it is certainly an auspicious day, for we have come to Kailasa to beseech you to get married. You may not seek a wife or any pleasures of marriage, but this creation needs a mother," said Brahma, a bit nervously and

---

7   Tapasya – Or Tapa. Deep meditation with extreme self-discipline
8   Pashupati Nath – Lord of all animals. Another name for Shiva
9   Namaskara – Or Namaskaram, a Hindu greeting

without meeting his eyes with Rudra. When one knows one's words are not entirely selfless, it's difficult to put up an act under a gazing eye. "But what will I do with a wife? Who would want to marry a yogi who is predisposed to Yog? Also, marriage seems like a bondage to me. You know how I live, don't you!" Rudra was quick to respond. "We know the woman for you Aadi Purusha," said Brahma, beaming with a smile and looking toward Vishnu. "O Hara, we know the woman who would be your *vairagya* when you are a yogi, and your maya when you are *grihasta*[10]," said Mahavishnu with a face like a sea of calm. That got Rudra's attention, and he smiled. "We are talking about my granddaughter, Daksha's daughter, Sati. She is…." Brahma could not finish, Rudra interrupted him, "She is Durga, Bhawani born for me. Who else can bear my seed within her womb!" "And the three worlds will rejoice this union for yugas and yugas," added a joyous Narayana.

Narayana and Brahma left Kailasa. On the way back Brahma wondered, yet again, that the meeting went more like Mahavishnu and Mahadeva both wanted this more than him. Perhaps even the pain in his own heart, both from the love for Saraswati and shame from Rudra's unspoken contempt, was part of this design. He conjectured if there was something he missed to see. Again! But he did not delve as long as it met his plan and made him contented.

I was smiling. This time from deep within, but then again, I knew the perils of love. One day, when Sati was observing her fast, Rudra appeared before her. He looked

---

[10] Grihasta – Householder. Someone married, living a family life

so magnificent that Sati stood there stunned, not knowing what to do. This was the moment she had been preparing for and now that it had arrived, she was stumped and tongue-tied. Shiva right there, in front of her, nonchalant and effortlessly majestic. Beaming at her with a gaze that made her feel exposed. "Mahadeva!" she tore her gaze away from him, lowered her head and kneeled at his feet. Shiva kept his hand on her head and said in a voice so tender that her heart raced. She had to struggle to make sense of what Rudra was saying, "Sati, ask what you seek." "You! I seek you, Purusha," said Sati, keeping her eyes down at Aadi Yogi's feet. He chuckled and pulled her up by her shoulders, "Be my wife!" A blushing and lovely Sati with large, beautiful eyes set on a dusky golden face looked straight into Rudra's eyes as her hair swayed on her svelte collar bone and slender waist. They stood transfixed.

"I will meet you at your father, Daksha's house shortly Dakshayni," announced Rudra to a shy Sati.

A few days later, Rudra summoned Brahma. "Brahma, Sati worshipped me and to honor my promise to you and Vishnu, I went to her. She asked me to be her *vara* [11], and I agreed. I had promised you both after all," narrated Rudra to Brahma without taking a breath pause. This was a first! Brahma finally found himself in a position of power. Despite Rudra's best efforts to hide, and Rudra's efforts, no less, Brahma could see his disquiet as clear as day. Such is the sovereignty of love. Rudra was smitten by Sati, without Kama's arrow. And it was the definition of equipoise, Rudra

---

[11] Vara – Bridegroom

before him, pining for a woman, unable to center himself. At that moment, Brahma was also reminded how he was cursed by the same Rudra to remain without worship in the three worlds because of that one little lie he told. It's amazing to see how the mind works when you see someone powerful tumble in love. Love makes you vulnerable. So powerless. So needy. Fortunate are the ones who are graced by acceptance. The ones who lose in love regret the expression of vulnerability. Sometimes for their lifetime. But no one will be spared!

Soon Sati was married to Shiva. It was a celestial wedding where all the rishis, devas, gods, and goddesses were invited. The wind blew fragrant. The stars aligned in perfect positions. The gandharvas and kinnaras danced to the heavenly music. Brahma performed the marriage rituals, and an anguished Daksha along with Prasuti gave away their daughter to Rudra. Rudra rode out to Kailasa with Sati before him atop a delighted Nandi jingling his bells. As they arrived, Nandi and all the ganas left Rudra alone with Sati. Rudra hadn't realized at that moment that the entire creation waited with bated breath to hear them make love. This was going to be the cosmic union, the entire galaxy wanted to witness. This was the consummation that races in the future would rejoice and worship. Rudra and Sati were both new to intimacy; psychologically as well as physically. But I and my Mahadeva wouldn't be denied the pleasures of the flesh in these incarnations. This was the unspent love older than the universe itself.

Sati made herself comfortable on a large, flat rock outside Rudra's cave. She stretched her arms in the air, taking

in the fragrance of Rhododendron, and glanced sweetly at her husband with mischief dancing in it. Then she closed her eyes in bliss, reclining her perfect back with the support of her silken arms, and lolled her head backward as her long black tresses stroked the rock below. She could hear the whispering of the gust through the sparse Blue Pines carrying the message of Sati's arrival at her mountain abode. Rudra picked a straw, sauntered towards Sati and traced sunlight falling on her half-asleep face. He plucked a clump of wildflowers growing through the gravel and weaved them one by one in Sati's locks, while pecking on her pacific face like a bird. Then Rudra picked Sati in his arms and put her gently on her back. He touched her petal lips tenderly, ran his fingers on her slender neck, all the way to her bare collar bones.

Now Shiva and Shakti began exploring each other, making silent notes about each other's pleasure penchants. Every touch released a thousand birds from the cage. Every kiss unfolded the wants they didn't know were coiled inside them. Sati opened her eyes, moaning with pleasure, when Rudra asked her, "Without you Devi, Shiva is *shava*[12]. Now that I am in Rudra's body and you in Sati's, tell me did you ache for me as much as I did for you?" Sati, priming Rudra, cooed, "I do not come into flower without you. You are my Purusha and I am your Prakriti!" Rudra turned intense at Sati's expression, "Say my name Sati, why aren't you saying my name!" he asked impatiently. Sati now roared like a tigress, "O my Shiva, your Shakti has awaited this day

---

[12] Shava – dead body

from the beginning of this universe. I have yearned for your scent on me, longed to unfurl like a floret for you, Rudra!" "Hearing my name from your lips is consent. Knowing that you desire me makes me powerful in the way nothing else does, my Sati." Sati chuckled, "The lord of the cosmos didn't experience power before this!" "All other power is worthless. I can enduringly wait across eons to hear my name from your lips. This consent unrestraint me Sati," said Rudra. He got up with the speed of a cheetah, picked Sati by her waist like she was a flower, made her sit on his lap with her legs wrapped around him into the lotus position and started to kiss her slender neck. The crescent moon sitting on Shiva's matted hair shone a beam down on Sati's kohl body. The most elegant lovemaking between Prakriti and Purusha led to the wildest consummation, the music of which touched the end of the *brahmaand* and Shiva was enthroned in the temple of Shakti's divine body. Rudra, who had not spent himself before, stayed inside Sati for twenty-five divine years. This would later be worshipped as *Shivalinga*[13], the symbol of the cosmic union between Shiva and Shakti, the masculine fused into the feminine. Unified and inseparable, in each life form.

All celestial beings showered flowers and heavenly scents on this most awaited union. The sky wore extraordinary colors and birds sang songs of joy and prosperity. Kama stayed with them for a long time and Vasanta came early, never to leave. All flowers of every season bloomed together.

---

[13] Shivalinga – Or Shivalingam, is an aniconic symbol of Shiva and Shakti

There were mango blooms on one side and almond blooms on another. The meadows turned green with never-ending flower beds of springtime. The mountain lakes blossomed lotuses as if they were emulating the Shiva-Shakti union. The winds were seductive with the spiced scent of bergamot, cloves, and tangerine. The entire Kailasa appeared to be drunken on *Som Rasa*[14].

---

[14] Som Rasa – Alcoholic drink

MAHAMAYA

CHAPTER 5

MAHAMAYA

The Goddess of Wealth, Wellness and Liberation

Mahamaya – Also known as Maya, Maha Lakshmi, Sri, or Narayani. When compared to Saraswati, this form of Mahadevi is somewhat contrarian in her disposition and demeanor. Yet, she is truly the lone voyage towards consciousness that one needs to take efficaciously to reach the gates of Vaikuntha. She is indeed the other name for Vaikuntha. She is the deliverance.

I am the mother of all. Of both knowledge and ignorance. Of all three *gunas*[1], the *Sattva* of balance and harmony, *Rajas* of passion and action, *Tamas* of darkness and imbalance. Therefore, I must tell you to not think of asuras as demons. But then anyone can be a demon, including devas when tested at the hands of time.

---

[1] Gunas – Attributes, qualities

Asuras, the people driven by intuition, led by their Guru Shukra and devas driven by reasoning, led by their Guru Brihaspati, were deliberately pitted against each other. Asuras were the beings of Patala Loka, which is where all the wealth of the universe has always resided. The riches of the earth such as oil, coal, diamond, gold, silver, gemstones, minerals, seeds, and spores for all vegetation, even soil as also many other elements have always been buried, subterranean or in the *lokas* below the Bhu Loka.

Asuras lived below the Bhu Loka, and devas lived above it. By virtue of that design, devas will have to continually fight asuras to release the goddess of wealth from the depths of the Patala Loka. The only reason why asuras were assumed demonic was their loathness to part with these treasures. But then, asuras were configured by Brahma to protect the treasures and devas were designed to procure, produce, and nurture. It was always meant to be like that. This war is perpetual and vital to the workings of the world.

All through the life of this planet, henceforth, the same series of actions will repeat itself. Every time it will be accomplished, there will be ferocity of brute force. There will be explosions and tunneling in the heart of Prithvi when the gems, coal, oil or metals will be extracted. There will be immense Agni and ruthless pounding whenever the metals will be smelted or crafted. The crops would be baked by Surya and then flogged and thrashed. Varuna and Chandra would get into dangerous duels to produce the hydropower, just as Vayu and Aakash would do a colossal dance for wind energy. Even the smallest unit of matter will

MAHAMAYA; The Goddess of Wealth, Wellness and Liberation ■ 57

have to break into fission to generate *parmanu shakti*². Look at Surya, who has been burning incessantly by fusion for ages and will do so for many more, all because that's where sits the foundation of the enterprise called the universe. So, this is how and why there will be vehemence, even violence between asuras and devas, which will become an acceptable routine. The asuras will resist and the devas will persist.

It is for the same reason that only this force and counterforce together could churn the ginormous Ksheer Sagar enough to upheave the treasures from the *Patala Loka* and bring Devi Lakshmi out for the *samsara*³. Asuras, the beings of passion and heightened excitements, who failed to understand the science of balance or commerce, would never give up the alluring Lakshmi and would always remain tightfisted about her. This is exactly what makes an asura. And this is why Sri Hari Vishnu conspired the great *manthan*⁴ of the ocean of milk in the name of *amrit*⁵.

Wars after wars between asuras and devas, there came a time when devas fell and did not come back to life like they always did. Indra had lost all his three *lokas* to asuras. This was the result of a curse by the perpetually annoyed rishi Durvasa. Things got worse because Indra was sloppy enough to keep the floret garland gifted by the rishi on his elephant's head, who happened to throw the garland to the ground, perturbed by the fragrance or perhaps a bee

---

² Parmanu Shakti – Nuclear power
³ Samsara – World
⁴ Manthan – Churning
⁵ Amrit – Elixir of life

inside it. That garland belonged to Sri Hari and was gifted to Durvasa, who in turn had given it to Indra as a blessing. This made Durvasa livid, and he hurled a curse at Indra. As I said before, words were as good as promises kept by the ones who uttered them, and for that reason, the cosmos supported them. Now the cosmos's support isn't anything supernatural, it's a method. As more and more people keep their word, more and more they are forced to be liable for their actions and decisions. It is cyclical in nature and difficult to disrupt once put into action. This's the beauty of *dharma*.

Subsequently, Durvasa told Indra, "Self-conceited, foolish Indra, you will soon lose your vigor. So will the other devas. You will lose your kingdom, the three *lokas*. And eventually, your misplaced arrogance."

Brahma advised Indra to meet Sri Hari. Indra narrated the whole story to Narayana. "Obeisance Sri Hari, Obeisance! I have made a blunder. It was the beast, not me if one thinks of it. My dear lord, I didn't even know the garland belonged to you," cried Indra and prostrated in front of Narayana. The astute Vishnu spoke, "You have not offended me, Indra. You cannot, even if you attempted to. But you have offended the learned sage Durvasa. Now, to bring things back to order, you have no choice but to make amends. Get asuras as allies to churn the intergalactic ocean of milk, Ksheer Sagar, my home. The upheaval of the Milky Way will bring the elixir of life to the surface, which seems to be the only way to save your kingdom." "I will do as you ask Narayana, but asuras are magical beings. What if they get the ambrosia before we get our hands on it?" quipped Indra to cover up his anxiety. "Asuras are surely very capable of it, but I will make sure that they don't. Devas' reasoning keeps the sense of balance in place, but it fails to do things magical. Asuras' madness and sheer prowess of unpredictability complement devas' rationality. We need both. But unfortunately, we will have to deceive them to get your Swarga Loka, Bhu Loka and Patala Loka back from them. You have left me no choice," Vishnu detailed to Indra in a stern tenor.

Indra knew this would lead to another battle with asuras but hopefully after devas have consumed the elixir and have become invincible. He swallowed his pride and went to Bali, the king of asuras, and proposed that they join hands with devas to churn out the amrit. This was not a very difficult task. Who wouldn't be tempted by celestial riches and immortality? Indra promised them an equal share of the divine treasures, asserting the fact that neither the devas nor the asuras could do this on their own. "O King of Triloka[6] Mahabali[7] Bali, join this pursuit. All we need is your equal participation, mount Mandara as the churning rod and the great serpent Vasuki as the rope around it." "Yes, something tells me this is what we should be doing," affirmed Bali. That something was Vishnu's voice relayed in Bali's subconscious as his inner voice. I could hear what Bali could, through the collective consciousness between me and Sri Hari.

The great Mount Mandara was uprooted. It turned out to be heavier and larger than what they expected. They had

---

[6] Triloka – The three worlds
[7] Mahabali – Someone with great powers

to keep it down hurriedly, crushing many asuras and devas. They used all their devices and technology but could not carry it forward. This needed an intervention by a creator god, consequently, Mahavishnu picked it up and carried it to Ksheer Sagar on his *garuda's*[8] back. Once that was done both Indra and Bali went to Vasuki, the serpent king in Patala Loka and offered him a share of *amrit* in return for being their churning rope. Again, not a difficult task, Vasuki rallied along and soon began the churning.

The devas were positioned towards Vasuki's head but asuras would not have it, they contested, "Why should we be holding the snake's tail?" Sri Hari smiled at Indra, and he immediately shifted with his clan to the tail end of the serpent, giving the head to the asuras. That is the thing with insecure beings, they are so skeptically focused on others that they forsake their own blessings. The clever ones can see their unfounded envy and leverage from this pessimism.

The churning started slowly and clumsily, but soon they achieved the pace and began churning rapidly. Shortly they realized that with every swivel, mount Mandara was sinking into the bed of the ocean and becoming shorter. That was when Vishnu transformed into a giant turtle, dived into the bed of the ocean, and slid under the mount to support it on his shell. He secured the mount with one of his enormous hands to make it stable, and with the other, he hurled Vasuki's tail. Now it was the blue one everywhere, vast, and immeasurable, and the golden Mandara twirled

---

[8]   Garuda – A kite or an eagle, the mount of Vishnu

beautifully. The sound from every spin was so deafening that no one could hear much, and no one cared.

The reason indeed as to why Narayana was involving himself to this extent was unknown to all of them, except me. His own destiny was to emerge out of the depth of the ocean. It was time for Narayani, Maha Lakshmi to manifest herself. While Sri Hari was about to bring Devi Mahamaya out of the ocean, it was preordained that he will not be chasing after her like everyone else. Perhaps for this very reason, quite unlike Lakshmi's natural self, she will always be drawn toward him. For that is the only way for the *srishti*[9] to work. The feminine is devout to only one at a given point of time, and unless she is committed, the masculine would struggle to function with full potential. Narayani had to be Narayan's enabler and on that rested the fate of the universe. So, Narayana will have to devise a way to make the disloyal and delightful delusion called Maya find a place in Vishnu's heart forever.

Both devas and asuras were completely obsessed by Devi Lakshmi. The unachievable Mahamaya, her heavenly demeanor, her amaranthine youth, the prowess to make every dream come true, her divine glow, her vitality and unearthly beauty, even her fickleness, made her deliciously attractive. Although asuras lived in proximity to her as she too was *Patala Nivasini*[10], but all they had garnered were the riches, not wealth.

Back at Ksheer Sagar, Vasuki was hauled so violently that he started to throw up fire, fumes, and venom over

---
[9] Srishti – Universe
[10] Patala Nivasini – The dweller of the Patala. Another name for Lakshmi

the asuras close to his head. Mahavishnu took care of that as well. He made rain and blew such cool breezes that the ocean started to swell. The vigorous churning continued. The entire Milky Way started to go in circles around the devas and asuras. And then rose the fuming black *Halahala*[11]. The primeval venom that was benumbed at the bottom of the ocean fluids mounted up and up, enough to cover up the sky and eat up the sun. Vishnu dropped everything and rushed straight to Kailasa. "Mahadeva, only you can save this creation now!" called out Vishnu, pointing at the obscuring sky. Shiva looked at Shakti, who did not look incredibly pleased. This was not a part of the plan, but Sri Hari knew how to get Bholenath's[12] attention. "O the wearer of serpents, if you do not contain the *Halahala*, its green fumes and raging darkness will swallow the universe. Before the ocean throws up the good, it must heave out the bad. Who else can contain it, if not you!" Shiva pressed my hand softly but tellingly and rose taller than the Kailasa. He reached for the sky, started to collect the fuming *Halahala* in the cup of his hands, and quaffed it in a gulp. The poison seared his throat, and it turned blue. Shakti sprang to her feet and grabbed Shiva's neck to contain the poison in his throat, so the rest of the body remains unaffected. A few drops that driveled from his lips were licked by snakes, lizards, scorpions, spiders, and insects. Shiva got a new name, *Neel Kantha*[13].

---

[11] Halahala – Or Kalakuta, the venom that came out of samudra manthan, churning of the ocean
[12] Bholenath – A benevolent form of Shiva
[13] Neel Kantha – The one with the blue throat. Another name for Shiva

Right after the *Halahala* was taken care of next appeared Alakshmi, a devi who did not look pleasing to the sentiments. A converse of expected Lakshmi, her elder sister Alakshmi wore filthy clothes and unkind expressions. She had a long nose as if she poked it in everyone's matters. Drooping breasts that reached her navel, sagging belly and abundant thighs, all suggesting her ill-health and lethargy. Squabbling and sore red, disturbed with anger, holding a broom to sweep all propitiousness away, her birth divided the world into auspicious and inauspicious. One could tell Alakshmi was the bringer of grief and poverty of minds, souls and homes. She illustrated how a wrong enabler can take a doer to nadir. No one welcomed her except some with evil and sinful disposition, and in due course, she found herself dwelling in sorrowful places.

At the site of *manthan*, Ksheer Sagar coughed up Som Deva next, also called Chandra. His birth gave way more meaning to the night falls on earth. Its waxing and waning will be the genesis of the Vedic calendar, a prodigious influence on the health and life of the entire creation, as well as the practices of *Sanatan Dharma*. Then came up some belongings of Narayana, like his Kaustabhmani a divine jewel, his bow Sharanga and his conch Panchjanaya[14]. Also emerged some heavenly animals, Uchhaishravas, the seven-headed horse of light that was gifted to the asura king Bali; Kamdhenu, the wish-granting cow which was gifted to the seven sages who would make the best use of her milk; Airavat, the multi-tusked white elephant that Indra took. Kalpavrisksha, the

---
[14] Panchjanaya – Vishnu's conch

wish-granting tree with Parijat flowers, the scent of which befitted the heavens, surfaced as well, so that too was given to Indra. Then appeared a lovely and drunken goddess of wine, Madira, who was taken by Varun Dev, who then named her Varuni. Also appeared hypnotic *apsaras*[15], who chose to make a life with *gandharvas'* celestial arts.

Then peered out the gorgeous god of Ayurveda and medicine Dhanavantari, the very picture of good health of mind, body, and soul. He was youthful, brilliant blue, long-armed, lotus-eyed, dressed in a yellow garment, every bit like Vishnu. And most notably, he arose with a chalice of amrit in his hand. But right then, appeared a radiance that strayed everyone's attention away from Dhanavantari at once. Ascended the incarnation of auspiciousness, Sri Lakshmi. Narayani, a luminous white beauty that no one had seen enough before, stood in front of them in a scarlet and gold raiment. Spectacularly vibrant, pleasing to eyes and minds, calming, and nearly intoxicating to watch, she was every bit propitious. The sight of her removed everyone's attention away from the ambrosia. *Gandharvas* and *apsaras* broke into dance and music. Vedas appeared, and the chanting echoed. Vasanta showered flowers on her. Ganga and other sacred rivers drizzled water on the goddess of fortune. There was a fever in the air when she laid her eyes on Narayana, who displayed a properly enigmatic smile. She walked up to him, took off her *vaijayantimaal*[16] made of rare immortal blue lotuses and draped it around his neck. Mahalakshmi

---

[15] Apsaras – Celestial beauties who are singers and dancers in Deva Loka
[16] Vaijayantimaal – The elemental necklace associated with Vishnu and his incarnations

MAHAMAYA; The Goddess of Wealth, Wellness and Liberation ■ 65

had made her choice. Narayana wrapped his arm around her slender waist and ambled away.

That was when asuras woke up to the reality of what had materialized. They moved towards the amrit, but before they could do anything, their eyes gravitated to an even more voluptuous and breathtakingly beautiful woman. The enchantress was blue, lustrous, and moved like a seductress. This was Mohini, Vishnu's female form. Both the devas and asuras were love-struck in a blink. She took the chalice in her hand and made asuras sit on one side and devas on the other. Mohini started to pour out the amrit to devas first while winking at asuras, suggesting so much more than just the *amrit*. While the rest of the asuras waited for her to come by, Rahu did not. He disguised himself as a deva and drank a share of *amrit*. As soon as the *amrit* was distributed amongst the devas, Mohini transformed back into Vishnu.

An inevitable conflict broke out. Asuras were driven back to the Patala Loka and devas were again invincible. Later, to make compensations, Shiva imparted the Sanjeevani *Vidya*[17] to asuras, the knowledge of bringing the dead and lost back to life. This is why the venerated God of Patala Loka can be no one else other than Mahadeva. The idea was never to cheat on anyone. It was to bring back the social order and Mahalakshmi out of the Patala Loka.

Vishnu took Mahalakshmi to Vaikuntha on his ride *garuda*. Once home, Narayana introduced Narayani to Aadi-Shesha, the one who remains despite everything

---

[17] Vidya – Correct knowledge

and anything. The tamas form of Vishnu, Anantshesha helps him balance the world and devours it at the end of the *manvantara*. But he himself is interminable, so he is Ananta. Shesha expanded his coil to make room for Lakshmi, while keeping his blissfully stationary posture, the *sthirsukhamasana*[18], and welcomed the propitious Mahalakshmi in his circle.

The newly wedded couple, Lakshminarayan, laughed uncontrollably about Vishnu's Mohini *roopam*[19], when he took his preferred position, *Ardhashayana*[20], and Lakshmi sat next to his feet and rubbed them lovingly. "What happened my dear Narayani, what are you doing to my foot?" "Just wiping your lotus feet clean, Narayana," responded Lakshmi impishly. Vishnu sat up to listen to his wife more closely. "I did not fail to see my elder sister, my antithesis, Alakshmi at the manthan, Hari. I am mindful that if all is well-tended and there is health of body and mind, she will be where she wants to be, but it will certainly not be our home, Vaikuntha." "So, you are nursing my feet, Devi?" smiled the almighty Vishnu. "Do not get me wrong my Srihari, Alakshmi is my sister, a constant reminder of what not to be. I will always have her on my mind and that, by itself, is my submission to her. As it will be for many other women." Vishnu got curious and asked an unrelated question, "Shri, you know that you are desired by one and all. Don't you? I saw how every eye; every heart was

---

[18] Sthirsukhamasana – Strong, steady and stable yogic posture
[19] Roopam – Form
[20] Ardhashayana – The lounging position Vishnu takes atop Shesha

inundated with lust when you emerged out of the Milky Way. They completely disremembered the ambrosia until you broke the spell by garlanding me. I cannot think of anyone in this entire creation who would not crave you. Then why did you select me?" Lakshmi threw her elegant head backward and broke into laughter that sounded like bells of fortune, "You know very well that I am the goddess of wealth and desire. I will always invoke insatiability and yearning in every heart. But then that is the test I throw at every interaction. All creatures of flesh choose the wealth of the external world and not the inner kingdom of prosperity. But that is acceptable to me. Once they have manifested their material desires, or not, if they happen to rise enough to see that the joy material possessions bring is transient, the pleasure that desire brings is ephemeral, the happiness that gluttony brings is fleeting, they will come closer to me. If they do, they will get to see that I am the goddess of Liberation, *moksha*[21], the doorway to Vaikuntha. But if they do not, then all they get from me is *maya*. A twisted and tangled life of *maya*. And you Narayana are the conspirer of this maze as much as I am. Yet you ask like you do not know, my love," and Lakshmi giggled.

"It wasn't me asking Lakshmi, it was Saraswati on my *jivha*[22] as my *Vac Shakti*[23], but of course the thoughts were mine," Vishnu teased Lakshmi as he put his tongue out with Saraswati sitting on it. Her eyes closed and her hands

---

[21] Moksha – Salvation
[22] Jivha – Tongue
[23] Vac Shakti – The power of speech

in *dhyana mudra*[24]. Lakshmi felt a pang of envy, she rushed to Vishnu's heart and occupied it abundantly. Vishnu gurgled with laughter and held his heart firmly, "Now stay there forever, for people will address me as Lakshmikantam, the lover of Lakshmi." Shri had made Narayana's heart her home, giving him the name Shrinivasa, the abode of Shri.

---

[24] Dhyana Mudra – A meditative hand gesture

SATI

CHAPTER 6

SATI

The Goddess of Love and Renunciation

Sati – The word Sati comes from the word Satya and translates to verity or truth. Also known as Aparna, the form of Mahadevi who endured in the worship of Rudra, without swallowing a single leaf. Or Dakshayni, the daughter of Daksha Prajapati, she is the Goddess who lives by sacrifice and renunciation. She renunciates in life as well as in her death.

Ages went by, when on Sati's request, Sati and Rudra moved to the higher reaches of the Himalayas. Sati asked for a home like any married woman does and Rudra, who didn't feel the need for it before, asked her to elect a location between Mount Meru close to Indra's Amaravati, Kailasa near Kubera's secret city, or Himalayas, the abode of devas and rishis. Sati chose the Himalayas with ancient trees, lakes, resplendent flowers from the heavens and glorious animal life. That was where she met Mena, the mountain king Himalaya's wife, who loved her

like her own daughter. Little did they know what fate had planned for them or why destiny had made Sati elect the Himalayas for her home? Fate is born the day a person is born. No one alive or in a body can escape it.

Meanwhile, one day, Sati was cooking for Rudra, although he did not need material energy from food. Rudra, being a Yogi, drew his energy from the cosmos and could go on without food and water for interminable periods of time in and out of *samadhi*. But food cooked by Sati was a love language. As soon as Rudra arrived, Sati began preparing to serve him. He walked up to her, she turned towards him and said cheerily, "I have cooked for you Rudra, allow me to feed you." Rudra blew a soft kiss towards her, put the ladle away from her hand, picked her in his arms as she stared at his face, and took her to their love-making spot. All silently. He held her face in his palms and started to kiss Sati like the bird pecks on food in the morning. Sati could not help giggling and looked at Rudra in amazement. Quite like most other days, Rudra made slow and unhurried love to Sati, leaving her swooning and sweet-smelling like jasmine in the monsoon. Then he rolled over, allowing Sati some time to gather herself, and intonated, "Now that I have had this Bhog, tell me what you have cooked for me my love." "This Bhog?" Sati got inquisitive, she slid herself onto Shiva's shoulder and asked, "Now wait for a little while longer, first tell me Mahadeva, what is love? What is it that you feel for me?"

Rudra, known for his eternal equanimity and little need for communication in words, looked at his beloved, smiled devotedly and phrased, "I know you look for

satisfaction on my face when you cook for me. It is not just food but dollops of affection that you blend carefully in the cauldron. And then you feed me from your own hands. With your fingers on my mouth and the other hand on my chin, you turn into Annapurna before my eyes, and I feel a river of love flowing inside me. Anyone can bring me food, but no one else can bring me fulfillment like you do." Rudra then added, "Also, when you make me the subject of your intimate desires, you cannot fathom how fortunate I feel to be the man to a woman of your radiance, elegance, and beauty. When your presence and our nearness ignite passion within me, you become Kamakshi. I feel a massive surge of love for you. These two feelings are best described as love in its primal form, *Bhog*."

"*Bhog*?" Sati sat up, tying up her hair with her nimble fingers into a braid she probed, "Is that all love is?" Rudra laughed knowingly, stroked Sati's face and emphasized, "Yes *Bhog*, although it is a primal need but very foundational. Do not underestimate it, Sati, it is extremely gratifying for me but becomes apparent only for the body. Do I move to the next form of love now?" Rudra asked Sati. "Yes, I can barely wait Mahadeva," replied Sati, moving towards Rudra's feet, and facing him directly now.

"The second form of love that fills me is when I feel an assured influence over you. The dominion you gifted to me out of sheer grace. A mighty powerful woman who runs the planetary systems, holds the universe together, rides a lion, dreaded by the evil, adored by the gentle, whose mind is swifter than lightning, becomes a simple girl in my company. How dignified you are to disremember all that authority and surrender yourself in my arms. It is you who allows me to question you, pester you, take you for granted and even dominate you at times. It is mesmerizing to see Bhagwati turn into a demure Gauri. Only for me. But then, it is still more enthralling how at times you turn into Ambika and wield brutal weaponry to defend me or tie sacred threads on my wrist to protect me from evil like a mother would to a child. Both these forms grant me a certain sweet power over you. This influence makes me feel the love beyond the body..." explained Rudra as a completely beguiled Sati watched his face.

"To watch you switch from Gauri to Ambika and back to Gauri, makes me feel the love beyond the body. Love for the heart – *Shakti*," said Rudra. He winked at a speechless, gawking Sati and continued, "Let me now give you the third form of love I feel for you."

Now shining in the reflective glow of Rudra's deep observations of her, Sati enquired, "So there is a third form too?" Rudra nodded with a smile, "Yes, the final and the most significant one. Yet somewhat incognito!" "And what's that?" asked Sati curiously.

"When you turn into your primeval form as Kaali, unafraid to show your darkness, untamed tresses, stripped self, intoxicated in ferocity and dance on top of me, it becomes an unmatchable mix of raw power and defenselessness at the same time. Your fearlessness of being derided or judged is hypnotic to my mind. That is also the time you become Saraswati and show me the mirror of truth. It is you who empowers me with the grit to see the undressed prancing reality. And in that moment again, I

feel a gush of love, the love of a beautiful mind – *Darshan*."

Sati placed her face on Rudra's foot and said, "*Bhog, Shakti, Darshan*. One needs to be a Shiva to know a Shakti." Rudra kept his hand on Sati's head and exclaimed, "Just as one needs to be a Shakti to know a Shiva."

Sati and Rudra had lived a perfect marital bliss in the mountains for a thousand years when Sati suggested that they go out to explore the world. Subsequently, they traveled to the plains. There, they met a devastated Ram in the Dandaka *Vana*[1], looking for his abducted wife. Rudra did not intervene in the progress of the story of Ramayana-to-be, but he blessed Rama for his certain victory. They met many rishis and munis, together saw the changing landscapes and climates on their way. They discussed the variety of trees and rivers and clouds. Talked about the *atman*[2] and its progression, the cycle of life and death, the inseparability of pain and joy like night and day, and much more.

Sometime later, at a yagna[3] in Prayaga, Rudra and Sati were invited where they were offered a seat of honor. Daksha Prajapati was also invited there. His grief, which everyone mistook for antagonism or bitterness, had eaten him up completely by now. Daksha himself did not know he was grieving, and the demon of dejection from his daughter's choice of man had been gnawing at him consistently. He had lost his beautiful beloved daughter whom he considered a blessing by me, his Ma Bhagwati, directly. Daksha had

---

[1] Vana – Forest
[2] Atman – Soul
[3] Yagna – Pronounced as Yagya, is a ritual performed in front of a sacred fire

lost that blessing to another man. Was it because Sati chose a man greater than him, or was it because she loved this man far more than she ever loved Daksha? He did not know but felt scorned by this deficit in his love equation. His grief, not anger, had made him bitter. His agony looked for opportunities to attack Rudra and wound Sati knowingly or unknowingly.

Rudra and Sati saw Daksha enter the premises but did not get up to greet him. They could not leave their seats during the ceremonies. Sati may have smiled at Daksha as a daughter would to a father, but Rudra didn't, for he bounced back the same sentiment that he was receiving from the other end. Daksha was furious. He started to spit fire. "What does he know of respect and culture, this Rudra with no parentage and pedigree! Uncouth the keeper of the company of beasts, serpents and drunken, debauched ganas," cried a seething Daksha before he barred Rudra from the yagna. Some rishis, including Bhrigu, who was once put in his place by Sati, supported Daksha, but most of the gathering was thunderstruck by his absurdity. Nandi kept looking at Shiva for approval to speak but when he did not get one, he couldn't stay quiet, "Daksha, you fool, what *yagna* are you talking about? Rudra is the *yagna*. How can you ever expel him? Wherever he will go, *yagna* will follow him. Oh, you are bringing shame to yourself and all other Prajapatis. The Vedas that you prattle about have taught you nothing about your own inner truth. Your insolence is unintelligible!" Nandi spoke for his friend and deity, to Daksha, "Daksh, the filth that you spew comes from the nightfall at your heart. This visceral bitterness will one day

obscure all your light, and you will wear the face of beasts that you so detest, mark my words." There was a profound hush at Nandi's retort. Rudra looked in Nandi's direction, suggesting him to stay calm and not speak anymore. Daksha stormed out, his mind festered with hatred and insult. All he wanted now was to square up.

After some time passed, Daksha announced his own Ashvamedha *yagna*[4] at his place in Kanakhala, on the banks of Ganga. Everyone was invited. Mahavishnu was beseeched to preside over it. Brahma too was bidden by his son, along with his Vedas, who by now were given bodies of their own. They worked with Brahma and whoever else had inquiries for Vedic resolutions on the matters of the world. All the rishis and munis were sent invitations to join the ceremony with their families. There were devas, asuras, lokpalas. The Saptarishis[5] were there and so were the gandharvas and nagas. Also invited were the kings and royal families. It was a gathering of all worlds in the universe, but Rudra and Sati were expressly excluded.

An event that large cannot be kept hidden and Daksha knew that very well. One day, when Sati was talking to the parrots on the tree above her head, she saw a convoy of *vimanas* in the sky. One of them was her sister's. She found out about the *yagna* from her. Sati could not believe that her father had not invited her, and her Rudra. Her heart felt constricted, and her eyes welled up. Rudra saw Sati

---

[4] Ashvamedha yagna – A ritual wherein a horse accompanied by the king's warriors is released to wander for a year
[5] Saptrishi – The seven sages

from a distance as he was chatting away with his ganas and asked her for the reason. Sati apprised him and said, "Let us go, Rudra. I am his daughter, after all. We should go to Gangadwara." Rudra took Sati on his lap like always, not knowing this would be the very last time, "I cannot, my love. Your father did not invite me because he does not want me there. You are his daughter; you can go if you so desire, and I cannot stop you. If you do, please take Nandi along. Your *sakhis*[6] can go with you and so can some of the ganas. But I cannot. It is not appropriate." He held Sati's tear-smudged face and kissed her wet eyelids.

This was Sati's first trip from Kailasa without Rudra. And the last. Sati's *sakhis* packed up her things. Nandi wore his finery. Rudra came out with Sati from their cave as she embraced him, and he kissed her forehead. Then he secured the pomegranate flowers in her knotted hair and told her to come back to him at the soonest. As she mounted Nandi, her pet parrot came and perched next to her, without its partner. Sati left for Kanakhala. It all happened so fast that both Rudra and Sati felt a bit of a chafe in their hearts. But as I said before, departures are never announced. If we foretell them, no one would like to leave. I, Kaali, influence them.

At Gangadwara, everyone got seated one by one and the *yagna* was just about to begin when Rishi Dadhichi got up and asked about Mahadeva and his Shakti. Daksha retorted "All those who are worthy of being here are already

---

[6]   Sakhis – Girl friends

here, Dadhichi. I have not invited that Rudra or my daughter Sati out of choice." Some people in the gathering agreed with Daksha which peeved Dadhichi further and he stormed out of the yagna. He yelled at Daksha as he left, "You have invited your downfall, you dimwit. And you will meet it in this very yagna!" Soon entered Sati.

She greeted everyone around cheerfully, but they responded nervously. Prasuti and Sati's sisters came to her but could only welcome her halfheartedly because Daksha was watching them from a distance. Sati went impulsively to greet Daksha, but he didn't so much as look at her. She noticed that the share of offering for Shiva was absent. She could now gather what was going on. Shiva was right, it was all designed to insult him. She also noticed many eyes trailing her. A shadow loomed over her face. Her tresses came undone and swung loose behind her like a robe, releasing the red pomegranate flowers at the *mandapam*[7]. Standing at the *mandapam*, Sati yelled at her father, "Father, why are you inciting Rudra! He is the lord of the universe. And my husband. I am your beloved daughter!" "Huh daughter! Beloved daughter! I do not care for you or your nobody husband. Do not talk to me of him."

Bewildered Sati then looked at Vishnu, "And you Hari. You are sitting here knowing fully well that my Rudra, your Lord Shiva is not here. So, your words of worship for him meant nothing?" Vishnu stayed quiet. "And you Brahma, Mahadeva has blessed and exonerated you so many times. Have you forgotten? And all of you, devas! Have you no

---

[7] Mandapam – An open temporary pavilion used for offering prayers

sense of loyalty?" boomed Sati in plain anguish, "All those who are silent without a protest are partakers of this ghastly plot. I should not have come here. But now that I am here, I cannot go back to my Rudra." Daksha retorted, "Oh don't keep mentioning Rudra's name. You are our daughter and will always be. Stay here. You will be given a share of this yagna but stop this wailing now. It is an auspicious day at your father's house." Sati had a strange mix of fury and distress on her tear-smeared face. Nandi looked at his precious Sati with anguish. He felt helpless in the midst of this strange power battle between the father and the daughter. He had said so much to Daksha at the last *yagna* that now there was exasperation and remorse for the loss Daksha was incurring with his behavior. All the ganas who had accompanied Sati were too shocked to even move.

Sati now could see to what extent the father she had known had fallen. She regretted the decision to come to the *yagna* and ached for her Rudra. It no longer mattered that it was her father's place. She had come uninvited and was paying dearly for it. Her father had become apathetic towards her, so much so that he could say such poison-laced words to Sati, all so uncaringly. Sati's mind kept questioning when and how did this relationship become so depraved. Why couldn't she see it coming? But she was her father's favorite daughter. Was she too occupied in her own life and happiness? What did she fail to see? But again, it was too much humiliation and hurt to live with. And what would she tell Rudra? How would she face the ganas and her sakhis who witnessed this? How would she meet with the same devas and rishis later in Rudra's presence? How will they

have the nerve to meet Rudra? Oh, they will, for lack of courage makes people cunning. But she will surely die of chagrin before anything else. And if she must die, then why by means of shame? Sati gathered herself and announced with a speech that reverberated, "Listen Prajapati, I abhor the truth that I am your daughter. I cannot change that reality till I am breathing through this body. But I do have a choice to abandon it and renounce the relationship with you. For Rudra, I will be born again to a father who I can love, and who would love my Shiva. I will be Rudra's wife again, but I relinquish being your daughter." Pregnant silence prevailed in the auditorium, as a deathly calm covered Sati's distraught, but still, face.

Sati sipped some Ganga water, sat in *Agnistambhasana*[8], covered her face with her garment, balanced her *Prana*[9] and *Apana vayus*[10] and entered *dhyana*. She raised her *Kundalini shakti*[11] from her *Muladhara*[12] to *Anahata*[13] to *Ajna*[14]. I Bhagwati, embodied as Sati, was soon levitating. In a few moments, her Ajna between the eyebrows illumined with *Udana*[15], the third *vayu*[16]. Before anyone could comprehend anything, she emanated a blinding bright light. She turned into a ball of fire soaring above the ground as everyone in

---

[8] Agnistambhasana – The fire log yogic pose
[9] Prana Vayu – Inward moving breath
[10] Apana Vayu – Downward moving breath
[11] Kundalini Shakti – The serpentine energy released in the body using specific meditative techniques
[12] Muladhara – The root chakra
[13] Anahata – The heart chakra
[14] Ajna - Pronounced as Agya. The third eye chakra
[15] Udana Vayu – Upward moving breath
[16] Vayu – Air

the arena watched, gasping in terror. When the fire went out, her lifeless, blackened body dropped on the floor. There was a hush. Even the wind ceased in horror. And like this, unexpectedly Sati turned out to be the supreme sacrifice at Daksha's yagna. Seeing this, Prasuti her mother, fell unconscious in shock. This led to shrieks and screams everywhere.

"We cannot go back to Mahadeva without you Mahadevi, we are coming with you," screamed one Gana after another, hacking and killing their own bodies. Some of them started to chant, death for Daksha. Bhrigu and some others started to protect Daksha and attacked the ganas with their occult powers. Ganas were getting burned, feared killed next to their dear Sati's dead body. Soon the place turned into a battleground. But someone had to tell Rudra. Even the thought was mortifying.

Shaken and grief-stricken ganas jabbered something incoherently to Rudra. "Sati immolated herself, Mahadeva. She could not take the shame her father subjected her to," Narada informed Rudra without meeting his eyes with him and sobbed like a baby. Rudra looked at Narada in disbelief. He was quiet. He lost his balance for a moment and dropped to the ground in *Veerasana*[17]. The earth quaked with his fall. With both his hands on his thighs, he looked up at the sky and roared so hard that the mountains trembled, causing avalanches. His matted hair unleashed itself and Ganga gushed out of it. The wind started to blow a sound of mourning. The trees howled. The Himalayan cats yowled

---

[17] Veerasana – Kneeling yogic pose

long wails. Rudra's matted hair blowing with the wind scrubbed his blood-spitting eyes repeatedly. Mercifully, the third eye was shut. Panic-stricken and distraught Rudra sprang to his feet, pulled some tufts of his hair and broke into *Samhaara Tandava*[18], the dance of horror and death. At some point during those convulsions of agony, he thrashed the *jata*[19] in his hand on the mountaintop. Ascended Virbhadra towering over the mountain. Next emerged Bhadrakali to enable Virbhadra, like all devis do.

Rudra told the personification of his grief, "Go Bhadra, annihilate Daksha, his *yagna* and everyone else who is there. Do not spare anyone! Whoever was there is an accomplice, no matter gods, devas, rishis, gandharvas, yakshas or anyone else. Do not spare Yama. How dare he let this happen!" Virbhadra, with his innumerable hands, heads, and armory, was an army in himself. He led Rudra's army of ganas, bhootas, vetalas, pretas, rakshasas, bhairavas, kshetrapals and others. With Bhadrakali went all her devastating forms and *yoginis*[20] to summon *kaal*. With every breath Rudra exhaled were born more and more ferocious ganas. Shiva was birthing creatures like Brahma. It soon became a sea of an army led by Virbhadra.

As the army started from Kailasa, the earth started a seismic activity, the sky breathed fire and there were meteor showers. The sun looked pale as if it was bamboozled. All scavengers began to make their way toward Kanakhala.

---

[18] Samhaara Tandava – The dance of annihilation
[19] Jata – Tress
[20] Yogini – An aspect of Mahadevi. There are 64 of these sacred feminine forces.

Jackals, hyenas, coyotes on the ground and vultures, ravens in the skies. A swarm of flies, locusts and moths covered the yagna arena. They virtually made a sheet over the *yagna samagri*[21], sacrifice vessels and the *kund*. Brahma, as the head priest, was horror-struck. The *mandapam* erected by Vishwakarma and palaces constructed for guests started to fall apart like twigs. The winds turned ill after so much weeping. Brahma fled to Satya Loka. He knew Mahakaal[22] was on its way. Personified *mantras*[23] despondent with Daksha, cried in protest and absconded from the *yagna shala*[24] into the sky.

When Daksha saw his father, Brahma, abandon him, he went running to Mahavishnu, "Only you can save me Narayana, save me!" Tears coursed down his face, just like Sati's a little while back. The air was filled with screams, "It is time. This is Mahakaal coming for us. Dadhichi's words are soon coming true!" Even Vishnu wasn't untouched by this terror. But he was the only one looking at the scene playing out in front of him with a *tathasta*[25] *bhava*, as a spectator without getting affected by the elemental omens. "You have called this upon yourself Daksha. Sati has killed herself in this yagna *mandapam*, because of your apathy towards her and your disregard for Mahadeva. Do not for a moment imagine that Shiva will tolerate the loss of his love." Narayana was speaking assuredly, "I will fight him, if

---

[21] Yagna samagri – Holy offering at yagnas
[22] Mahakaal – Bringer of kaal. Another name for Shiva in his destructive form
[23] Mantra – A sound, words or phrase repeated during meditation
[24] Yagna Shala – The place built for the purpose of yagna
[25] Tathasta – Neutral spectator

need be, for I have promised to protect this *yagna* of yours, but who am I to protect you from a lover's wrath? I too am culpable for being here. Here where Parashakti had to immolate herself." Daksha and many of his guests started to have inexplicable convulsions. They vomited blood. Their faces turned purple with fear and their bodies trembled, sweating profusely.

Bhadra, enabled by Bhadrakali, and her nine forms, crossed the threshold of Kanakhala. Vishnu blew the thunderous Panchjanaya to gather Indra's massive and highly decorated army, and devas to fight against Virbhadra's army of ganas. But he knew, fight they shall but they stood no chance. Virbhadra was Rudra's that part, which was stabbed directly in his heart, and with that exposed, mutilated, and hemorrhaged, he was only expected to do a macabre dance. Bhadra will stop at nothing. Mahakaal had lost what he valued the most, and felt no distress in losing anything anymore and that is a dangerously drunken place to be in. A power in that place is always invincible. And this was Shiva, god of gods, Mahakaal.

As soon as Virbhadra's army reached Gangadwara, right at the gate, Nandishwara saw Indra of that *manvantara* wearing his usual smirk ahead of his army. Nandi did not wait for anything. Filled with anguish at losing his valuable Sati, and having watched his Rudra in excruciating agony, he leaped at Indra. A torrent of ganas and kshetrapals charged on devas. And Virbhadra moved inwards toward Mahavishnu. On his way to the *yagna* shala, he hacked, pierced, stabbed, clubbed, hewed, plucked, gouged and tore away many a deva. He challenged them by their names and asked them to confront him.

When Bhadra reached Vishnu, they had a quick dialogue where he declared that he would not like to fight Vishnu and implored him to step aside. Vishnu responded by saying, "I have always been Hara's Hari and will continue to be. My supreme love and devotion towards Shiva are not a thing of words. But I am bound by a promise to Daksha, as the protector of his *yagna*. To fight is my only choice, Virbhadra." Then commenced a fierce battle between the towering Virbhadra and the vast Blue One. The almighty Narayana's Saringa and Sudharshana were incapacitated, and garuda wings were singed one after the other. Bhadra was there to sweep everything clean with blood, while Narayana was protecting what still had a chance. The objectives were different. But who could stop that force of deep agony at Shiva's core, of which was born Virbhadra.

The *yagna shala* was destroyed in the rampage. The *kund*, gold and silver urns were flung in the air. The priests were thrown into Ganga. The ganas gorged on the food and vessels filled with milk, honey, and ghee[26] for the rituals and tossed away the rest. They vaulted, ran somersaults, and desecrated the sacrifice, making horrifying sounds. The same people who were either supporting Daksha or choosing to be silent spectators were now prattling nonsense out of fear. Many devas ran back to their homes without giving any fight. Some of them were caught in the air and hacked.

The bhootas and vetalas floated over the *yagna shala*. Bhrigu raised Ribhus from the *yagna* fire to fight the Gana

---

[26] Ghee – clarified butter used in Indian cooking

army, but he was tied to a pole and his beard was torn off. Agni's hands were cut off. Bhaga's eyes were plucked out so he could never bring another morning. Surya's head was kicked hard. Pusha, who was heard laughing at Rudra, was slapped so hard that his teeth fell out. Yama's mace was crushed. Chandra was thumped to the ground like a glowworm. Varun and Vayu were axed. Saraswati's nose was clipped off. Anyone and everyone who did not care to use their prudence, or a sense of judgment to stop what had transpired, were seen as collaborators to the crime with their silence. Anyone who did not oppose the injustice had to pay a price. No matter who and in what capacity. That was Mahadeva's sentence for tormenting the love of his life.

I, as Bhadrakali, was relishing the rivers of blood, quaffing, slaughtering, and hurling gore into the skies. Virbhadra and his ganas hurtled in the direction where Daksha was hiding. Bhadra saw him and dragged a whimpering Daksha out. His clothes soiled by his blood, from vomits and mud on the ground, he looked frail and frightened. But Virbhadra had not come to serve justice, he was there to avenge Sati's death. Bhadra gave a blow on Daksha's neck but, the yogi that Daksha was, his head remained on his shoulder. Bhadra did not like it one bit. He snarled, picked Daksha up and tore his head from his shoulder with his bare hands. Then he threw it toward Bhadrakali like an orb. I tossed it back at Bhadra and he kicked it back to me. We played with Daksha's head to our heart's content. The sky roared with our revenge laughter and with the trumpets of elephants I wore in my earrings. Bhadra kicked the deformed head into the *yagna* fire and walked out of the ravaged *yagna shala*. And so, did I.

Mahadeva appeared with Narada, he was calmer than before. He looked tellingly at Bhadra and Kaali. Everyone alive in that arena dropped on their knees or fell on their faces in the direction of Rudra. People who do not understand love surely understand fear. Brahma flew back from Satya Loka. Vishnu said delicately, "Obeisance Mahakaal, we have sinned by coming to Daksha's *yagna*, and more so by staying here despite his intentions. This is beyond forgiveness. We have been punished Mahadeva! If shame was a currency, we will keep paying with it forever. Mercy Mahadeva, show mercy!" Brahma, with folded hands, said with all humility, "Forgive us Mahakaal, Aadi Yogi. It was my son; I ask for your forgiveness." All the half-dead devas echoed Brahma's plead.

Rudra remained quiet, with a face still with bereavement. He made a hand mudra and brought the dead devas, rishis, and other beings to life, whole and restored. "Where is Daksha, bring his body," said Rudra. Bhadra appeared from somewhere and threw Daksha's headless body in Rudra's feet. "Where is the head?" Rudra asked, like he did not know. "Cooked in the *yagna kund* [27] my lord!" said Bhadra in a tone to suggest deservingly so. "Behead a sacrificial goat and let's give Daksha that head." Rudra brought Daksha back to life with a head that will continually remind him of his vanity, and about Rudra's love and terror both at the same time, till his last drawn breath.

"The only eternal ecstasy is the one of the *atman*.

---

[27] Kund – The vessel in which the fire is ignited and holy offerings are poured

Everything else leads to grief of the mind or body. There is anguish at birth, anguish in sickness of body, mind or soul, and anguish at death. Life is another name for anguish. Dhyana is the only lasting bliss," said Rudra, picking up his lady love's charred body in his arms. He walked and walked and walked for ages, clasping Sati's body close to him. With the passage of time and Sati's profound absence, his grief swallowed him. He was but a memory of Sati in Rudra's devastated body. So much so that he couldn't even see that the body was decomposed, and its parts were dropping hither and thither.

Vishnu came in to release his deity Hara from the clutches of the past. He disposed the charred remains of the body and took him back to Kailasa. Rudra then recommenced his *tapa* that would last for yugas together. Thereafter, he was either a yogi or a rogue doing unimaginable things.

BHAGWATI

CHAPTER 7

BHAGWATI

The Goddess of Feminine Prowess and Justice

Bhagwati – The form of Mahadevi that metamorphizes from a soft power to an exacting, merciless, fearsome warrior, also known as Mahisha Mardini or Durga. The Trishula[1], Sudarshan Chakra[2] and lethal weapon wielding tremendous devi mounted on a lion. She is a warrior queen who transforms from an unseen enabler to a doer when comes the time.

Now was coming the time for me to switch roles. I was to do something that I had classically enabled Hari or Hara for. There were malevolent forces coming forth that would require me to pick brutal weaponry and transform into a warrior goddess, because I and I alone, with all my enablement back with me, could effectuate it. It was time for the enabler to be the doer and the doer to be the enabler.

---

[1] Trishula – Trident
[2] Sudarshan Chakra – The divine discus or wheel of time owned by Mahavishnu

Asuras could never make peace with the fact that the devas ruled all three worlds. They could never appreciate the reason behind the design of the organization called the universe. The supremacy that came with the unsurmountable wealth the asuras always held, if they were also given sovereignty, the universe was sure to slip into a grave disbalance. Irrespective of the creator god's intermittent interventions and amendments, there were yugas in between when the worlds were reigned by asuras, who had hardly proven to be good rulers.

In one such *manvantara* was born Mahishasur. He was one of the most prevailing asuras of ancient history. Mahisha was a love child of a formidable, shape-shifting asura king, named Rambha and Shyamala, a princess who turned into a water buffalo because of a curse. Rambhasur took the form of a male buffalo as his expression of love for Shyamala. Born out of their union was Mahishasur, an asura with a buffalo head. Rambhasur had earned a boon from Agni deva that his son would be the strongest in the three worlds, that he would be the best shapeshifter born, a master of *maya* and completely invincible across the three worlds. Moreover, Mahisha grew up to be further powerful from his extraordinary *tapa*, which resulted in a blessing from Brahma. But like most asuras, he too was consumed by envy and rage for devas since his childhood.

Rambha and Shyamala were in love, but soon an actual buffalo discovered Rambha's truth and impaled him to death. The asura was strong with blessings from Brahma, but he didn't have immunity against animals. Rambha died, and the buffalo chased after the she-buffalo Shyamala. She ran to yakshas of

the *Pipal*[3] tree pleading for protection. Yakshas, who had been friends with Rambha for thousands of years, had developed special care for Shyamala too. They thronged around the she-buffalo and killed the raging buffalo in minutes. Then they built a pyre to cremate their friend Rambha's frayed and cloven body. As the blaze came about, Shyamala, calmly, walked into her dead lover's pyre and immolated herself. But something magical happened! A light emerged from the epicenter of the pyre, it was the half-asura half-buffalo love child of Rambha, who Shyamala was carrying in her womb. He stepped out of the pyre and bellowed, quaking the earth and the sky alike, while his dark black tail flipped hurriedly behind him. He had hooves and huge curved horns as big as tree trunks and he was massive, like a mountain. This was the fulfillment of Agni deva's promise to Rambha. Mahisha was born. But a moment later, another light appeared in the fire. It was a burned asura walking out of the pyre. He was the color of the raw flesh, acquainted faced, only more horrifying. Rambhasur was reborn. Did Agni deva put him back together, wondered the beings watching this unfold in front of them. Or was it because his soul was tormented, for he could not protect his lady love, that he came back to live in wretchedness? Or was it for the love of his son, a blessing just materialized from Agni? Or did his lady love give up her own life to bring him back? Whatsoever it may be, Rambha was soon to earn the name Raktbeej, the blood seed.

Soon Mahisha was rampaging the world. He had earned the boon from Brahma after a long and arduous penance, which lasted so long that the worlds had started to scald with

---

3   Pipal – Or Peepal. Fig tree

its effect. He beseeched Brahma, "Grant me immortality, *Pitamah*! I want to live fearlessly." Brahma explained, "Death is certain. We all have to die one day. Ask for something else Mahisha." "Then make me invincible. Make me the most powerful being across the three *lokas*. No man of any race in *Bhu Loka, Swarga Loka or Patala Loka* should cause my death," then laughing in pure arrogance that reverberated enough to reach me, he said, "There is no woman born in this multiverse who would dare think of causing Mahishasur any harm. Is there? So, let me die at the hands of a woman, *Pitamah*." "So be it!" blessed Brahma. It is the wishes, inadvertent and arbitrary, that make people's destiny. Don't they?

Mahisha did not take too long to conquer Bhu Loka. He and his army controlled by awfully ruthless commanders had butchered everyone in their way. And now he wanted Deva Loka. He sent a ferocious asura as a messenger to Amravati[4], "Indra, be Mahisha's liegeman and live a life of a vassal. At least you will get to live here and keep some shreds of your dignity. Or else choose a certain defeat and lose Amaravati completely, along with your famed pomposity," shouted the enormous asura.

Indra snubbed him off, "My dharma does not allow me to murder you, for you are a mere messenger. Go and tell that Buffalo Mahisha that he is blinded. He cannot see that he is amid a colossal loss of reason. I would like to set that right on the battlefield. Tell him I am coming for him." Indra said what he had to, but then hurriedly sought his Guru Brihaspati, who discussed with Indra his options.

---

[4] Amravati – The capital city of Swarga Loka, the realm of devas

They went together to Brahma to seek advice, who took them to Kailasa to meet Rudra, who in turn suggested that this being the matter of the worlds, Mahavishnu's involvement is of paramount importance.

The messenger informed Mahisha. Asura generals, upon Mahisha's instructions, immediately started to gather their army from far and wide in the multiverse for a war with devas. They also informed their Guru to come and guide them. Mahisha knew Indra's confidence came from the presence of Vishnu by his side. But Mahisha feared nothing, for he had double immunity, "Let us see if he will set me right or I will set that liar, debauch, schemer right! I can do it all by myself but now that I am the ruler of two worlds, soon-to-be the ruler of all three worlds, I will do it with the magnificence they would have never seen before," thundered Mahisha in amusement.

At Vaikuntha, Vishnu said, "To fight is our only option. It is almost always the only choice. All dialogs to evade it are futile. The battlefields keep changing. At most, the fight may alter its appearance, its location or method, but to fight is to stay alive. Therefore, we must go all-out. That is our *dharma*." Consequently, the most brutal armaments of all worlds and the mightiest warriors born in the three worlds stood on either side, lined up to slaughter each other. The devas, with their glorious armor, devastating weapons and rides that were a sight to behold and marvel, self-assured of their immortality, attacked the asuras. Asuras, with their mammoth sizes, ruthless weapons, and violent deportment, stormed on devas as if hell had broken loose. A fierce war broke out. The sky was covered by clouds of arrows, fumes,

and fire from explosives. Soon the field was a turbulent ocean of horrific shrieks by asuras, raging animals participating in the battle, thundering, and clanking of astras, and cries full of agony of limbs and heads coming off, eyes plucked out and bodies melting away. Almost immediately, there were rivers of blood flowing between the sky and earth. Devas summoned their deadliest of weapons and asuras now summoned Maya. Indra, Varuna, Yama had come across Mahisha multiple times in the field, but their weapons were nothing more than a tickle on his giant body. His dreadful commanders were like tigers in a field full of cows. They were plundering the battlefield and hacking the deva's army of gandharvas, kinnaras, yakshas, ganas and others. Through sorcery, occult and shapeshifting, Mahisha and his army had the devas fall in chaos and flee. After trying innumerable times and failing disgracefully, many devas bolted from the battlefield.

Mahisha was now battling Hari and Hara together. Hari was cutting across Mahisha's maya when he attacked garuda's wing who dropped to the ground grimacing in pain. Vishnu attended to him immediately. Now Rudra was engaging Mahisha directly, but his trident wasn't making a single dent in Mahisha's body. Vishnu sprang back and covered Mahisha in a wall of arrows, but Mahisha emerged unscathed. Then he struck Vishnu back with his Parigha[5], an iron bludgeon, and Vishnu fell to the ground with the impact. The earth shuddered. Upon watching this, some more devas left the field in utter panic. Mahisha hurled some dark *shakti* on Rudra, which could cremate a whole

---

5   Parigha – an iron bludgeon used as a weapon

planet. Nandi and Mahisha locked horns while Rudra dusted off the effect of the sorcery. Vishnu went up again. Mahisha attacked him as a buffalo who transformed into a lion. Hari prepared to cast his Sudarshan at the lion as large as a mountain when Mahisha swiftly transformed back into a buffalo and dug his horns into Vishnu's chest. Two fountains of Hari's blood sprayed out of his blue body. Garuda flew in like magic and took Vishnu straight to Vaikuntha, for treatment and recovery. Rudra gathered Mahishasur was unconquerable, and this was not coming to an end any time soon, certainly not in this battle, so he too took to Kailasa.

Now there was no fence between the asuras and devas. Mahisha's army crushed the devas army like a thunderstorm crushing an open grassland. The war that lasted for over a hundred years left devas terrorized, humiliated, homeless and robbed of all their riches and celestial possessions. Mahisha was invincible.

Devas roamed in jungles and deserts, hiding their face in shame and lived in caves. Then came a time when they went to Brahma again, "O generous *Pitamah*, how can you let this happen to your children? He sits on my throne in Amravati, wreaking havoc on all three worlds. He has taken away our benedictions from Ksheer Sagar *manthan*, our celestial animals. Even our women are his captives. What are we to do? Will you watch silently? If nothing else dear father, at least think of the order of this universe! After all, what has happened is a result of your boon to Mahisha." cried Indra after losing his conceit.

Brahma inhaled sharply, "Oh, let us not talk about the

manthan, Indra. Asuras were misled. Have we forgotten that? The tide has turned. Which is the very nature of time. It is loyal to no one. Let me be fair, for both devas and asuras are my children. As for the boon, I bless *tapa*, no matter what race, disposition, or gender. Quite like how Agni did, and now suffers from his own blessing. But having said that, what Mahisha has done with his powers, what he has done to you and other devas, is pure evil and against the way of the worlds. I do not know what to do, for he is too powerful even for the gods. So I propose we all take this up to Sri Hari once again." They all went to Vaikuntha, where Rudra joined the summit once again.

"We fought him and failed at it. So far, we have all been enabled by Aadi Shakti, Durga Bhuvneshwari. When she voices within our beings, she is Saraswati, she is Maya. When she devours, she is Chandika, she is Ambika. When she protects, she is Uma, she is Durga. In entirety, she is Bhagwati. Look at history closely and you will know that it was Bhagwati's grace all along that we fought many a battle and came out triumphant. All sorts of battles! Both inwards and outwards.", professed Mahavishnu. "Now is the time we follow the mother goddess to victory. Let us get together with folded hands, beckon the queen of the cosmos, offer her all that we have in us, and implore her to protect the worlds as we know it. Only Devi Bhagwati can slay Mahishasur," explained the Jagannath[6] Narayana.

I smiled at this and blew my breath at Vaikuntha. The fragrance in the air was calming to one and all. They somehow now knew that the bane was at its culmination

---

6   Jagannath – The lord of the universe. Vishnu

and the auspicious period was about to begin. Sri Hari had barely finished speaking about me when a bright ruby-colored light emanated from Brahma's brows and stood like a blaze in the heart of the room. Next emerged from Shiva's face, his Shakti like a pillar of silver light. It was dazzling and arresting as it merged with the light from Brahma. Then Vishnu's Shakti poured out from his face in a resplendent blue and melted itself in the mother dynamo upright before them. It was the unification of three enormous *Shaktis* of *Rajas, Tamas and Sattva*.

Now it was blindingly bright for even Gods. As everyone struggled to watch, bemused and awestruck, the devas emitted their Shaktis into the luminescence which was shaping up before them. The luminosity was me. From the formless pure energy, I the goddess of the universe, the mother of all causes, Durga was manifested. I stood there in front of them mounted on my lion, wielding eighteen arms, each carrying dreadful weapons of destruction. That form of mine was extraordinarily enchanting. It was so numbingly stunning that it redefined the very definition of beauty. Everyone in that room, including the *Trimurti*[7], was captivated and dazed. Sri Hari gathered himself and requested everyone to give up their best resources and weaponries on my feet. Vishnu gave me his Sudarshan *Chakra*, Shiva gave me his *Trishula*, Indra gave me his *Vajra*[8] and likewise, all the other devas gave me what was most precious to them.

---

[7] Trimurti – Brahma, Vishnu and Shiva together
[8] Vajra – Thunderbolt

"Kaal! Time is the only perpetual power. Look how it brings the mightiest to the lowest point and carries the hopeless to the top of the worlds," I declared to all around me and laughed blaringly. My laughter caused the ocean to rise and fall, the earth shook enough to displace the rivers and highlands developed cracks. Devas dropped on their faces before me. I blessed them and left for Amravati. Mahisha had heard my laughter. He did not quite like anyone's voice louder than his own. He asked his danavas[9] to find out who had the nerve of this measure. Asuras soon found the source. They saw me in my *tamas* form concocting for the war, drinking what they thought was wine from Kubera's goblet.

They scooted back to Mahisha and reported what they had seen. "She is so beautiful and so terrifying at the same time! She wears blood red, sits astride a lion, swirls, and sips wine like a true warrior. She has so many arms that we could not count out of terror. Or was it her refulgence, which blinds not only the eyes but also the mind! She wears exceptional jewelry. The kind we have never seen. Toys with her weapons and skulls. She has thick black tresses that hang like a cape behind her. She throws her head back and laughs, not sure about what. That is the laughter we get to hear in Amravati, my lord. Her beauty is petrifying!"

A soft smile broke on Mahisha jagged face, and he told his generals, "From the description of her, she seems befitting to be my queen. Go get her to me with veneration.

---

[9] Danavas – A race of Asuras

Do not harm her. Cajole her, tell her about me and urge her to come to Amravati and take her place next to me. If she denies, then bring her by force. But I repeat, do not harm her in any way." The generals went across, found Devi in a secluded place, spoke to her, and came back empty-handed. "She is not relenting, my lord. She told me to tell you the unspeakable. She said that your time is up! And that she is kaal herself. She said I should ask you to scurry away to Patala Loka where you belong. And that you are sinister and have put devas out of their home, denying them their share of *yagnas* and making the world an ominous place," reported the general speedily out of distress with his head hanging low. Some in Mahisha's court were enraged to hear this, while many others opined this was a woman's way to fuel his interest further but only a few thought it as a warning sign. A refusal is usually not understood by menfolk. They are either infuriated or stoked.

Vaskala and Durmukha were sent to me. The presumptuous fools, who were following their king's directives blindly, were slain by me. They were not willing to go back shorn of me, so I was left with no choice. I was tickled by their toys for weapons, but eventually, the little play had to end. Then were sent Chikasura and Tamrasura, who were both stronger than the previous duo and more unwise than them. I had no option but to neutralize them too. Despite me telling them repeatedly that it was not them I had any hostility towards, I only wanted Mahisha to vacate Amravati and leave with his asura clan, but they did not give in. Then came Asiloma and Vidalakhya, who were wise and understood the misplaced arrogance of their king. Notwithstanding that fact, they urged me to fight them because that was their *dharma*. I had to slay them too, albeit reluctantly. It was awfully demanding to get into these unwelcome skirmishes with people who did not matter or did not deserve to die. All because of one man's conceit, his vanity, his hunger for supremacy.

Finally came the day when Mahisha appeared in front of me. The shapeshifter came in the form of a flamboyant human wearing silk and jewels. He was still optimistic, despite so many bloodbaths and losses of his commanders and other asuras. Self-importance is a peculiar enemy. It lives within the conscience and eats up the insides slowly and soundlessly. The mighty and unsurmountable Mahisha who once defeated the Gods was so weak for a woman. In his poor mental health, he could not accept the naked truth dancing in front of him like *kaal*.

"Take me for your *vara*, Devi. We will rule the three worlds together. Your place is next to me on my throne and in my bed. I will be your slave forever!" said a visibly forlorn Mahisha. "You do not bear the eye to recognize me, you fool. I am Bhagwati, Aadi Shakti, Durga, the ultimate force of the universe. At the far end of the universe, above all other *lokas* is my throne in Manidweepa[10], where you can never even dream of reaching. What good is your little throne to me? I am formless and you are talking of pleasures of body to me. What depravity! I had to take this form only to rid the worlds of you. Go away and I will let you live. Go to Patala Loka, which is rightfully your home. You have brought

---

[10] Manidweepa – The abode of Mahadevi

enough muddle in the order of the worlds. The worlds are ominous place because of you. Leave or prepare to die," I boomed at him. Now a vexed Mahisha transformed himself into half a buffalo. He had finally accepted my truth. And by virtue of that, his own truth. He snorted, bellowed, flicked his tail, and scoured his hooves to the ground, posturing to attack. For now, I was only defending.

He sent a volley of arrows at me; I swept them away. Durdhara, Trinetra, and Andhaka joined him swiftly. One of them shot an arrow, which was but a slight sting on me. In return, I blew him up into thin shreds. Another one shot an arrow laced with sorcery. Only if he could see beyond the woman I was to his three material eyes, he would have seen I was the Maya he had tried to decipher and study for his lifetime. The third one tried to get into combat with my lion, who tore opened his chest.

Mahisha kept aiming arrows at me. I threw my *gada* at him, which hit him at the center of his chest and was felled to the ground. Now he picked a mace but again, my lion came in between him and me and raked him with his claws and talons. Mahisha changed his form to a lion, and they both got into a combat. I struck him with a poisonous arrow, forcing him to come back to his original form. But no, he turned into a bull-elephant, a mad elephant who was jilted and furious. My lion pounced on the elephant's neck, dug his talons in, gnawed at him and mauled him. Wincing with pain, he turned into a large bird, Sarabha. With talons and beak like blades, it hovered around me and my lion making an ear-splittingly loud cry. I cleaved its lightning-fast wings. Now it finally shape-shifted into a buffalo and bellowed, "Woman, I will drink your blood! I see you for who you are now!" "At last, you see me! What do you think I have been drunken on, Mahisha? This is Asura blood. And yours will delight me the most!" I laughed, brandishing the goblet Kubera gave to me.

Now finally, to finish the battle, I took the offensive and turned into an assailant. I picked my trident as Mahisha was changing forms every moment, from one being to another. I could feel my eyes spitting red fire. I aimed and struck it in Mahisha's chest directly. He fell to the ground insensible, with blood gushing from his chest. But he rose in the air rapidly and kicked me in my face with his hooves. Then he spiked me and hit me repetitively till I was covered in my own blood. Now my blood was dropping from my brows into my eyes and my hairline was marked crimson. My eyes, however, emitted a blue light, for I had the Sudarshan *Chakra* whirling over my index finger. I held it up in the air and announced to Mahisha, "You are irredeemable, Mahisha. Look, this is your *kaal* coming for you!" and flicked my wrist to release the *chakra*. In moments, his head was removed from his neck, liberating a geyser of blood. His body swayed and then dropped with a massive thud. And that was how *dharma* returned to the three worlds.

Mahisha committed too many criminalities for one lifetime, but the biggest of all was regrettably corrected only by his death at my hands. And that was his profound inability to see the enabler behind every doer, the feminine within every masculine, the application inside the paraphernalia, the flesh and blood holding the bones together, Shakti behind Purusha.

UMA

CHAPTER 8

UMA

The Goddess of Penance and Marital Permanence

Uma – Also known as Parvati and Maha Gauri, or Shail Suta, the daughter of the mountain. The form of Mahadevi whose dominion is not of wars, wins or public affairs but of her wholeheartedness and commitment towards her loved ones. She is solely the most potent lover who stimulated a rogue Rudra out of his ascetic isolations and transformed him into Sundar Murti[1] Shankara[2]. She is the consort, wife and mother whose powers reside in her devotion.

After losing Sati, the same Kailasa that blossomed, chirruped, and smiled back at Rudra, when it was his love nest, was now a withered and weepy cold dessert. Only if he could undo his feelings which had left him half-finished forever. Only if he could bring back the

---

[1] Sundar Murti – A beautiful form of Shiva
[2] Shankara – The householder form of Shiva

day he agreed to marry Sati and gave up the life he had known before her. There were times when he fell silent and submitted to his fate, and there were times when he howled in pure agony, haunted by the moments spent with Sati. Grief reveals itself in strange ways. Rudra was burning from within and did many obnoxious things that would not have transpired had Sati been with him. He was tormented to the point where many called him delirious or a rogue. Rudra needed a sanctuary, so he tried going back to his original love, *Yog*. One step at a time, he moved towards his safe house and along took his memories of Sati. *Yog* took him back without any protests. His heart boomed with emptiness, but gradually Rudra walked, talked, and lived *Yog*.

Mena and her husband, King Himalaya, had been worshiping me for a long time. They were a couple bursting with love and reverence for each other, hoping to build a family together but could not. Meanwhile, Tarakasur had been creating massive disruption for devas. He did an unprecedented *tapa* to get Brahma to bless him. There was no conjecturing needed when he asked Brahma for what almost everyone asks for. Material life! He had earned himself two boons. One, that he will be the strongest of all beings there are. And two, that he would die only at the hands of Rudra's son, who everyone knew had travelled light years away from material world.

Devas got together to worship me, for they did not know how else to reach me. They were accompanied by Brahma and Mahavishnu in their prayers, who knew about my abode Manidweepa but then it was me who

once took them across the galaxy on my *vimana* to show them a glimpse of other universes, other Vishnus, and the other Brahmas. They also saw the other Rudra. And my home. When they reached close to my bedecked throne at Manidweepa, they were startled to see their own bodies transform into female forms. But that is a story I will tell some other time.

Consequently, I appeared in front of devas black as ever, mounted on my lion. They all dropped on the ground, "O Bhuvneshwari, Jagadamba Durga, please be born on Bhu Loka! Be Rudra's wife again. O Omniscient Mahadevi, you very well know what is happening with him. Rudra must become Shankara. And Tarakasur needs to be neutralized". I responded, "Mena and Himachal have been worshiping me for twenty-seven years in Aushadhiprastha[3]. Also, when Sati died, she had wished mutely to be born as Mena's daughter. Everything has fallen in the right places now. I will be born," and I disappeared. Then I went to Mena and asked her to choose her boon. Overawed, she asked me for a hundred strong and valiant sons, and me as her daughter. "So be it!" I affirmed. It was time anyway I took a form to be with my Shiva. Himachal and Mena together gave birth to a hundred gallant mountains before I was conceived by Mena. It was a difficult pregnancy. And it had to be, for she was carrying me inside her womb. Himachal loved and cared for his wife like she was the chest of a treasure. On the night of labor, first I streamed out of Mena as a vision for a human eye and then as a human child. I, Durga Bhawani,

---

[3] Aushadhiprastha – The capital city of Himavat, kingdom of Himachal

was born as a human baby.

A dark girl child with rare lotus blue eyes was named Parvati, the daughter of the dignified parvat Himachal. Just like *prakriti* does not need education and has primeval knowledge to orchestrate every fragment in the universe to perfection and precisely in time, the girl too was born with ancient knowledge from her previous birth as Sati. She knew the purpose of her life and *tapa* came naturally to her. As a little girl, she meditated on Shiva and continued the penance from her previous life, only more severe and prolonged. So laborious for her tender age that she gained the name U-ma from people's admiration and wonder. Strenuous enough to not consume even a leaf for months together, gaining herself the name A-parna.

Meanwhile, Rudra was moving locations every so often, or was he unwittingly coming closer to Uma's location as she was coming of age! Once, when Himachal heard that Rudra had camped in his area, he went to pay his respects and took Rudra's greatest devotee Uma with him. He requested Rudra to let him assist while his camp was in the area. When he introduced his daughter Uma to him, Rudra broke into cold sweats. One look at her and he recognized instantly that Uma was his Sati. The minute Uma offered to help with daily chores at the camp, his heart fluttered with bliss it had forgotten. That was all Rudra wanted, to be around his Sati who was now Uma. He accepted with a nod, but at the same time, the agony of losing Sati was as raw as ever. Aadi Yogi Shiva, the lord of annihilation was terrorized by the misery and despair that love was capable of bringing.

Uma's presence wasn't making things any simpler for

Rudra when Kama was sent by devas with Rati and Vasant to do their enchantments on Rudra. Kama covered himself behind a bush, looking for the safest opening to shoot his love arrow at Rudra. He watched as Uma mopped the entire camp. Next, she took baskets full of flowers and fruits and kept them near Rudra. Then she brought some hot water from the fire built nearby and walked towards Rudra. Kama took his position. Rudra had been in *dhyana* for weeks. Sati was wiping his feet with a warm damp cloth when Kama saw this as an opportunity and shot the arrow. He assumed with Uma's scent everywhere and beauty so bewitching close to him bodily, Rudra's attention would not go elsewhere. And he was partly right. Uma's touch on Rudra's body challenged his Dhyana, for only she owned a power that great. It was a tender reminder of his intimate moments with Sati. The sweetest of memoirs become ruminations of agony when one's love is slashed brusquely. Which is what had happened with Rudra and Sati. Rudra's third eye opened in a flash and the fire leaping out of it charred Kama. In moments, he was but a pile of ash. A shaken Rati shrieked in pain and wailed endlessly. Uma had already dropped what she was doing and quietly left the camp as Rudra watched her go. The pain of watching her leave. Again!

This was ordained, it had to happen, Rati," said Indra, who was watching everything. Rudra, frustrated with these plots, said, "How did it come to this? This whole conspiracy was unnecessary. I am Shiva! Bhagwati and I are beyond the need for Kama, Rati, or Vasanta. We have been lovers from the beginning of time, long-long before any of you were born. And we will be lovers forever. Together or separated,

we are devoted and unfailing. Look what your antics have brought upon you all. Now how can love depart from this already mortal world! Kama will have to live in spirit. He will be born in a body again in the age of Krishna, as his blue son Pradyumna. That is when you too will be born, Rati, and you both can be together."

Uma continued her searing *tapa* in another place in the wilderness. A *tapa* that the universe had not seen before. The refulgent fire of which touched other *lokas*. She was burning from within and with her was burning the entire cosmos. No one dared to say anything to Rudra this time. Brahma and Vishnu were the ones to plan and plot the last time and were still paying in shame. And devas were too scared after watching Kama's end. So, Narada went to Shiva and told him as it was, "Obeisance Aadi Yogi Mahadeva. I am here to tell you about Tarakasur. He is burning your creation, Aadidev[4]. You are aware, he has boons, and he cannot be neutralized unless your son does it. If not for yourself, then for this creation, but please marry Devi Uma. O Purusha, Chandra is from your mind and Surya from your eyes, Prithvi from your feet and Agni came from your mouth, your breath is Vayu, and your head is Aakash, time is your motion Mahadev and Dharma is your heart. Oh Shiva, save your own creation."

Rudra did not want them to beg or plot anymore. He told Narada, "Leave it with me. You know what happened the last time I married. Let me understand Parvati's mind once. I do not want to go through the same misery again."

---

4   Adidev – The first deva. Another name for Shiva

Shiva went disguised as Jatila, and tested Uma's love for him. He confirmed what was apparent to the entire cosmos and was stumped to find the depth of her adulation. Or was he simply reminded of Sati's love for him? This was his Sati, now as Uma. Rudra sighed, "I am done pretending that I do not need you. Truth is, I turned into a rogue without you, my love. I am somehow imperfect, insufficient, incomplete, a little less than whole without you Uma", said Rudra bowing his head to Parvati. A *yogini's* penance, her immortal love, one life after another, was about to turn Aadi Yogi into a *bhogi*[5] once again. Uma's resolve was about to turn Rudra into Shankara. She knew it would be their unfailing, passionate, committed, and infinite love that would inspire human hearts for many a yuga. For also it was only their unification that could birth a life potent enough to keep the universe going. "Take me as your wife, Rudra. Go to my father and ask for me. This time we will be together forever!"

Uma went home to announce the end of her *tapa*. Rudra being Rudra could never follow the customs as they were. He took the form of a dancer named Sunartaka and performed for Mena and Himachal. They were muddled and transfixed in equal measures. At the end of the performance, Rudra asked for Sati's hand as alms. They figured it was Shiva after he had disappeared. Many more muddles later, finally Rudra was sent a letter of betrothal to confirm his wedding with Uma. Mena had put together the best of jewelry and finery for Uma while Himalaya was busy

---

5   Bhogi – An indulgent person

inviting the guests and having the city readied and dressed up like never before. All the mountains, rivers, rishis, and royalty were invited. Shiva, on the other hand, had put Narada in charge of invitations and mediation between the groom's side and the bride's side.

After all the rituals that Vishnu personally oversaw this time, Rudra's wedding procession started from Kailasa. It was the largest and the mightiest wedding parade anywhere in the universe. Narada had reached Uma's house beforehand to help and assist Mena and Himachal. As the convoy reached the gates of the city, Mena watching from the terrace of her palace saw magnificent Devas making the entry one after the other on their divine rides. Erudite and radiant rishis and munis were showering blessings and singing hymns. She saw Brahma and Saraswati on a swan, followed by Vishnu and Lakshmi on *Garuda*. Their luminous bodies, perfumed presence, unearthly jewels and silken garments, Mena could not have imagined anything like this. That is the limitation with familiarity and appropriateness. When something unfamiliar aligns with people's classification of what is appropriate, they accept it. When it does not, they reject it. Mena was overflowing with gratitude, her hands folded on her chest and eyes welled up with absolute joy, until a moment before she laid her eyes on Rudra. Right behind Vishnu, was Rudra. He arrived riding a snuffling Nandi, surrounded by his demented, deformed ganas, aghoris, pretas, bhootas and many other terrorizing creatures.

What Mena saw was a five-headed, nine feet tall Rudra with three frenzied eyes on each face. He was hump-backed, coated with thick ash and snakes hissed around his neck,

biceps, and ankles. He wore an elephant skin dripping with blood, fastened by another snake on his waist. His dreadlocked hair was sloppily piled up on his head with a piece of moon stuck on it. He was holding his *Trishula* and a skull, with Pinaka on one of his shoulders. In place of his family, he was surrounded by ganas. Some of them did not have any bones in their limbs that came out of unusual parts in their bodies. Some were missing limbs altogether. Some had multiple faces. Some had none. Some had no eyes, while others had ten of them. Some had deformed faces with features in the wrong places or should we say unfamiliar places. Some had only one eye hanging by a tentacle on top of their heads. Some were green in color, and some were totally white. Some had horns. Some had fangs. They were not only distorted but seemed profane and spoke a language no one understood. They sounded abusive and uncouth. As they reached the wedding arena, the air was full of shouting, yodeling, and howling. Some of the betalas were floating in the air, hissing, and making frightening sounds. There was also Chandi lurking behind in her most horrifying form.

As Hari and Lakshmi, who were right ahead of Rudra, alighted, and garuda turned back, the snakes draped around Rudra's body started to flee. Bolted off the snake around the waist of Rudra, making the hide on his midriff drop to his feet. Now Rudra stood there at the entranceway of his soon-to-be father-in-law's house majestically naked. And the drunken ganas yodeled harder. Witnessing a trail of horrifying scenes without batting an eyelid, Mena fainted. What ensued was a commotion. The ladies in the gathering

started to move backward out of revulsion.

Uma was informed about it by one of her *sakhis*, "Your mother has fainted Uma. Rudra looks appalling!" Mena was attended to. Vishnu himself was next to her. Meanwhile, Uma requested Narada to arrange a private meeting with Rudra before the wedding ceremonies began. Parvati beckoned me in her consciousness and then wore an equally petrifying form with Chandrakhanda, a piece of moon on her hair. She looked every bit like me and wielded ten arms. Holding some weapons of destruction, as also some gears of peace, she prowled to Rudra. "My eternal love Shiva, what do you choose? Tell me." Rudra was not at all surprised to see Uma as Bhagwati. "I choose you, in every form, Bhagwati. And so do you. However, I had to know if Mena and Himachal would appreciate me with all my oddities. Will they gladly give me their daughter knowing who I am, or have been in your absence? I want them to know my foulest. And it is only fitting that they do. So, I have exposed to them all I could. Did you not say this time we will be together forever! I am only confirming that, Uma," elucidated Rudra. Uma beamed at this, "My parents in this life have loved me over my two lives. They are virtuous people and I understand them completely. Now that they have seen the terrible Rudra, I implore you to reveal the gentle and benevolent Shankara. I urge you to make this marriage procession nobler and come forward as my groom. Give them a sighting of my Sundar Murti!" Mahadeva accepted it graciously.

Rudra was then dressed up by Saptarishis' wives. He turned up as a groom he should have been in the first place. He stood tall and glorious, with his head at the same level as those of the horses in the procession. Shankara wore silks, gold, gems, and unguents. He also adorned a gentle and cheery face like a Magnolia. With an emotionally moved and teary Narada on his side, he went to Mena, who was standing next to Hari at the gateway. She saw her magnificent son-in-law and wept with joy, "Oh, how blessed I and Himachal are, lord of the lords Rudra!" She did Rudra's aarti with fire and welcomed him inside the palace. By the way she was watching Rudra, one could tell that her heart was bouncing with bliss.

    There were Vedas and Mantras personified singing hymns. The sky was resonant with the music by gandharvas. Apsaras who had come down with Indra were dancing gracefully. Everything was auspicious when I arrived as Parvati draped in a scarlet silk raiment. I wore a dot of vermillion and saffron on my forehead and I knew I was glistening with diamonds, rubies, emeralds, and pearls. My body as Uma was scented with musk and sandal. The lotus and jasmine buds woven in my hair were livelier than ever before. The wedding ceremonies began and lasted for a few days. Uma locked her eyes with Rudra every so often, and his impatience was not obscured at all. We stole glances wherever and whenever we could and there was so much cheer around Himachal's house. He was seen dripping tears of joy at many rituals. The royal cooks had arranged the most lip-smacking food for every ceremony. Flowers and festoons, *Omkara*[6] in the mornings, lamps, and stars in the twilight sky, it seemed the heavens had come down to Himachal's abode. To conclude, at the end of all the

---

6   Omkara – The primordial sound from which the whole universe was created

wedding rituals and prayers, Rudra marked Uma's hair with vermillion. Vishnu was overseeing everything. Rudra did all the offerings to Brahma, including pots full of grains and a cow, the principal gift to the brahman who was the official priest for the wedding. As Saraswati, Lakshmi and all the seven rishi wives teased the newlyweds with suggestive yarns, Mena and Himachal performed some more rituals to send off their beloved daughter.

Rudra assisted Uma as she mounted Nandi, who was grinning giddily at the commencement of Shiva-Shakti re-union. She merrily took Rudra's Damaru above her head and played it, to declare her involvement in his things of joy. My lion watched this with me from above, tickled at Uma's understated conquest. Then Uma held her favorite blue lotus in one hand, suggesting her blissful reliance on her lover and husband, Rudra. And a trident in another hand, signifying her detached individuality. Authority in one hand and compassion in another. Powerful yet stoic daughter of the august Himachal and lovely Mena, Uma, also called Parvati was the goddess of the discipline of discovering one's individuality within the permanence of marital bliss.

Over time, Parvati and Rudra had two children, Kartikeya and Ganesha. Kartikeya, who at the tender age of seven, with the help of divine weapons from Gods and most significantly the one presented by his mother Uma, a spear called Vel enshrined by my *shakti*, slayed Tarkasur.

Parvati doted on both of her sons, cherished them, protected them fiercely, and raised them to be the ideals for the worlds to emulate. Kartikeya was the tallest keeper of *dharma* and a warrior that the worlds had never seen before, and Ganesha was the personification of applied intellect and guiding light for the worlds. But neither of them was conceived or carried by Parvati in her body. Uma carved the very definition of motherhood, which has little to do with conceiving or birthing a child. But then, that is a tale for another time.

AMBIKA

CHAPTER 9

AMBIKA
The Warrior Goddess

Ambika: Also known as Kalika, Chandika, Chamunda or Durga. The form of Mahadevi when she steps out of her blissful love nest, puts her own life aside and wears an awe-inspiring, indomitable, often blood-curdling form to protect her creation from evil. She is the deliverance from manumission and maladies of mind and body.

The wheel of time spun around, but the disposition of people born with flesh and blood did not vary too much. Men of all races and species have one thing in common: they seek power, pleasure, and immortality. Not necessarily in the same order though. Hunger for these desires bring sickness, more so when God's own protegé become drunk on power, pursue pleasure, and come back to threaten them. Such was the account of

Rambhasur, an erudite albeit not so wise *tapasvi*[1]. He was reborn from his own pyre, did more of tapa until he was blessed by Mahadeva with a rare boon and was named Raktbeej, the blood-seed. Each drop of his blood dropped on earth was a seed that would birth an entire new Raktbeej.

Manvantaras later were born two asura brothers, named Shumbha and Nishumbha, who sought nothing unfamiliar. They chased the same unquenchable desire for deathlessness. And power, which they presumed was the fiefdom of men. The brothers performed excruciating tapa at Brahma's Lake in Pushkar, which lasted over ten thousand years. They did not eat, sip water and barely breathed. I am always astounded by how they give up living for yugas in *tapa*, only to gain more yugas, when there was so much more they could have accomplished with their lives, or tapa.

"Death is inevitable! I too will die the day this multiverse has lived its age. Ask for something else, asuras," said Brahma, repeating himself to two new asuras. "Then *Pitamah*, bless us that no man of any race or kind, of any world, a beast, bird or fish should cause us death. Let us exclude women, as no woman born anywhere can cause us any harm," said the naïve asura brothers. Amused Brahma granted, "So be it!" thinking that this too shall be put to a proper end by Rajeshwari Durga. Brahma too, like me, was reminded of Mahisha's life, his ominous desires, the gloom he fetched and its culmination at my hands. He could clearly envisage the age of misfortune that was to unveil

---

[1] Tapasvi – An ascetic

itself with Shumbha and Nishumbha's wishes.

History has a wicked habit of repeating itself. Shumbha and Nishumbha did precisely what Mahisha had, even though they smugly believed they were the first ones to attain a boon like that. Another horrid irony about history is that its lessons are generally lost. Barring the creator who has lived long enough to see all seasons through the aging of the universe. The brothers conquered Bhu Loka, developed an ocean of an army of danavas and rakshasas of all sorts, and all the worlds. Even the human empires of the earth joined them either to placate their insatiability, or for the fear of asuras. The indestructible Raktbeej too joined the asura king with his enormous army of two *aksauhinis*. Subsequently, they invaded Amravati as well, overcoming the devas who fought valiantly but lost and fled chagrined. Once again, asuras declared themselves the rulers of the three worlds and the era of asuras began. Once again, they became the masters of the elements, time and destiny.

Yet again devas roamed in jungles and deserts for thousands of years, humiliated and frightened of getting hunted down. When they couldn't live with the dismal failure anymore, they gathered the courage to see their guru and sought direction. Brihaspati told devas the story of Mahishasur and the great war between the devas and asuras of the earlier *manvantara*. "Uma, Rudra's wife, and Himachal's daughter, is Bhagwati on Bhu Loka in her full form. She lives in the Himalayas, with Rudra. Go and meditate on her. If there is a power who can bring you salvation, it is her! She is the Goddess of all Gods. She is kaal herself, she births and ends time." I heard Brihaspati and not so far along, I

heard devas' chants of my *beej mantra*[2] till the end of the universe. And so did Uma.

The dark devi Uma, immensely beautiful and infinitely fearsome in equal measures, made herself apparent to devas astride her giant beast. Upon hearing devas' account, Uma grew blacker. She shuddered, rumbled like lightning, and exuded another devi, who was identical to her, only white like Champaka flower. "Suras, I am Kalika, and this is Ambika, the warrior goddesses that your universe will never forget from this day on!"

At Amravati, the same inanity repeated itself. Yet again, the asuras mistook Devis' loveliness for weakness. Yet again, their puny minds could only envision devis as objects for desire. Yet again, drunk on their transient power, they failed to see the truth of Durga's sovereignty. Only this time Ambika expressed interest in marrying Shumbha, but with a condition. She announced a test for the worthy groom. "Tell Shumbha to conquer me in the battlefield first!" giggled Ambika, telling Shumbha's messenger Sugriva, who was foolish enough to propose the empress of the galaxies to be the queen of some worlds by marrying Shumbha.

This was the beginning of the bloodiest and grisliest war in many *manvantaras*. The mighty Dhumralochana was sent with an army of sixty thousand to fight with two goddess warriors. Right after he was done speaking his profanity to Kalika and lifted his Parigha to attack her, she simply roared at him revealing her fangs, and Dhumralochana was reduced to a mound of ash. So were most of his soldiers.

---

[2] Beej Mantra – Seed Mantra. Sounds endowed with powers

Next, Shumbha sent Chanda and Munda with the goal of bringing the lovely Ambika, and killing her dreadful aid, Kalika. But before they could comprehend much, they were tethered by their necks in a noose of light. And Kalika cleaved their heads off their shoulders, earning herself the name Chamunda. Out of Devi Ambika was then raised Bhadrakali, the same name of terror that smote the city of Kanakhala to a pulp at the death of Sati.

Millions of asuras were hacked and there were rivers of blood flowing. Bhadra was quaffing it ravenously and hurling it at other asuras for amusement. Amravati was a sludge of blood and gore. Now was sent the mightiest of all, Raktbeej, with one *aksauhini* large army. Also, Shumbha and Nishumbha followed him with their elitest of warriors, Kambojas and Kalakeyas to fight the three women, Ambika, Kalika and Bhadra. That was when the *shaktis* of the gods and devas materialized on the battlefield. Brahmi of Brahma, Vaishnavi[3] of Vishnu, Shiva's Maheshwari, Shankari of Shankar, Kaumari of Kartikeya, Indrani of Indra, Varahi of Varaha, Narsimhi of Narshimha and Shaktis of Yama, Kubera, Surya, Som, Vayu, Agni, Varuna and every other deva ascended at the battlefield. The asura warriors were watching stunned, gaping at so many warrior goddesses hacking and hewing heads and limbs like bottle gourds in a farm. They stood horrified.

Kalika had now grown darker and to the size of Bhadrakali. Together they were ululating, drilling terror in the hearts of the asuras and feeding on columns after

---

[3] Vaishnavi – Another name for Lakshmi, a form of Mahadevi

columns of their army. Ambika was demolishing *aksauhinis* with a deluge of lethal arrows. Brahmi was sprinkling enchanted water from her *kamandala*[4] which burned asuras to ashes. Narsimhi was ripping asuras' chests and tearing their hearts out. Maheshwari's bull was crushing, impaling, and kicking hooves into the asuras' faces. Vaishnavi's firewheel was beheading thousands without an alarm, and her mace had mauled legions. A warfare of this measure and ruthlessness in battlefield was unprecedented. Asuras could not believe what they were witnessing.

That was when Raktbeej saw Vaishnavi. He attacked her as she was gliding above the battlefield on her garuda. Vaishnavi released the fire wheel at him, which sliced his chest, unleashing a fountain of his blood. He boomed in laughter as every drop of his blood that touched the earth birthed a new Raktbeej. Each one as malicious as him. In a moment, there were thousands of new ghastly Raktbeejs. This was the rare boon he had earned from Shiva becoming apparent to all. Now anxious Indrani attacked him with her Vajra and another scarlet stream of blood erupted from him, making more of Raktbeejs. There was panic! Ambika said to Kalika, "Devi, you will have to drink every last drop of Raktbeej's blood. Not a single drop of his ominous blood must impregnate Bhoomi. As I and other Shaktis hack the army of Raktbeejs, to the last one of them, you need to prevail over them like *Akasha*[5]. We must close what Shiva had once started with this protégé of his!" As Kalika heard Ambika, her

---

4   Kamandala – A small water container with a handle on the top
5   Akasha – Sky

roaring laughter sent a wave of horror across the battlefield. What ensued was an unbridled and tumultuous wrath.

    Ambika and all other Shaktis shredded each and every Raktbeej to ribbons, as Kalika slurped their blood till their bodies were pale and hollow. Then Ambika and Kalika reached the original one. Ambika thundered like lightning with her lotus face glistening with streaks of blood all over it and removed Raktbeej's head from his shoulder. Kalika grabbed both the head and body, drank hungrily, drained it dry and flung his headless body in one direction and head in another which went tumbling down the mountain. Ambika raised her conch and blew a blast as Kalika, now swollen with asura blood and gore, was dancing the dance of death. There was devastation all around, but Shumbha and Nishumbha's conceit was not still gratified. They attacked Ambika and Kalika.

    Ambika and Kalika now fused into one Chandika. She rode up on her lion, boomed like the storm clouds at the end of the world, and hurtled towards the brothers with her crescent moon axe up in the air. Her dark wild mane reddened with asura blood, her boundless eyes wide open and fiery, taking in the sight of her Shumbha and Nishumbha were stunned. They had not seen anyone so marvelously awe-inspiring and fearsome at the same time. Their weapons were now inoperable. She axed Nishumbha's one limb after another before beheading him and did the same to Shumbha. In a wink, the tale of the mighty asuras had come to an end. However, Chandika would not stop. She went hacking and squashing the asura soldiers and beasts in her way. Her roars and snarls had already caused volcanos

to erupt and mountains to give way. The fish had swum down to the bottom of the ocean and birds had emptied the skies. The whole creation was terrified but Bhagwati had transformed into Chandika. With blood dripping from her lips and skulls in her hands, her macabre dance was not concluding.

Shiva, who had been watching, laid himself down amongst the corpses surrendering to his devotion for me. I Bhagwati, mad in a drunken fever stepped on his chest. The fever left me in an instant when I recognized amongst *aksauhinis*[6] of carcasses whose heart was throbbing under my foot. Rudra crooned, and I heard it in my consciousness, "Mercy, the empress of the cosmos, the goddess of all Gods, Bhagwati. Mercy Chandika! Mercy Ambika and Kalika merged in one, the Warrior Goddess mercy!" Self-conscious Chandika was stunned out of her intoxication.

That was when Shiva took her in his arms and bathed her in Ganga water. As the grime, pain and gore of the war came off her exhausted and distressed being, Maha Gauri glowed like the blooms of night jasmine through a shroud of stormy deep darkness.

---

[6] Aksauhinis – A battle formation comprising 21,870 chariots, 21,870 elephants, 65,610 horsemen and 109,350-foot soldiers. A total of 218,700 soldiers

THE AGE OF TIME

Yuga – a period of time, an age

Maha Yuga – a cycle of four yugas i.e., a Chatur Yuga, which lasts 4,320,000 solar years (12,000 divine years)

Chatur-Yuga – Krita/ Satya yuga followed by Treta Yuga followed by Dwapara yuga followed by Kala Yuga that lasts for 4,320,000 years

Krita or Satya Yuga – The first yuga of the Chatur Yuga that lasts for 1,728,000 years

Treta Yuga – The second yuga of the Chatur Yuga that lasts for 1,296,000 years

Dwapara Yuga – The third yuga of the Chatur Yuga that lasts for 864,000 years

Kala Yuga – The last and fourth yuga of the Chatur-yuga that lasts for 432,000 years

Manvantaras – One age of Manu. A total of 71 Maha Yugas

Sandhi Kaal – recovery period after the end of a manvantara

1 Kalpa – 1 day of Brahma or 14 Manvantara and 15 Sandhi Kaals

GLOSSARY I

A

Aadi – The first one

Adidev – The first deva. Another name for Shiva

Adi-Shesha – The first Shesha, the serpent Vishnu sleeps on

Aadi Shakti – The first Shakti

Agna – Pronounced as Agya. The third eye chakra

Agnistambhasana – The fire log yogic pose

Akasha – Sky

Aksauhinis – A battle formation comprising 21,870 chariots, 21,870 elephants, 65, 610 horsemen and 109,350-foot soldiers. A total of 218,700 soldiers.

Amravati – The capital city of Swarga Loka, the realm of devas

Amrit – Elixir of life

Anahata – The heart chakra

Anant – The one with no end

Anant-Shesha – Endless Shesha, the serpent Vishnu sleeps on

Apana Vayu – Downward moving breath

Aparajita – A flower blue in color

Apsaras – Celestial beauties who are singers and dancers in Deva Loka

Ardhashayana – The lounging position Vishnu takes atop Shesha

Ashvamedha yagna – A ritual wherein a horse accompanied by the king's warriors is released to wander for a year

Asura – Daityas and Danavas. Children of Diti and Danu with Kashyap

Atman – Soul

Aum – or Om, the sound of the universe

Aushadhiprastha – The capital city of Himavat, kingdom of Himachal

B

Beej Mantra – Seed Mantra. Sounds endowed with powers

Bhogi – An indulgent person

Bholenath – A benevolent form of Shiva

Bhoomi – Earth

Bhu Loka – Planet earth

Brahma – The creator god responsible for the creation of the universe

Brahmaand – Universe

Brahmi – Another name for Saraswati, a form of Mahadevi

C

Chamunda – The fearsome form of Mahadevi, responsible for bringing the end of the universe

Chitta – Also written as Citta. Mind, which is not brain. Or consciousness

D

Daitya – A race of Asuras

Damaru – A two headed drum

Danavas – A race of Asuras

Dasaavatars – ten primary incarnations of Vishnu

Devas – Also called as Suras or Adityas. Children of Kashyap and Aditi

Dharma – Cosmic principles and laws which govern the universe

Dhruva – Polar Star

Dhyana – Meditation

Dhyana Mudra – A meditative hand gesture

E

Ekarnava – The primordial ocean

G
Ganas – Shiva's companions
Gandharvas – Celestial musicians and singers
Garuda – A kite or an eagle, the mount of Vishnu
Graha – Planet
Grihasta – Householder. Someone married, living a family life
Gunas – Attributes, qualities
Gyana – Also written as Gnana, but pronounced as Gyana, meaning knowledge
Gyaneshwar – God of knowledge

H
Halahala – Or Kalakuta, the venom that came out of samudra manthan
Hara – Another name for Shiva
Hari – Another name for Vishnu

I
Icchit Mrityu – the death of choice

J
Jata – tress
Jagannath – The lord of the universe. Vishnu
Jivha – tongue

K
Kaal – Time. Another name of Shiva
Kaali – The dark one. The feminine form of Kaal. Another name for Mahadevi
Kamandala – A small water container with a handle on the top
Kinnaras – Part human and part bird. Classical lovers

Ksheer Sagar – Ocean of Milk, broadly understood as Milky Way

Kund – The vessel in which the fire is ignited and holy offerings are poured

Kundalini Shakti – The serpentine energy released in the body using specific meditative techniques

Kusha – a long, pointed grass considered very pure

Kushmanda – The mother goddess. Another name for Mahadevi

M

Mahabali – Someone with great powers

Mahadeva – God of devas. Another name for Shiva

Mahakaal – Bringer of kaal. Another name for Shiva in his destructive form

Mahamaya – The conjurer of illusion. Another name for Lakshmi, a form of Mahadevi

Mahavishnu – Another name for Vishnu

Manas-Putras and Putris – Sons and daughters born from the mind

Mantra – A sound, words or phrase repeated during meditation

Mandapam – an open temporary pavilion used for offering prayers

Manidweepa – The abode of Mahadevi

Manthan – Churning

Maya – Another name for Lakshmi, a form of Mahadevi

Maya – Illusion. The word also used as the opposite of Vairagya. Or the supernatural power wielded by gods and asuras

Moksha – Salvation

Mount Meru – Also called Sumeru, the center of the material, metaphysical and spiritual worlds

Muladhara – the root chakra

Mul Prakriti – The cause of all nature

Muni – Thinker or sage

N

Narayana – Another name for Vishnu
Narayani – Another name for Lakshmi, a form of Mahadevi
Nagas – half-human half-serpent
Namaskara – Or Namaskaram, a Hindu greeting
Neel Kantha – The one with the blue throat. Another name for Shiva

O

Omkara – the primordial sound from which the whole universe was created

P

Panchjanaya – Vishnu's conch
Para-shakti – The all-pervasive Shakti. Another name for Mahadevi
Parigha – an iron bludgeon used as a weapon
Parmanu Shakti – Nuclear power
Pashupati Nath – Lord of all animals. Another name for Shiva
Patala Nivasini – The dweller of the Patala. Another name for Lakshmi
Pinaka – Shiva's bow
Pipal – Or Peepal. Fig tree
Pitamah – The grandfather. Name for Brahma the great grandfather of the universe
Prajapati – Creator
Prakriti – Nature. Another name for Mahadevi
Prana Vayu – Inward moving breath

R

Rajas – Qualities of passion, activity and movement
Rajeshwari – Empress. Another name for Mahadevi
Roopam – Form

Rudra – Shiva's name when he was in a body on earth
Rudraksha – a stone fruit
Rishi – Sage

S

Sakhis – Girl friends
Samadhi – A state achieved in meditation
Samhaara Tandava – the dance of annihilation
Samsara – World
Sandhya – Another name for Saraswati, a form of Mahadevi
Sattva – Quality of goodness, calmness and harmony
Shakti – Energy. Another name for Mahadevi
Shankara – The householder form of Shiva
Saptrishi – The seven sages
Shatrupa – Manu's partner, created by Brahma, as was Manu. Sometimes used as another name for Saraswati
Shiva – The creator God responsible for the destruction of the universe
Shivaa – Female form of Shiva. Another name for Mahadevi
Shivaangi – The one who is a physical part of Shiva
Shivalinga – or Shivalingam, is an aniconic symbol of Shiva and Shakti
Som Rasa – Alcoholic drink
Sri – Another name for Lakshmi, a form of Mahadevi
Sri Hari – Another name for Vishnu
Srishti – Universe
Sthirsukhamasana – Strong, steady and stable yogic posture
Sudarshan Chakra – The divine discus or wheel of time owned by Mahavishnu
Sundar Murti – A beautiful form of Shiva
Swayambhuva – Self-existent. Not born from parents. Asexually born offspring

T

Tamas – Qualities of ignorance, inertia, laziness
Tandava – a dance performed by Shiva
Tapa – Or Tapasya. Deep meditation with extreme self-discipline
Tapasya – Or Tapa. Deep meditation with extreme self-discipline
Tapasvi – An ascetic
Tathasta – Neutral spectator
Triloka – The three worlds
Trimurti – Brahma, Vishnu and Shiva together
Trishula – Trident

U

Udana Vayu – Upward moving breath
Ushma – Energy. Another name for Mahadevi

V

Vac Shakti – the power of speech
Vaijayantimaal – the elemental necklace associated with Vishnu and his incarnations
Vaikuntha – The abode of Vishnu and Lakshmi
Vairagya – Dispassion and detachment
Vaishnavi – Another name for Lakshmi, a form of Mahadevi
Vajra – Thunderbolt
Vana – Forest
Vara – Bridegroom
Vasanta – Springtime
Vata – Banyan, the tree
Vedas – A body of scriptures, comprising Rig, Sama, Yajur and Atharva Veda codifying the ideas and practices of dharma
Veerasana – Kneeling yogic pose

Vidya – Correct knowledge

Vimanas – Aircrafts

Vishnu – The creator God who birthed Brahma, responsible for the preservation of the universe

Y

Yagna – Pronounced as Yagya, is a ritual performed in front of a sacred fire

Yagna samagri – Holy offering at yagnas

Yagna Shala – The place built for the purpose of yagna

Yakshas – Spirits of trees, lakes, mountains, oceans et al

Yog Maya – The creation enabling form of Mahadevi

Yog Nidra – Yogic sleep

Yog Nidra – Deep sleep induced by Yog

Yogi – A practitioner of yog

Yogini I – The female yogi

Yogini II – An aspect of Mahadevi. There are 64 of these sacred feminine forces.

PART II

THE EYE FOR DURGA

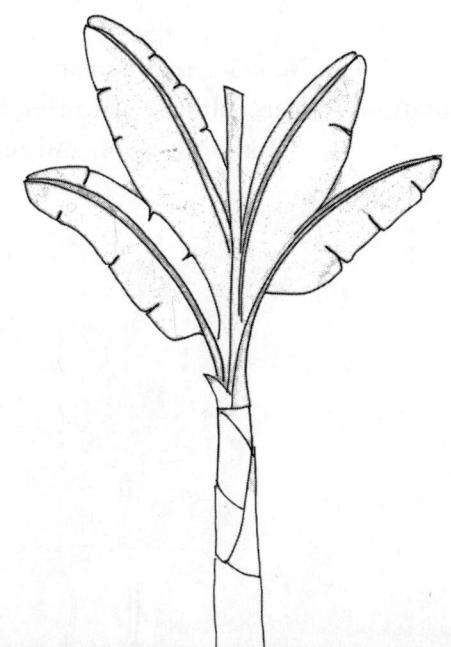

KUSHMANDA
The Mother

Yaa Devi Sarva-Bhuteshu Shraddhaa-Roopenna Samsthitaa |
To that Devi who in all beings abides as Faith,

Yaa Devi Sarva-Bhuteshu Maatri-Roopenna Samsthitaa |
To that Devi who in all beings abides as Mother,

Namas-Tasyai Namas-Tasyai Namas-Tasyai Namo Namah ||
Salutations to Her, Salutations to Her, Salutations to Her,
Salutations again and again.

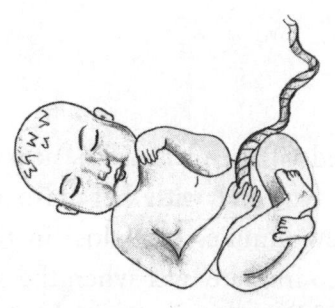

KUSHMANDA

CHAPTER 1

KUSHMANDA
The Mother

In a thinly populated village of Ladakh, near Turtuk in Leh district, lived Kushma with her husband, Zopa. They were the last few families of Baltis[1] in the region. Most of them chose to migrate over when the region was under the territory of Pakistan. Though things changed after India won back Turtuk in 1971 but the region became a permanent area of conflict between the two countries. The cold harsh region saw action during the Kargil war and remains under threat of invasion till the present day.

Kushma was pregnant with her first child, and she had entered the last leg of her pregnancy. An inherently tough and happy woman, blessed with marital bliss and cheer in her heart, she was spending her time eating well under the loving care of her husband. Zopa'a father had died long ago, and his mother passed away a year before. He made a living from working with Dorjey, a travel agent in Leh, who took

---

1 Baltis – an ethnic group of Tibetan descent who are native to the Pakistani-administered territory of Gilgit–Baltistan

tourist groups to Pangong, Nubra and places in and around Leh. Typically, Zopa would walk across a mountain to reach the motorable road, from where the bus would pick him to assist the group. Whensoever he left for work, Palmo, their neighbor who was also Kushma's friend, would promptly come by to give her company. Like all villagers, Zopa too had borrowed a pushcart so he could wheel Kushma to the midwife when it will be time. The midwife lived on the other side of the mountain across the Shyok river.

One afternoon at lunch, Zopa told Kushma, "*Matchon*[2] Lahmo has aged. She will take her time to trek across the mountain, don't you think, Kush!" "So, you are again thinking about it! I realize we are not a very populated village, but your child's birth will not be the first one here. Everyone here was delivered by *Matchon* Lahmo. They have managed. So shall we," Kushma comforted him. Zopa wasn't very convinced, but he didn't want to discuss this with Kushma anymore and pass on his worries to her. He had played out the future so many times in his head and worried about it so much that it had made him edgy. Therefore, Zopa decided to persuade the elderly woman to move in with them until Kushma delivered. One morning, right after his first meal of *Khambir*[3] with eggs, Zopa said, "I should be back before the sunset Kushma, with or without her." "Who? Without whom? *Matchon*?" shouted Kushma after a harried Zopa. Zopa nodded towards Kushma, pushing the cart along to fetch the old woman on it. Kushma stood with her gaze

---

[2] Matchon – address for aunt from mother's side in Ladakhi
[3] Khambir – a traditional Ladakhi bread

frozen on her husband till he crossed the willow grove, and she could not see his silhouette anymore.

The village was thinly populated with only five houses. One of them belonged to Palmo, who was also like an elder sister to Kushma. Palmo would climb up her terrace and call Kushma's name rapidly. Kushma would holler back, then one of them would go to another one's home and they would sit together in the sun while it lasted.

After Zopa left to bring *Matchon*, Kushma continued like any other day. She finished her chores and went to soak in the sun with Palmo. The remnants of slush from the snowfall a few nights back were still there along the cold bends and crooks of the village. Kushma brought the shaggy goats out towards the sun and fed them chattering to Palmo about the new knit they saw on Tara's son's cap, "She did not share the right stitch for us to copy her pattern, Kushma. I tried the stitch, it does not work," quipped Palmo and laughed Kushma. "Is it. Let me show you something new," Kushma started to teach Palmo a new pattern. She was knitting a pair of socks for the baby to come. "You have to finish this Palmo, if the baby is born before I complete the knit," winked Kushma and smiled with the light of a thousand suns. Then they had some lunch and stretched themselves in the sunshine.

Both were later chatting over the sips of *gur-gur* tea[4] when Kushma felt a sudden movement inside her. "Oh, so you like this tea heh?" she mumbled to her unborn baby. But before she could gather much, she knew it was time.

---

4   Gur-gur tea – The butter tea

Her water broke, and it was dripping along her legs. Palmo noticed. Without any delay, Kushma babbled to Palmo, "Quick, pack some of my clothes, a shawl, and some water. Also, a torch. It is on the shelf near my bed. Look for a bag hanging on the peg behind the door. It already has a piece of cloth in it. Throw everything in that bag. And put the goats in their shelter, douse the fire in the kitchen there was some tea left on it. Pick the matchbox too, just in case." Palmo dashed around to follow all instructions and soon emerged with a bag dangling in her hand. She asked, "Should I keep a *khabdan*[5] too?" Kushma laughed uncontrollably with both her hands on her belly. "What for? You want to lay down and gaze at stars on the way?" "Only you can crack jokes in such moments! Just in case we need it, I thought." "Okay, drop it in the bag, now let's get going," announced Kushma. Saying so, she turned around and led the way as Palmo was latching up Kushma's house.

Palmo then darted to her house to inform her mother-in-law and joined Kushma back, who was ahead of her. Palmo's mother-in-law had handed her a stick for Kushma's walking support. She uttered shakily, hurriedly but inspiringly, "Women are strong because they have to be! I am confident you both will make it. The village men will return over the weekend. Still, I will make some calls and check if anyone is on his way back. Meanwhile you both make headway." Together Kushma and Palmo, began to hike up the mountain, which was against the direction of the sun and a thick layer of snow rested on it. In an hour or

---

5   Khabdan – Ladakhi carpet

so the sun dropped over the horizon and cold wind swept the valley.

The first hour was manageable. Palmo held Kushma's hand whenever she felt a spasm coming and gave her water intermittently. Then it got dark, Palmo pulled out the torch from the bag and walked behind Kushma, throwing light in her path. She told Kushma stories of her own baby's birth and how her husband fainted right next to her foot at her first proper scream. Kushma teeheed at Palmo's jokes, but as she walked up, the spasms became stronger. A couple of hours or so later, the intervals between the spasms started to turn shorter. And a little later, even shorter. The uphill climb on the rocky mountain became arduous with every passing minute. Palmo wiped Kushma's sweat and proposed if taking a break would help. Kushma denied, "There is no need for the *khabdan* yet!" breaking into laughter yet again, precisely a moment before a big-long spasm. She took a deep breath, and once it passed, she said, "Truth is, my dear, I may not be able to get back on my feet once I lay down. And my water is draining fast. I hope the baby is alright inside. Also, the night is dark, and the mountain could get wild. In this condition, I will be a sitting duck. What will you do all alone!" Kushma carried herself with absolute resolve well into the dead of the night before she declared she could not anymore.

Palmo perspired in fear, running her mind in all directions, contemplating what to do. The snow under her feet was melting, making her feel very-very cold. She was out of her wits and felt like crying. But of course, she could not when it was indeed Kushma who was going through this utter darkness. Palmo was afraid to look at Kushma's face, who now half-dragged beside her and could barely stand on her two feet. Palmo pulled Kushma's arm around her shoulder lest she might drop on the gravel and rocks covered in snow. When Palmo felt a tug at her shoulder after a few steps, she barely had the courage to look at Kushma's face. Yet when she did, she saw Kushmanda's face radiant, with a silent smile reaching the whole creation around her. She stood grand, although pale, her temple beaded with sweat drops, but her eyes glinted, head was held high in the midst of white wall of mountains. It seemed like the darkest hour had ticked away. And just at the same moment, as if on some invisible cue, the cloud cover floated away and the rising sun filled the valley at once, tearing through the darkness. Palmo squealed in utter surprise, "Has the sun come out already? It is not even 6." The morning light bathed Kushmanda, and the sky reverberated with a loud cacophony of birds. But rising above it all was the ethereal sound of Zopa, calling Kushmanda's name and running down the hillside with the cart and the midwife atop it, hugging a bag in her lap.

Mesmerized with the sight, for a few moments, it seemed to Palmo that it all happened because of Kushmanda's smile. She kept on looking at her friend as the sun rose to become a brilliant orb to erase last night's remembrance. As if the dark night never happened. The *khabdan* ultimately came to use. Zopa helped Kushma lay down on it next to a big rock behind some dried-up shrubs and an apricot tree. He made some fire near his wife to make her warm. Palmo assisted Matchon. Kushma soon gave birth to a beautiful and healthy baby girl with Zopa by her side.

Palmo helped *Matchon* swaddle the baby. She had only one thought on her mind, "I hope the baby grows up to know the value of this life. I wish she never, even mistakenly, unsees Kushma or her awe-inspiring resolve as a mother."

Kushmanda: The primeval force of the universe signifies the import and irreplaceability of motherhood. Her rather unshareable, private, and demanding duty through conceiving, carrying, birthing and upbringing a creation, all while raising a mother within herself makes her Parashakti, the all-pervasive energy. Kushmanda is Mahadevi's humble presence in the life of her creation and what we know as the psychological, emotional, spiritual and physical strength of a mother.

BHUVNESHWARI
The Empress

Yaa Devi Sarva- Bhuteshu Chetanety-Abhidhiiyate |
To that Devi who in all beings abides as Consciousness,

Yaa Devi Sarva-Bhuteshu Kshaanti-Roopenna Samsthitaa |
To that Devi who in all beings abides as Forbearance,

Yaa Devi Sarva-Bhuteshu Lajjaa-Roopenna Samsthitaa |
To that Devi who in all beings abides as Modesty,

Yaa Devi Sarva-Bhuteshu Tushtti-Roopenna Samsthitaa |
To that Devi who in all beings abides as Contentment,

Namas-Tasyai Namas-Tasyai Namas-Tasyai Namo Namah
Salutations to Her, Salutations to Her, Salutations to Her,
Salutations again and again.

BHUVNESHWARI

CHAPTER 2

BHUVNESHWARI
The Empress

It was October of 1931 and the winter had begun in the town of Balloki, famous for Balloki Headworks, 70 km away from Lahore. Zaildar[1] Pandit Dinanath Bali's youngest child, a girl, was born. He already had two sons, Ramlal, and Rajhans. His wife, Kaushalya had been suffering from pneumonia for over a month and now with the childbirth, she had become too weak to feed the baby girl. The very same day, their cow, Billo, also delivered a heifer calf. Her milk couldn't be touched for that was saved entirely for the calf. *Zaildar's* elder son Ram said, "*Pita ji*, let us bring Mangla back home. The baby needs milk," referring to their other cow that was sent to Patwari's home. Patwari's son had typhoid and needed an extra supply of milk. Looking at the newly born baby girl sleeping next to her mother, Zaildar spoke, "Bring Mangla back *puttar*[2] if you

---

[1] Zaildar – landowner, in charge of a Zail, an administrative unit for a group of villages during the British Indian Empire

[2] Puttar – son in Punjabi. Many times, used for daughters too

like, but I am afraid it is not the newborn's turn to survive. You know, after every healthy born, my next child does not make it. Particularly the girls. But if mother goddess wants her to survive, then she will, come what may!" The infant mortality rate was 145.6 for every 1000 live births and over 2000 mothers died for every 1 lakh childbirths in India around those times.

The baby girl was born weak and did not get the attention and mother's milk she deserved because of her mother's ill health. The household had a baby feeder made of bronze with a tube-like thing secured at its mouth with rivets, but a maidservant's child took it for a toy and refused to return it. Consequently, the baby was spoon-fed Mangla's milk by a maidservant and given some basic care. But the girl was already demonstrating tenacity. She started gaining strength with every passing day and her mother started to recover as well. Kaushalya was a fair-complexioned, petite, modest, and docile woman with a cool temperament. While Zaildar was a tall, handsome man with a wheatish complexion, long-curled mustache, and hot disposition. "This girl is a fighter, boys! We will call her Bhuvneshwari, queen of the universe!" announced a delighted Zaildar to his two sons in the courtyard of the house. Bhuva slowly became her father's favorite child. She was the only daughter after two sons and inspired the kind of love in his heart that he had not experienced before. Zaildar called her *Khamb*, which is Punjabi for wings, for she soared like a bird all day. Bhuva grew up in a busy household where the kitchen was kept alive all day by her mother, and her father used

to hold meetings in his *baithak*[3] which was an embargoed silent zone for children. But exceptions were made only for Pitaji's[4] *Khamb*.

Ramlal was a kind young man, but a little distant and self-absorbed. Little did anyone know that he would assume *sanyasa*[5] in the future. The younger son, Rajhans, was a loving boy. He was extraordinarily fond and protective of his sister. He and Bhuva would horse ride long distances, pluck jujubes on the way and come back home, with both their pockets and hearts overflowing. "Bhuva, I am coming for you!" declared Raj one day, serving his turn to look for Bhuva in the game of hide and seek. He walked towards the Bailkhana[6], where all the livestock was kept and cared for. He believed that the young Bhuva would be found hiding behind her mare, Goma. But it seemed Bhuva had grown up and knew how to hide well. Raj looked through the *Bailkhana* and gestured towards the servant bathing and attending to the cows Mangla and Billo, the newborn calf, the buffalo Shama, the horse Bahadur and the mare Goma. The servant, who knew about this routine between the brother and sister, smiled and pointed towards the granary, which was next to the *Bailkhana*. The dog Bhura, who was never kept under a leash, was also romping on a heap of fodder. Raj made his way toward the granary. It had large earthen, wooden, and brass vessels lined up against the walls to store wheat, maze,

---

[3] Baithak – drawing room
[4] Pitaji – father in Hindi
[5] Sanyasa – a form of asceticism marked by renunciation of material desires
[6] Bailkhana – cowshed

rice, ghee, whey and things like that. It had stone grinders on one side, and some other such manual equipment. The room also had many wooden shelves for brass jars filled with dry spices and condiments like turmeric, dry ginger, red chilies, saffron, jaggery and whatnot.

"Where are you, Bhuva!" called out Raj when he could not find her in the granary too. "I am here, Bhai[7]," stuck out a little hand dripping with *ghee* from one of the large vessels, as the other hand was clutching the rim with all the strength to keep her small head afloat. Raj saw two black eyes on top of the pot gaping at him. He hurried to grab her, "Why did you have to jump into *ghee* of all things, Bhuva," the container was as tall as Raj. He dragged her out, but the vessel toppled, and in a minute, he too was bathed in ghee from head to toe. The servant in the *Bailkhana* heard the racket and came in rushing, "*Bibiji*[8]! You need to get here," he called out for their mother. Kaushalya saw her kids unable to stand on their feet, gliding in a puddle of *ghee*. She put them out one by one and twisted Raj's greasy ear, "Is this your playground? Look what you have done. All this *ghee* was made over a month. Wait for me to tell *Panditji* about it." Kaushalya used to address her husband as *Panditji*, as they were a brahmin family. Raj did not utter a word. "It is my fault Ma. I thought this pot was empty. I climbed up the stool and hopped in it," explained Bhuva as her mother grabbed her little hand and towed her towards the bathroom. "I had the vessels swapped, you silly girl!"

---

[7] Bhai – brother
[8] Bibiji – an address for older women in Punjabi

clarified Kaushalya as Raj followed his mother, looking like a young goat dressed in a kurta pyjama.

When Kaushalya narrated the kids' adventure to her husband, "*Bhaagwan*[9], my girl is a survivor. Don't you see, what I see? She is a warrior, both strong and smart. She kept her head afloat. *Khamb*, you keep soaring. We will make more ghee, don't you worry about it!" said a gleaming *Zaildar*, taking his little girl on his lap. Bhuva was growing into a curious and creative little girl bursting with ideas and energy. She was kind, polite and especially loving toward animals. Her love for languages was exceptional. She could not read or write yet, but she could speak Urdu, Hindi, Punjabi, English and a bit of Sanskrit. Balloki did not have any schools for girls and *Zaildar* wanted his daughter educated properly. When Bhuva turned ten, he decided to move his family with all their servants, cattle and dog to Lahore. His eldest son Ram was already studying in Lahore University and Raj was in class nine. The new house in the big city of Lahore was next to a mosque with a large green dome on top of it. Amongst the many trees in their expansive verandah[10], was an old Gulmohar, upon which was tied a swing. The tree seemed so tall to little Bhuva that the rope was long enough to take her close to the dome every time she went up the swing. The young boys on the terrace of the mosque sometimes waved animatedly at her. The horses, cows and buffalo were given a new part of this building, and

---

[9] Bhaagwan – the holder of Bhagya, destiny. Typically used by husbands to address their wives in Punjabi
[10] Verandah – porch

the latest addition to them was a camel named Durg.

Bhuva recognized that her education had begun quite late. She got to see the Lahore girls and their fashion sense for the first time, and felt under-confident, especially when speaking in the class. For this reason, she was withdrawn in the school, but she focused her energies on understanding things conceptually. Bhuva grappled and found her feet. Raj helped her at every step of the way. He even wrote essays, summaries and did her homework many a time. One day, Bhuva could not keep to herself and told the teacher, "My brother wrote this for me, I didn't," expecting a thrashing, but the teacher appreciated her honesty before the class. This made Bhuva feel assured for a while, but soon she figured that she was, in fact, written off as a truthful but dull student. Quietly but surely, she kept learning and became independent. Bhuva could soon do without her brother's help. But she could not gather enough nerve to stand up and speak for herself.

Years went by and then came the time to send the students' names for university programs, through what was called the golden examination. A list of students was drafted where Bhuva's name did not feature. The class was now divided between the smart ones and the weak ones. Despite all the hard work, she was not noticed. Now Bhuva knew that her teachers thought of her as a fraud, since her honest acceptance in her early years at school. Plus, her quiet demeanor was not helping her case. There were elements about her that she could change, but then there were fundamentals that were an essential part of her design and could never be altered. One of which was

never to ask for attention or try too hard to make herself visible or prove herself. Bhuva knew both her capabilities and her limitations. She was her father's daughter, a survivor, she accepted both, especially her limitations. One day, when the class was told to write an essay on Moonlit Night, Bhuva picked up her notebook and went to the desk at the far end of the classroom, away from all the girls. This was to ensure that the teacher took notice of it. She was the first one to finish her essay and handed her notebook to the teacher. When the teacher read it, she hurried to the principal and accepted that she had made a mistake. But it was too late, the list was already sent to the university.

Ram had joined the army and Raj was now working with The Imperial Bank of India. The freedom movement was now at its zenith. Lahore was quite the epicenter. Furthermore, the tension between the Hindus and Muslims was leading to intense riots every now and then. It was upsetting for the day-to-day functioning of colleges but that did not affect Bhuva much. By this time, the longing to do something for soon-to-be independent Bharat had birthed in her. Bhuva's father had always encouraged Bhuva to study medicine and treat the undernourished and suffering people of his beloved country. He himself took a keen interest in Ayurveda. The average life expectancy in 1946-47 was 32 years. 23 percent of the population was afflicted with Malaria. Every day more than 500 children were disabled because of Polio. TB and Smallpox were rampant. The country needed major healthcare overhaul.

Finally, India got independence in 1947. But it came with a major judder. British India was divided into two independent states, Hindu-majority India and Muslim-majority Pakistan. And just like that, one day, a few people sitting in a room somewhere far away from Punjab drew a line on a piece of paper, which effectively tore apart the blood-laden, beating heart of the land of Heer and Ranjha. On the other hand, the British successfully marched their army away with almost no loss. Bhuva was preparing for her Matriculation Exam, but the schools were abruptly shut down. The nation was burning and so was Punjab. Bhuva's headmistress coached the girls before the schools were closed, "Do not let anyone touch your living body. If you find that you are surrounded and there is no escape whatsoever, you must have the courage to immolate yourself!" Bhuva kept a cannister full of kerosene in her reach, a matchbox in her pocket and wore at least three layers of salwar suits[11]. The layering was to buy time if the girls got abducted and sexually assaulted. The Hindus living around Bhuva's house were leaving. The British had no resources after the second world war, and they were leaving India in an absolute chaos, but Zaildar assured his family, "You have read history. Upheavals and struggles are part of life. It will all settle down. Do not worry. This is our motherland, and we must be devoted to her."

What Pakistan will be was based on the principle of contiguous Muslim majority areas, for which they were using an undependable 1941 census. Lahore had over

---

[11] Salwar suits – an Indian traditional dress for females

60% Muslim population, which made it an undisputedly Pakistani area. Hindus and Sikhs were minority, yet all the commerce through businesses, industries and banks was owned by Hindus, like the rest of Punjab. Hindus owned twice the area of land in Lahore and paid twice the amount of taxes, but none of this mattered. Hindus-Sikhs argued with the boundary commission about their socio-cultural contribution, but they did not know that a decision was made way back in February 1946 within Wavell Plan, which said, since Amritsar will be with India, Lahore would be with Pakistan. However, *Zaildar* and his family did not leave their home.

By now, Bhuva's entire neighborhood was vacant. One of *Zaildar's* close Muslim friends, Din Mohammad, used to send his sons over to bring *Zaildar's* family to their house for safety. One day, Din Mohammad's son Abdul Rahim came over unexpectedly and said, "Chacha[12] ji, my Abbu[13] is not thinking straight. His love for you has blinded him. If you come to our side, I am afraid I will not be able to protect you from other Muslims. My religious brothers do not want Qafirs[14] in the area. Abbu refuses to believe this, just like you do not. But I cannot protect you anymore." *Zaildar*, still in disbelief, said, "Why don't you all come over here to our place, *puttar*? How does it matter if we are here or there? We will all be together." Abdul looked blankly at *Zaildar's* unflinched eyes, gave up and went back

---

[12] Chacha – uncle
[13] Abbu – used as an address to father in Muslim families
[14] Qafirs – the ones who reject or disbelieve in God as per Islam

home. A little later, a Dogra soldier, on his routine rounds, walked into the house. He was astounded to see *Zaildar* sitting in his drawing room, reading a newspaper like any normal day. Horrified, he said, "*Zaildar* Sahab[15], you are still here?" Next, he saw Kaushalya and both the kids. The soldier now yelled, "I am alone right now. I cannot protect all of you. Also, the Balochi army is coming to occupy this area. Leave right now! I will drop you to the camp. Fast!" *Zaildar* stepped back wordlessly and asked his family to go with the soldier. Two days later, Pandit Jawahar Lal Nehru and Sardar Baldev Singh visited the camp. And the day next, *Zaildar* came up and took his family back home. That whole night was consumed by skies roaring with the slogans of *Ya Ali*, splintering metal, and ringing swords in their collapsed neighborhood. Bhuva's mother did not sleep a wink. She was a bundle of nerves, petrified about her daughter. Kaushalya bolted all doors that opened into the courtyard, pulled at those locks repeatedly to be sure, checked on her daughter, the kerosene can, her younger son and her husband the whole night. By morning, she had made small pendants of poison for Bhuva and herself. She had decided death from poison would be quicker and less messy.

As the morning sun rose, the same Dogra soldier appeared from somewhere. This time, he was spitting fire. The family was fuzzy because of lack of sleep and anxiety. "*Zaildar* Sahab, do you want your daughter taken away? Bhushan's daughter was abducted. Her naked, damaged body was found at the end of your lane last night. I will

---

[15] Sahab – sir

not be able to save you. I am all alone. It is a mob out there. I beg of you, leave. Leave at once!" There were wet clothes on the clothesline. A room full of food supplies for an entire year. Kaushalya's jewelry in a box under her bed. "Let me take my sewing machine," yelled Bhuva out of nowhere. "Okay, okay, I will carry it for you, but leave. Now!", approved the soldier. Kaushalya, Raj and Bhuva left abruptly for the camp with the soldier carrying their sewing machine on his shoulder. *Zaildar* still did not join them. He looked impaired at his family like he was stoned. Kaushalya looked at him imploringly, breaking into tears, but he did not relent. There was no time for any dialogue and the minds were dysfunctional. "*Panditji*, release the cattle!" was all Kaushalya could say with a voice that trembled. *Zaildar* nodded as he gazed at his family.

Hindus and Sikhs on one side and Muslims on the other, the most unprecedented mutual genocide ensued. Both Punjab and Bengal, adjoining provinces of India's borders with West and East Pakistan, saw concentrated carnage. Hindus were being forced to convert, there were massacres, arson, mass abductions, and savage sexual violence. Some seventy-five thousand women were raped, and many of them were then disfigured or torn limb from limb. Bhuva and her family, sans *Zaildar'*, were now in the camp where they found other people known to them. "We shifted to this camp when they burned down our house in Gawalmandi. We are leaving for Amritsar. Here is some ration that we are left with. You can keep it," a woman said to Kaushalya as Bhuva was listening to their conversation.

After five days, it was their turn to leave their homeland. A truck covered by a heavy canvas was filled with people to be dropped at Amritsar. The Muslims to Lahore were given food in Wagah and the Hindus leaving Lahore at Attari.

Bhuva, with her family and other Hindus from Lahore, was dropped at Amritsar Khalsa College in an open ground under the vast sky. Most people were empty-handed. Not a rag to sit on, nothing to change into. When Bhuva looked around her, it was a sea of harrowed men, women, and children. Some looked calm only because they could come out alive. Some were sitting on their haunches, weeping continually at their powerlessness, or the loss of family back in Lahore, now in another country, Pakistan. Many were screaming, wading through the crowds, looking for their missing persons. Some looked delirious, still talking about their homes and dreams. It was an inexplicable scene of plundered mankind living together under the sky, for days and nights, with no place to relieve themselves, change or bathe. There was no water or food, no plans for tomorrow, and utter hopelessness.

Most people of east Punjab, with homes and hearth back in Pakistan, except some supremely privileged ones, were now reduced to beggars. They were now labeled refugees in their own country. Locals were troubled by the influx of these deportees in their cities of northern India, for they too would now share the resources with them. But then some locals would come with food to distribute amongst these people who had lost all that they had built,

BHUVNESHWARI; The Empress ■ 161

and with that, their respect. "*Beta ji*[16], here, take this packet of biscuit," someone came and tied it on the end of Bhuva's *dupatta*[17]. She was both hesitant and stunned. Bhuva had been floating through the last few weeks, dazed, and confused. Some more women came by, with baskets full of *parathas*[18] and offered to Bhuva. The whole camp was starving. As she put her grubby hands out, tears trailed down her cheeks. She looked at her hands and wondered if this was the freedom, she had been fancying. She broke into a river of tears that drowned everybody around her. The circumstances, the absence of her father, no news of her eldest brother, who was last working in Quetta, her mother's quiet fragility and the darkness looming large were now planted in her heart. Forever!

Raj used to spend his entire day looking for an accommodation in Amritsar, but there were only so many houses in that town and a deluge of people had entered north of India. "Bhuva, come with me. Today is your matric exam," whooshed in Raj. "But the roll number, *Bhai*?" "They have allowed students from Lahore to sit through the exam without it." Bhuva got to the examination center, wrote down her home address with a lump in her throat and sat for her exam. Students were cheating extensively, and the supervisor was seemingly ignoring it in view of the grueling circumstances. Raj was outside, waiting for his little sister, who had grown up overnight. He quickly solved

---

[16] Beta ji – a respectful denotation to address a kid or someone younger in Punjabi
[17] Dupatta – a long Indian scarf worn with salwar suit by Indian women
[18] Parathas – an Indian flatbread fried in a pan

some questions and sent those through a boy. Bhuva saw the boy keeping a piece of paper on her desk, but she threw it away nervously. She had not forgotten Lahore. If anything, it had only become more pronounced in her subconscious, like the first lover. The boy kept it back and looked into her eyes this time. She again tossed it away. Once she came out, she realized it was her brother who sent the answers, but she was proud of her decision, regardless. Later, they heard that there was an attack at Lahore University, and the fire gulped it all. The students never received the results.

Raj finally found a house, and the family moved from the camp. It started to rain heavily as they reached, and the roof of the house poured like tea from a tea strainer. All they had was one broken bed in that dilapidated house. They managed for a few days before Raj found another one in Chitta Katra. These were the houses vacated by Muslims. Some more Hindu families moved into other houses in the same lane. This house was one-third the house in Lahore, but at least they had found an asylum. "*Bhai*, someone would have occupied our house by now. Isn't it? What are the chances that it is the same family that left this house here? But they are so much more fortunate than us. They will not have to worry about supplies for at least a year. Or water. There is a clean water supply, even a handpump. A kitchen jam-packed with brass and bronze. Our wardrobes neatly stacked with Ma's saris that I hoped to wear someday, Pitaji's coats and pagris[19], my dupattas that I tied and dyed. Beds and chairs covered with my embroideries and doilies

---

[19] Pagri – turban for Indian men

on the tables lovingly crocheted by Ma. Only God knows where Pitaji is. I hope he has kept Ma's jewelry with him. Oh, I hope like hell that they are kind towards Goma, Bahadur, Mangla, Billo, Shama, Durg and Bhura. Or do you think they would have left already? Ma asked Pitaji to release them. But I am glad we had the good sense of letting the servants go well in time," ruminated and mourned Bhuva, as Raj looked at his sister's face remorsefully when they were interrupted by someone's entry at the main gate.

"Panditji!!!," Kaushalya let out a scream and whimpered as she ran short of tumbling toward her husband. She had been wordlessly holding a whole barrage inside her. Both Raj and Bhuva wept to see their mother finally expressing her suffering. Their father's *pagri* was missing, nor was he wearing his jutties[20], and his face was colorless with betrayal. He was slapped, kicked, and pushed out of his house by force. His *pagri* fell off his head and his jutties went missing. They did not allow him to pick his valuables. He was entirely sore and emptied. Not only about leaving his home behind but also from the awareness that the ship of faith had sunk. His Muslim brothers threw him out and threatened to hack his already distraught body. Some others cut their losses and threw the Hindus to butchers. The soreness came from the lost belief in what he thought was their sweet world. Gangs of killers set villages aflame. Old and young men and children were butchered to death, while young women were carried off to be raped. They cut off pregnant women's breasts and babies were hewed out of their bellies. Infants were found

---

[20] Jutties – a type of footwear common in North India

roasted on spits. More than fifteen million people had been displaced, and about two million were dead.

Some common friends and relatives on *Zaildar's* way to Amritsar, and in the camp told him about his family's whereabouts. "It was worse than the Nazi camps. This partition will remain in the consciousness of the people in the subcontinent as memories of unthinkable violence. The largest forced migration of people in human history without a war or famine. I am grateful to the Dogra soldier who saved my family. So naïve I was!" said Bhuva's father, howling and hugging her in his arms.

A few days later, they read an announcement in the newspaper that Bhuva's eldest brother had left Quetta and had safely reached Jaipur. Now everyone had only one thing to say - marry Bhuva off. However, former *Zaildar* Dinanath Bali did not want it. He had dreams for his daughter, for which he had no resources or money to fulfill. He hoped to wait and build back his life but could not promise anything. Every other day someone or the other was getting their daughter married. The idea was to merge families and become stronger in the process. After having left Lahore, wealth, pedigree and even education ceased to matter. Almost everyone was a pauper. Families were coming to Panditji with marriage proposals for Bhuva. After a lot of pressure from Pandiji's sister and other relatives, he had no choice but to agree. His earlier choices had broken his backbone already. His sister proposed her relative's son, Prem for Bhuva. They too had migrated from Lahore. Bhuva had no opinion. There were far too many battles to fight, and she did not want to add to her family's despairs.

Her father and brother did not want this alliance. They did not think the boy was an ideal match for Bhuva's caliber, but Raj too was having a tough time with his job. The bank, which was still under British authority, wanted him to join back in Lahore, which was impossible. He was trying to get to the head office in Calcutta, but the process was sure to take time with so much mayhem in the country.

Bhuva got married. It was a quiet and small wedding. At one point, Pandit ji[21] was found sobbing in a corner of that tiny house. Not because his daughter was leaving him, but because she was leaving with unfulfilled dreams. He was brokenhearted and inconsolable after Bhuva left home. He went eerily silent after that day and couldn't get himself to eat. When Bhuva came with her husband to see her family a day after the wedding, she muffled to Raj, "I don't know what is wrong with Prem Ji's health, he keeps coughing all day and night, Bhai." "I will have him checked. Do not worry!" said Raj, hiding his apprehension. It took Raj over a month to find a doctor in Delhi. By then, Prem and Bhuva went to another wedding in the family. Prem's coughing had become violent. Raj and Prem traveled to Delhi, by which time Bhuva was already pregnant. Prem was diagnosed with TB. Their worst fear had come true. The doctor suspected that he had got it from the camp, though Bhuva, who had been living with him, wasn't showing any symptoms. They tried whatever medication was available and possible, but Prem's health was worsening and so was Prem's mother's behavior towards Bhuva.

---

[21] Pandit ji – a Hindu scholar. Generally used as an address for Brahmins

Bhuva requested Raj to send her the only treasure they had brought with them from Lahore, her sewing machine. Prem had lost his job because of nonattendance. Bhuva started to stitch and embroider clothes for people. The household needed money. Meanwhile, Panditji fell sick. No one could diagnose his illness except Bhuva. He had lost the desire to live. And one morning, he gave up, "My Khamb!" he mumbled before his last sigh. Kaushalya was now a walking corpse, waiting to meet her husband again. Bhuva was in her 7th month, heavily pregnant, when Prem succumbed to TB and passed away. She was a widow at 17. Life did not give her the luxury to mourn anyone. She tutored neighborhood kids, embroidered, and stitched to make money for the family. Ram, her eldest brother took to sanyasa, and Raj was given a branch to work from in Amritsar.

Bhuva birthed twin boys two months later and her mother-in-law refused to see their faces for a long time. It was a lone battle, which she had to endure to raise the boys. Raj pursued Bhuva to come back home. But Bhuva declined. This was her battle. And she was her father's daughter, a survivor. When Hindus around her house saw her circumstances, they figured out a way to help her. They sent her food as brahmin's share at every ritual. Bhuva crushed *Batashas*[22] from the temple to sweeten her tea and saved every rupee for her boys' future and education. She had to feed herself, her mother-in-law and her two sons. She cooked only once a day, saved good food for her children, and kept her eyes on her goal. This was far from

---

[22] Batashas – a sugar cake served as a holy offering in temples

what Bhuva had imagined for herself, but she accepted it with dignity. She had learned to accept limitations as much as her strengths exceedingly early in her life. And this life, with all its deprivation was after all her contribution to the struggle for free and independent India, she had always prayed for. Freedom for India was a fight fought by many in countless ways.

Sometimes strength is not about slaying the adversary or a victory in its conventional form. Sometimes a conquest has nothing to do with winning. Sometimes it is not so transactional and short-termed. Sometimes it is a long war that lasts a lifetime. Sometimes victory is only about endurance, about the nerve to survive, about keeping your head afloat. Sometimes, the fortitude, the morale is all the conquest there can be.

PS: Based on true events

Bhuvneshwari: The guardian, the silent queen, who sews the universe together but remains unseen. Her effect lies in her modest, unassertive morale. An eternal force that nurtures and holds the universe together with her unbending sense of duty, wisdom, and virtues. The form of Mahadevi whose role is to sustain and enable others' accomplishments while her sovereignty is visible only to the awakened.

SARASWATI
Wisdom and Dispassion

Yaa Devi Sarva- Bhuteshu Buddhi-Roopenna Samsthitaa |
To that Devi who in all beings abides as Intelligence,

Yaa Devi Sarva-Bhuteshu Shaanti-Roopenna Samsthitaa |
To that Devi who in all beings abides as Peace,

Namas-Tasyai Namas-Tasyai Namas-Tasyai Namo Namah ||
Salutations to Her, Salutations to Her, Salutations to Her,
Salutations again and again.

SARASWATI

CHAPTER 3

SARASWATI
Wisdom and Dispassion

Brahma, a senior colleague to Saraswati, both by age and experience, had become somewhat of a big brother to her. They had been working together for over five years now. Their workdays began with Brahma ordering two cups of tea, messaging Saraswati to tell her about it, and slurping tea together before launching themselves into work. Saraswati, a maverick and a natural problem solver, rarely found herself in the need of someone's aid. But if she did, it would most likely be Brahma. He had been someone she would bounce off her ideas with, not just to do with work, but life at large. Brahma had also been the one she would dash to for seeking technical support and solutions, which was more than once a day. He was ever so happy to see her and always prioritized her over others. He was protective of Saraswati and watched out for her. Together with decades of work under their belt, they complemented each other's skills so well that they made a formidable team. The equation between them, unlike most corporate situations, was based on honesty,

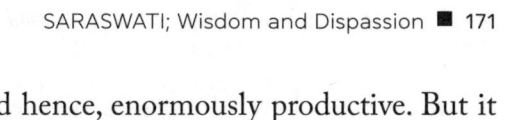

trust, affection and hence, enormously productive. But it was not like this from the beginning.

Four years back, Saraswati got this role. Her expertise and success preceded her, which probably got her the position in the first place. Brahma was one of the key decision-makers in Saraswati's appointment at the organization, still for some reason he was not quite sure about her. In the first year, he seemed visibly anxious every time they both were in the same room. It was difficult to tell by an onlooker if it was simply edginess about reliant performance or something more. Brahma would suddenly turn unreasonably assertive with her. Or he would call a team meeting, make a bunch of team members sit around as he would talk down to her, and everyone would watch listlessly. Saraswati had smelled his lack of confidence in her, expressing itself in various ways. She loathed this tension in the air but was amply sure that it was affecting Brahma more than her. If someone asked what, she did not have an answer, but she was certain that something about her affected Brahma. There were times when she responded firmly, without sounding bitter or disrespectful. At other times, she ignored it and walked away with a smile.

By the time she entered the second year, some of her colleagues had observed this circus too many times. Some had even advised Saraswati to forget about his seniority and confront him. It was not a case enough to be raised to HR, but it was exasperating, nonetheless. Saraswati, for that matter, was not the one to complain about trivial matters, open a contest or show disregard. Moreover, with decades of work experience she well understood the intricacies of

the male ego where oftentimes silence was more forceful than quarrel. Her weapons were diplomacy and dialogue. By the end of the second year, she had found firm ground beneath her feet. Her markets were set, fool-proof systems were in place, and the team was functioning like a well-oiled machine. She was continuously rising and doing better with each passing day. But Brahma was still uptight. What made it worse for Brahma was that Saraswati was too self-assured, poised, beautiful, astute, imaginative, and erudite, both with her work and communication. In fact, her communication skills were enviable.

One day, in a project meeting with Brahma, Saraswati manufactured an opportunity for herself to talk about their respective life paths. Brahma got interested. She was not sure if his interest was for the reason that they were talking about something away from usual work, or that this talk presented Brahma the opportunity to read her mind. Or both. Brahma participated wholeheartedly. The discussion then narrowed to their career paths within the organization, and then came to a point where Brahma asked, "Would you ever consider taking my position within this organization, along with your own? It is possible, really. I know that your last role was like that, I mean a combination of what I do and what you do. Would you like that opportunity?" Saraswati knew it was a test. This was the insecurity Brahma functioned from. She dived at the opportunity, yet calmy she said, "My preferred career path, Brahma, does not go in that direction. Even if someone offered it on a platter with dollops of other benefits, I doubt that I will pick it. I am sorry, I do not mean to undermine what you do. It has its

own complexities, but it does not interest me. I would rather widen my own area of work, increase the complexity within it and make it more strategic than what it is today. I have ideas and plans, trust me." Saraswati vehemently denied any wishes to tread on Brahma's toes. Brahma kept observing her face intently as she talked. He even reconfirmed her response in few other words and ways and seemed somewhat reassured. "So, what is your coveted career path Saraswati?" She promptly explained it in great detail, winning Brahma's confidence almost immediately.

Since that day, things shifted between the two of them. Brahma now started to dig into her said area of interest. He followed Saraswati's thoughts on social media, in meetings, in one-on-one conversations, and in their day-to-day lives. The same woman whose presence used to loom over him, had now started to trap his senses unknowingly. The more he learned about her, the more he could not help himself but support her. He saw no reason to not do that. Soon he not only encouraged Saraswati's interests, but his own started to intersect with hers. Brahma invited her to many conferences, talks and public platforms. He even drove her to places of her curiosity. Most of the time, their conversations revolved around Brahma asking her questions about life and its minutiae and Saraswati responding to them. She knew quite plainly that he treasured listening to her. Why, she did not know and did not want to.

Now Saraswati was comfortable with this new arrangement where their relationship was that of model colleagues who were lasting allies or perhaps great friends. Before she could fathom much, her every success became

his delight, and her every loss turned into his dismay, inside or outside of work. She found Brahma celebrating her wins more than she herself did. She valued this relationship out of sheer respect and care she received, despite the past, despite the implicit truth behind the talk that changed everything between them. Saraswati cherished what she had developed with Brahma. And wanted it to stay just the way it was, not a smidgen more or less than that. It was perfect for her. And for the organization. But it was not so for Brahma.

He, by now, had Saraswati all over his mind. Their talks became the most significant part of his day. Her voice, words and reactions started to make or break his day. If she was safe or not. If she ate or not. If she was happy or not. His emotions for Saraswati magnified as days passed. One day, on a message from him, Saraswati sensed it. She got anxious. No, not for herself. She was concerned about Brahma. He was somewhat like a big brother that she did not ever name, because the thought sounded like a silly old-fashioned label. Especially so in a corporate setup. If he was falling in love with her, he would be devastated to learn the truth. As for her, he was the dearest and the most dependable friend and guide, that she would not have liked to lose. This was no less than the feeling he had for her, but he would never appreciate it, or be satisfied with it. Or value it.

The last thing Saraswati wanted was to hurt Brahma's feelings. But a talk was imminent. The next morning at their tea session, she asked quite plainly, "What did you mean by those messages, Brahma? Why do I sense different emotions?" Brahma was astounded but did not deny anything. He promptly and unabashedly accepted his feelings for Saraswati

without getting into many details. He could barely find words, fumbled like a teenage boy in love, yet he was adequately clear. Brahma least expected the question so plain and straight. Softly he said, "I do not expect anything from you, Saraswati. Not even reciprocation. I hope you do not think of me as some pervert. I did not write or say to you anything to suggest that either. It is purely emotional, the love of the mind", he looked enquiringly at Saraswati, shakily took a breath and added, "Have I ever made you uncomfortable? I will never step into your personal space. Physically or otherwise. You have my word. I repeat, I do not seek anything from you. But I am only human and cannot help what I feel."

Saraswati was comforted, yet not too pleased about Brahma's emotional state. However, for her own peace, the fact that she was not expected to love him back was like a mountain taken off her chest. But of course, she did not know for how long. She did not state her mind to him, nor did he ask, but said, "You have never made me uncomfortable. That is a fact. But I feel this could become complicated in the future. For you, Brahma. Or worse, painful. And usually, such pains get passed on. Especially to the one causing it. That is me in this case!" He seemed awkward after all that he had already said, and promised, "Listen, I am sorry that we are having this talk today. You do not have to worry about it. I am no child, leave this with me. Nothing changes. You do not have to concern yourself with anything. Nothing, absolutely nothing will change."

That day, Saraswati went home all muddled but somewhat assured that she was not responsible for anything, or accountable. At least nothing in the near future could

fall apart. The next couple of months went well. They even traveled together for work and Saraswati gathered that Brahma's expectations from her had not at all altered. Nothing was different except the mindfulness deep within her. Which she was hiding successfully.

Few weeks later, on a normal working day, an old work acquaintance of Saraswati reached out to her. They connected back after a while and got talking over a few days. Brahma made some observations about Saraswati and asked her. She shared some bits with Brahma, like she always did, about other colleagues and people common between them, but not what she believed was private to them. In her head, she was clear that just the way she could not talk about Brahma's private matters to any of her friends, she would never talk about them to Brahma either. And this was not anything new. She always maintained the format. But in this particular case, Brahma did not quite like it. He felt left out. He believed that the place he had in Saraswati's life, where he had declared a stoical love for her, and she had expressed a loving friendship, was replaced.

Brahma desired an involvement in Saraswati's life where his opinion was sought on important life events, especially new relationships. He wanted it devotedly and directly from Saraswati. That was what his heart demanded. Brahma started to burn within. He also started to lose interest in work. He pried on Saraswati, conjectured, imagined, and subjected himself to more and more agony. Simply said, he was sore, and that created a bigger chaos within him than what existed. If Brahma had his way, he would put an end to this new friendship Saraswati had found, with immediate

effect, and bring things back to normal between him and her. But life does not ask for approvals before moving ahead. Saraswati started being watchful. This made Brahma even more inquisitive and perturbed. So, Saraswati sought space. Brahma turned panicky and agitated. He began looking physically unwell and pale. He became irregular at work. The office would keep looking for him most days, which was very unlike him. Saraswati felt utterly helpless about the situation.

Soon things between them went back to where they were five years back. Brahma became distant. Not because of anger, but because of unrest in his mind. He looked through Saraswati in the office corridors, meetings, and cafeteria. He seemed anxious, once again. Only this time, he looked pale, not red. He could not have exhibited his turbulent heart at work, so a disquiet substituted his weaker emotions. Saraswati tried to reach out, explain her side, or make a normal conversation, but Brahma was beyond reach. He went into a virtual hiding. He could not function very well with his own self, as a result of which he stopped involving her in work. He could not bear the sight of having her in the same room and not in his life the way he wanted it. If he was pressed to get Saraswati in the meeting, he would sit far away from her, not just physically, but also from her line of sight. Once again, the colleagues noticed. They noticed the fall of a great team, and a greater friendship, that they had once hoped to emulate.

Saraswati once again tasted Brahma's lack of confidence in her, expressing itself in various ways. She once again detested the stiffness in the air. She once again was amply

sure that it was affecting him, more than her. The cause was quite different this time around, but effect was similar. She did not want to attempt fixing things. Not immediately. Saraswati did not have the heart to risk it further, lest he thought she was bitter or disrespectful. Because she was not. All she had in her heart was empathy and reverence for Brahma. Empathy for his disquiet. And reverence for his unique influence in her life. But more importantly, she did not think it was appropriate to contend a good man when he was at his weakest. Therefore, Saraswati decided to wait. Even if it meant a lifetime. Sometimes deserting the battle is to honor your relationship. Sometimes keeping a relationship is not as vital as keeping its integrity. Sometimes the integrity of a relationship is not in keeping it. Nor is it in letting it go. It is in standing by. Saraswati resigned from the job.

Five years later, Saraswati was at a leadership summit. Jaded from the session, she walked out of it and went into the adjacent room where she was supposed to be the next speaker. What she saw was Brahma on the stage, taking a session. She looked into the agenda and realized that his name had been there. Although she never quite liked him as a speaker, her heart was filled with a certain warmness. The next session had to be a surprise mix of speakers from different industries debating on the subject, "AI in Metaverse & Augmented Workforce vs Cyber Security". Saraswati gathered herself. She knew she was one of the panelists. The Master of Ceremonies started to announce the names, and she found that Brahma was a part of it too. And he was on her side of the panel. The moderator had

informed Saraswati beforehand that this was an exclusive format they were experimenting with this year. They did not wish for the speakers to come too prepared. The idea was to keep it as authentic as it can be, for the media to get some unrehearsed and stimulating accounts to publish.

Saraswati walked up to the stage and shook hands with all the participants, including Brahma. She smiled at him, and he smiled back at her, but he was stunned to his core. When the debate began, Saraswati took the lead only so that Brahma gets some time to adjust to her presence. With a little rickety and somewhat awkward start, they soon found their balance. They saw themselves aiding each other's thoughts with illustrations and completing each other's sentences. They had picked exactly from where they had dropped. Together, Brahma and Saraswati dominated the stage. The session was a big success. "We knew you were colleagues in the past. But this was amazing! Unprecedented even!" said the moderator to the two of them once the session was over.

"We are back on the same page!" said Brahma, looking at Saraswati as they walked towards the tearoom. "And I have been on a stand-by for this, Brahma," responded Saraswati. "When passion sneaks in, it brings unrest, and friendship departs. But the good thing is, passion does not last, friendship does. And you and I Brahma, are a thing forever."

PS: Based on true events

Saraswati: The form of Mahadevi that reigns the dominion of words and their absence. She takes little interest in love, matrimony, or parenthood, which occasionally to an inquisitive

and rich mind makes for a magnetic attribute. She is driven by her duty, led by truth enough to separate milk from water, and detached by her strength of ultimate reality. She is another name for imagination through wisdom and consciousness and by virtue of this, she is low on patience about the lack of it.

SHIVAANGI
Marital Felicity

Yaa Devii Sarva-Bhuteshu Kaanti-Roopenna Samsthitaa |
To that Devi who in all beings abides as Loveliness and Beauty,

Yaa Devi Sarva-Bhuteshu Lakshmi-Roopenna Samsthitaa |
To that Devi who in all beings abides as Good Fortune,

Namas-Tasyai Namas-Tasyai Namas-Tasyai Namo Namah ||
Salutations to Her, Salutations to Her, Salutations to Her,
Salutations again and again.

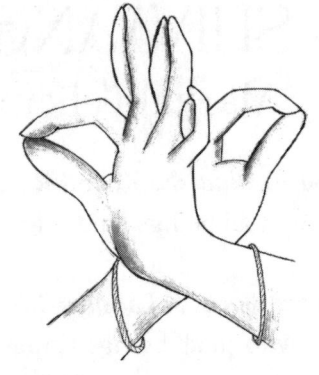

SHIVAANGI

CHAPTER 4

SHIVAANGI
Marital Felicity

Daksha Khanna, a global name in the pharma industry, cared only about two things, owning more and more patents, and his youngest child, his daughter Shivaangi. Daksha also had two sons, Buddhi and Urjah but he loved Shivaangi the most and was quite blatant about it. His wife Pratibha corrected Daksha whenever she felt he was unfairly prioritizing Shivaangi over the boys, but nothing much changed. Shivaangi had grown into an elegant, refined and well-educated young lady. She was level-headed enough to not misuse the power Daksha's love had conferred upon her. She was training for Odissi and took her Guru Sunartaka and his instructions like religion. Sunartaka was preparing Shivaangi for a solo concert in the next season. But then, an equally large part of Shivaangi's life was her full-time role in her father's business. Unlike her brothers, who were more interested in productivity, shareholders and increasing the global footprints of Moon Pharma, Shivaangi took a keen interest in research, development, and sustainability

initiatives. And that was how she had discovered Shiv.

There was not a single news piece written or recorded on Shiv, any of his published research papers, or an interview that Shivaangi had not consumed and filed with herself. Shiv Kapoor was a microbiologist from MIT, living in Los Angeles, running one of the fastest-growing healthcare companies in partnership with an American. It was clear from his interviews that he spoke as little as possible, to the point, with data, only when necessary and never to win an argument. Most recently, the world was frenzied about his latest discovery, an enzyme that could decompose non-biodegradable and hazardous waste at a very rapid speed. This enzyme formation was tested successfully under all types of weather conditions, temperatures, humidity levels and topographies. This was single-handedly the fastest solution to a cleaner planet, especially for the under-developed and developing countries. Shiv was interviewed not only for his discovery but also as a business owner, by virtue of which he was asked some truly rough questions, but no one had ever captured him rattled or agitated. Media had nicknamed him the Genius Yogi, who was always centered and un-flinched. To Shivaangi, as for many others around the world, Shiv was a refreshing change from the stereotypes of the business world.

There was soon going to be a Global Biotech Confluence in Zurich where Shiv was going to speak about his discovery in full detail. He had planned to make use of the platform to present the solutions using his new enzyme, which he had christened, The Sanjeevani. The event invitations were sent to state-sponsored representatives, global media, top scientists, and some select international pharma and healthcare companies, of which Moon Pharma was a part. Daksha Khanna was invited to it, and he had in turn nominated Shivaangi from Moon Pharma because this fell under the umbrella of sustainability. Shivaangi had never been this excited before, "Of course Dad, you know how I feel about environmental sustainability, and it will be a wonder like Shiv Kapoor opening the product to the markets of the world. I am thrilled already!" Shivaangi did not care to wait for her father's response and bolted out of the room, leaving both her father and brother, Buddhi, smiling.

Shivaangi flew out to Zurich. The next morning, after her swim, she took a quick shower, wore an emerald knee-length dress, paired it with nude pumps and handbag. Before leaving for the conference venue, she decided to grab some breakfast. So, she made headway to the restaurant. A lady from the hotel staff ushered her in and led her to an empty table. After parking her handbag on the table, as she turned around to get her breakfast, she saw Shiv cross her. He was talking to someone on his phone, earphones plugged in, and he held a plate in his right hand. He was tall, brawny at the right places, bespectacled, fair-skinned, sported a man bun and a dark, lustrous beard. He was wearing a crisp blue Saint Laurent, with the jacket thrown over his forearm, and magnificent hand-crafted half-brogue tan lace-up shoes. Shivaangi's eyes followed him inadvertently. "Oh, why did he sit on my table though!"

She requested one of the servers to send her some black coffee, pointing towards the table. She walked back, pulled a chair, and sat comfortably, "Hi Shiv!" Shiv looked up and

smiled at her. "Hey! Are you joining me for breakfast? Please do," lipped Shiv. "You are clearly not surprised that I know your name," said Shivaangi. "If Indians would not recognize me, I will be worried. That is the only part I like about this fame, in all honesty!" Shiv responded. Shivaangi's coffee arrived. "Sanjeevani is touted to become the biggest business there ever was. How…" Shivaangi was still speaking when Shiv interrupted her, "Can the knowledge of bringing what is lifeless back to life be a business? Sanjeevani is to make earth breathe, fully, again! Of course, there is a massive cost involved at every usage, which needs to be covered, but quite like the gift of life, this too needs to be earned, not bought. Don't you think?" Shivaangi was used to speaking the language of business, and how could she not, for unless one speaks commerce, they are seen as unpragmatic. Even foolish. Especially if it is a woman. Shiv now looking into Shivaangi's eyes continued, "That is why the patent! So, no one can import or sell without permission. And I did not think of competition because there is none." He smiled, "Oh, I think I must rush. Lovely speaking to you. Err did not catch your name," said Shiv. "Shiv. I mean Shiva-angi! Pleasure." Shiv left immediately. Shivaangi looked for her bag and found that it was on the table next to the one she was sitting on.

    The conference was as fabulous as it could have been with the Genius Yogi on a massive stage, standing in front of an enormous screen playing a demo video to explain the enzyme and its functioning with other molecules. There was a complete hush in the room. People were listening to his voice like they were verses from Vedas. After the conference, Shivaangi moved to the lobby for a cup of tea, when the media reached out to her for a sound bite. "Ma'am, do you

have any statement to make about this discovery by Shiv Kapoor? What will it mean for the Pharma industry? A new Business Unit?" Shivaangi was speaking to a journalist when Shiv saw her from a distance and walked up to her. Once she finished, "So you are my guest, and I did not even know your name. I hope you forgive me," said a visibly embarrassed Shiv. "That's ok really," Shivaangi smiled at Shiv explaining himself. "Truth be told, I never stay in the hotel where my company hosts any events. Not so much of a people person, you see! So, I did not expect to see any of my guests in that hotel. And then, I spend most of my time in the lab. Brad, my partner, keeps telling me to be more active in the real world and watch some TV," laughed Shiv. "Do not fret at all. You may not have found me in the news anyway. And if you did, it would be more for my concerts than Moon Pharma. I stay away from the press unless it is unavoidable," phrased Shivaangi. "Concerts! You have piqued my curiosity now, let us talk later in the day, shall we?" Shiv proposed and Shivaangi promptly agreed. They exchanged their numbers; Shiv resumed his dialogue with other guests, and Shivaangi with some of her connections from other parts of the world.

Shivaangi had no expectations of Shiv meeting her in the evening and thought of the earlier interaction as a nicety. But Shiv called her up. They started with a cordial chat at the restaurant of their hotel. Shivaangi was pleasantly surprised to know about Shiv's deep interest in Indian dance forms. "I trained for Kuchipudi. Do you know it was originally performed by men only?" Shiv said to Shivaangi. "So was Odissi actually, but now women outnumber men

multifold," Shivaangi chuckled. Shiv added, "I also play the Veena. So many times, I do not know what to choose, the science or the arts. I suppose that is why I was so keen to meet you today. You seem to be quite like me," grinned a visibly delighted Shiv. "Quite like me!" Shivaangi thought to herself. She had never expected to meet Shiv like she did. The man she had idolized for years. Nor had she ever projected him to be such an unassuming person. For the genius he was, he was extremely easy to get along with. Shiv and Shivaangi moved out of the restaurant to the lobby, then to the poolside and then to a 24-hour coffee shop inside the hotel. He had a calming effect on her. His acceptance and connection to his feminine side inside his massive masculinity were particularly mesmerizing. Shiv was a rare find. And they talked all night.

Next day Shivaangi flew back to India. She followed all the news on Sanjeevani till she stopped hearing so much about it. She gave it a year or two, thinking a process as elaborate as that would not get rolled out so quickly. But Shiv went out of her radar. So, one day, she looked up for his phone number and called him up, "Hi, is that Shiv?" "Hey Shivangi, is that you really? Wow!" Shiv said in a cheerful voice. "I will be straight forward with you. Where have you vanished? Why can't I hear anything about you or Sanjeevani?" questioned Shivaangi. "I am back in India. Up in the Himalayas. As for Sanjeevani, it is safe, is all I can say on a phone call. Come over. Meet me. Oh, but I should warn you, there are no fancy hotels in this area. But then, I will be delighted to have you as my house guest, if that is okay with you," Shiv offered. Shivaangi took her car out at 4 in the morning, refused to be driven by anyone else, and drove straight to the mountains to meet Shiv over the weekend.

After a non-stop drive of over seven hours from Delhi, as she reached close to her destination, the sky was red and gold. She saw an immense meadow that lasted till an oak grove on her left, with a perfect backdrop of lofty mountains speckled with snow. On the other end of the meadow was a stunning but small stone house. The house had a green sloping roof and a chimney blowing smoke to the far right. There was a wide, cobbled road leading to the house. Everything was bathed in golden light, the breeze felt like satin on her skin, and fragrant with wildflowers. There were no cars outside the house, just a battery-run cart, so Shivaangi parked her car under a tree somewhat away from the house. She stepped out of the car and heard some quacking. As she toured a few yards, she could not believe that there was a natural pond four times the size of an Olympic size swimming pool, brimming with fresh water on which floated merrily a raft of ducks. Also, there were dozens of chickens clucking about the lawns around the pond. The apricot, apple, and tangerine trees in the vicinity of the house were bursting with birds of all kinds, making an extemporaneous symphony. There were rose shrubberies, a vast bed of daisies and many other flowers she didn't know the names for. A little away, she could see profuse rows of vegetables growing. Some in bloom, some in the waiting. On her further left, partly hidden behind the stone wall at the end of the pond, was a rain-harvesting plant. When she turned around 360 degrees, she realized the tree under which she parked her

car was that of a Rhododendron, ablaze with red blossoms. On top of the house, she could see the solar plant. She was looking skywards when a large nicotine-brown mountain dog came rushing towards her, and behind him was Shiv dressed in a cotton kurta[1] pajama, "Hey Shivaa, I heard your car engine. Welcome to my humble abode. Meet Gana, my boy! Let us go inside. The sun is going down and it will soon become nippy." He tapped on Shivaangi's shoulder, gave her a side hug and then went to open the boot of her car to get the luggage. "Shivaa! Did you just give me a new name Shiv?" she said, bending on her knees to play with the dog but looking at Shiv. "You don't like it?" Shiv asked mischievously, making his way towards the main door of the house with Shivaangi's bag in his hand. "I do. I do. Terribly similar to your name though…" when she suddenly stopped at the sight of a large bull sitting beside the door. "Oh, that's Nandi. He is my friend. Perhaps the closest one." Shivaangi stroked Nandi's neck, and he responded, looking straight into her eyes and jingled his bells. He looked pleased.

Shiv built a bonfire in the evening after dinner and they sat next to each other in the lawn under the stars, "I had a fallout with Brad, my American partner. He wanted a large license fee during the patent period for Sanjeevani. The kind of fee under-developing or even developing countries would never be able to afford. Even if they could, it would affect their progress in other areas. Or worse, become the cause of corruption, scams and a whole political muddle. My original idea and the reason behind developing this enzyme

---

[1] Kurta – traditional Indian men's wear

was to make waste disposal so convenient that it becomes a solution for nations that are economically too weak to take enough measures for sustainability. But Brad's agenda was manufacturing complications, and no solutions. So, I broke off the partnership, paid him up for everything he asked for, and kept the patent with me. I am now in the process of building a new company and a new plant. This will take time, but the buyers are willing to wait. Meanwhile, I am also working on building a village model for sustainable living here, which can be replicated by other states and countries." Shiv took a deep-deep breath, "So that's my story."

"Wow! What are you made of Shiv?" asked Shivaa, enamored by the strength of his character, moving the tip of her finger on the brim of her now half-filled cup of green tea. "The same stuff that you are made of Shivaa!" and pointed towards the floating image of the crescent moon in the pond close by. Shiv moved closer to Shivaangi's face in the benign soft glow of the fire next to them. But Shivaangi's phone rang up. It was Sunartaka. Shivaangi was speaking on phone, but gaping at Shiv as he was dabbing geranium oil behind her ears. Then he grabbed her feet and rubbed them with his warm hands. Shivaa finished the call, dropped the cup on the grass, soared breathlessly at Shiv, sat in his lap, held his face and kissed him deeply. Shiv did not want to stop at that, but then Shivaangi said, "I have a solo concert in two months. My first. Would you like to come? Better still, why don't you come a day or two earlier? I would like you to meet my family."

"Knockout! I have not even begun wooing you properly, did not expect this to go so fast.," laughed

Shiv. "You have been wooing me for a decade now. All unwittingly. And after we met in Zurich, there was not a single day when I did not think of you," revealed Shivaangi. "Then why didn't you reach out? I thought that night of coffee and conversations in Zurich did not linger in your mind, as much as it did in my memory. I could not shake it off," explained Shiv. Shivaangi pulled herself closer to Shiv's lips, "Then why didn't you call me?" Shiv was tempted to kiss Shivaangi but giving details seemed more important, "My parents had passed away when I was two. I do not know anything about them. And then I was raised by foster parents, who too passed away a few years back. I have seen enough life to know that I may put you in trouble. I am not so sure that the great Khannas would like an orphan with an indefinite pedigree for their only daughter. I don't come from a known family, and you can see my house for yourself, and my life choices. I am a minimalist. Even if I have all the wealth in the world, this is how I will live. Five kurta sets in my wardrobe, no cars, no jewels, no brands, no mansions, nothing, nothing like the life you are used to living." "We shall see to that!" responded Shivaangi with confidence that made Shiv nervous with joy. The next morning, Shiv took her for a ride on Nandi, made her a headdress from wild daisies, rolled chicks in her lap as she giggled in utter bliss. Then he cooked for her and together they ate leisurely under the mountain sun while reading poetry. Their love blossomed.

A month later, Shiv came down to meet Shivaangi's family. "Who does not know you, Shiv? You are a phenomenon. It's a shame that your partner didn't know better. I like this new look of yours. Very Indian. Well, you make every attire look good," said Daksha, sipping his glass of wine and wearing a shine in his eyes. Shiv smiled politely as Daksha continued, "So, what do you plan to do? Let me offer this directly, would you like to partner with Moon Pharma? We could expedite things, you know. You have already lost two years from your licensing period. Allow us to help you!" "What do you propose, sir?" Shiv asked. "Just give us the license and allow us to manage everything for you. You can lead the research and leave the business to me," Buddhi and Urjja chimed in, "Yes, that sounds like a plan. We are going to be a family now, after all." "I will think about it and let Shivaa know, hope that's okay with you, sir. I shall head to my hotel now. Have a nice evening!" Shiva left abruptly.

Shivaangi heard about the meeting from her brothers and gathered things had gone dreadfully wrong. She hadn't expected her father to mention the patent of all the things in their first meeting. She called Shiv but there was no response. She left several messages, emails and made more calls but there was no response. Now she could not live with the fact that she had lost Shiv because of her father's insatiability. And what made it worse was that he justified this as his love for his daughter. Shivaangi left home and moved into a separate apartment. Her heart ached for Shiv. She threw herself into her dance recitals and made that the channel to express her grief.

Then came the day of her concert. Shivaangi had finished performing "The nine forms of Durga" to a packed auditorium and received a standing ovation. Sunartaka was

happy to his brims, watching her from the wings. Shivaangi went and touched his feet. "You had the audiences transfixed, my dear girl!", said a beaming Sunartaka, "now go meet your patrons". There were fans lined up on her path from the stage to the green room. Smiling, thanking, and getting clicked with them, she maneuvered her way to the room. She did not know her solo could be this successful. But all through the recital, she sensed as though someone was observing her very closely. It made her extra cautious on the stage, it felt like someone was watching her moves so attentively, that one wrong mudra on her part will break the whole spell!

She got to her room, content about the show, but relieved to be back in her space, alone. Shivaangi's happiness was incomplete. Her family was sent passes, but their pride did not allow them to join. But her emptiness was mostly about Shiv. Inside the green room, she stood in front of the mirror and took a good look at herself. The large red dot on her forehead was shining bright against her polished caramel skin like the rising sun on the horizon. The drape of her sari[2] was immaculately holding her bosom and ran up till her well-crafted collar bones. One necklace was wrapped close to the curve of her neck and the other dropped all the way down to her midriff. Her earpieces dangled weightlessly, leaving soft pecks sometimes on her jawline, other times on her cheeks. Her large eyes were well kohled but vacant. Her lips naturally pink and plump but wore no smile.

---

[2] Sari – a long piece of cloth traditionally worn by Indian women by draping around the body

She sat down to take off her right earpiece looking at herself in the mirror. "How I wish he was here today to see me perform. Wonder what he would have said. How I wish he helped me take off this elaborate jewelry," and she looked away from the mirror. Her internal monologue was suddenly broken by a knock at the door. Shivaangi looked towards it, still holding her right ear. It was Shiv, peeking in through the ajar door. Her eyes shimmered in disbelief, face shone up, and a radiant smile played on her lips. Shiv sauntered in and said impishly, "It is alright. I accept your apology. You do not need to hold your ear any longer." Shivaangi smiled harder with a crimson blush. But her eyes welled up out of incredulity and joy. Shiv walked close to her and began impulsively undoing her necklace, followed by another one. He held her perfect waist from behind, sticking his nose into her sweet-smelling nape and whispered, "You looked every bit like a goddess on stage today, Shivaa." Shivaangi closed her already flooded eyes, a tear coursed down her glowing face as she murmured, "So it was you watching me all along." She said a silent prayer and smiled like never before. Then she turned towards Shiv as he continued, "I did not bring any flowers. I did go to the florist, though. They are waiting for you on the bed."

Shivaangi: Mahadevi's name for resolute love, the ultimate force, the supreme motivator of the material world. No matter what the gain or loss, she willingly becomes a resounding naught when in love. No matter how hostile times become, she will always be Shiva's Shivaa.

MAYA
Wealth, Wellness, and Liberation

Yaa Devi Sarva-Bhuteshu Chaayaa-Roopenna Samsthitaa |
To that Devi who in all beings abides as Reflection,

Yaa Devi Sarva-Bhuteshu Bhraanti-Roopenna Samsthitaa |
To the Devi who in all beings abides as Delusion,

Namas-Tasyai Namas-Tasyai Namas-Tasyai Namo Namah ||
Salutations to Her, Salutations to Her, Salutations to Her,
Salutations again and again.

MAYA

CHAPTER 5

MAYA

Wealth, Wellness and Liberation

It was a busy morning at Welman Brothers, one of the most successful corporate law firms of the world. Kritika came up to Agni with two cups of coffee, cheerfully handed one to Agni, perched herself on his desk close to his knees while he swiveled on his chair, "So? Liking it?" She flipped the lanyard around Agni's neck, "I see, you have got your identity card. The coffee here is good. I am sure you will like it. And I am so glad you chose to join here Agni," she said, pressing his shoulder, "I must rush to the meeting room. Let's meet at lunch." Agni nodded and smiled vacantly. He was grateful for this role after he had to prematurely leave the previous law firm, and he did not want Kritika or anyone else to think otherwise. The reason was not entirely professional. His girlfriend for over two years, Pari, had walked out of his life and he had to let her go while he was still in love with her. She loved him too, but sometimes love is not enough.

Corporate life doesn't give you any room to lick and nurse your wounds in private, especially the wounds that aren't apparent to the eyes. Pari had met Agni in his office complex for the last time, and that was where they had decided to never see each other again. Agni had walked back to his office, but before he could reach his workstation, he curled up inside a hidden alcove under the staircase and sobbed till he could not breathe. He finished his day and went home, but the morning after, he could not get up from his bed. The same bed that he had shared with Pari many times. The eerie silence in his heart was so loud that he shut himself off in the hope to dampen it. Agni was worried that others would get to hear it. He kept his windows shut and curtains drawn so he never found out if it was a day or a night, for it did not matter anymore. Work didn't matter, goals didn't, and the future ceased to exist. He even considered taking pills and going to sleep forever. He soaked his pillow in rivers of tears without food or water, till his close friend Kritika found him in that condition.

"You have lost your job Agni. They have been trying to reach you for 15 days now. Where is your phone, your laptop?" Agni could barely keep his eyes open. He looked at Kritika, "How did you come in? And how do you know about my job?" Kritika got up to bring him a glass of water, which she had to wash first, as the kitchen was a mess. "Pari met me. She has given me the duplicate key you had given to her. And some more stuff of yours. Sorry I was worried sick, could not reach you on your phone, so used the key to take a look at you. Agni, your parents are preparing to come here. They could not reach you either. They heard from your office and informed me."

Agni sat up, sipped some water, and spelled out, "Did

any of us know when we worked together in the same team, and I fell hopelessly in love with Pari that it wasn't forever? I thought my feelings were forever, and so should be hers. But Pari was gone before she actually left, Kritika. I could not see it coming. Or did not want to. But I hope you, my best friend in this whole wide world and I are truly forever. As for Pari, I guess I need some time". Time. It does not heal anything. That is a myth. Both joy and sorrow from the past neither die nor kill. They just make visits. And time teaches us how to deal with those visits. Then there are memories. The memories to endure. With time, we learn to store them in a different place. A recessed place in our mind.

Agni took six months. There were some good days and some bad. He gathered his broken pieces. Nursed his wounds. Reflected on what could have been. And concluded that what belongs to him would never have him do reproductions of the past. Agni knew he can never be whole again, but who or what is whole on this planet anyway. He started to look for a new opportunity and that was how he reached this new workplace where Kritika was already working.

His calendar said he had to be in the Training Room for his Induction Program, so he found his way to it and grabbed a seat. Senior executives of the organization were walking in, one after another, to do sessions on their functions for the new joiners to comprehend the organizational structure, philosophy, and their contribution in the whole scheme of things. The head of operations had finished his presentation and, on his way out, he was heard talking to a woman whose voice, sort of, woke Agni up from his slumber. The six

months long torpor. Agni looked over his shoulder towards the voice to see who it was, but he could not, as the man was blocking the view and the woman was on the other side. His subconscious now followed the voice. Little did he know how very extended in his life that would be. He looked around the room and found most of them, women included, had their heads turned towards that voice.

Now he was too embarrassed to look that way, so he kept his face towards the dais. He knew the voice was coming closer. It was a woman in a cream organza sari, which was a little slack around her waist. She walked fast towards the screen holding just a phone in her hand and then she turned her face towards the audience. Was she luminous? Agni rubbed his eyes to check if he was dreaming. Or was he dead, and she was a goddess? When she spoke, Agni could hear her voice but could not get himself to hear her words. Why couldn't he decipher anything she said? And why was she glowing? Agni's eyes roved over her body. Inadvertently. He could see the softness of her waist and her perfect navel through the organza. The neckline of her blouse revealed her beauty bones on which danced a slender chain this way and that way with her each movement. She was wearing spectacles. How can a goddess be wearing spectacles! Agni rubbed his eyes again, opened the bottle of mineral water in front of him, and gulped a few sips. As she turned her back towards the audience to point something on the screen, he gawked at her toned and deep upper back. She was tall. A smile frolicked on Agni's lips. After months of despondency, this was the first honest smile. It seemed to Agni that she was about to wrap up the session and he was praying with all his

heart that she would not. She walked out of the room, and this time, Agni's eyes moved every inch with her.

It was lunchtime. Agni rushed out of the training room with a newfound energy in the direction of the cafeteria. Kritika was waiting for him there. She waved at him, and Agni joined her on the table. "Who is that woman?" Agni asked Kriti. "Who?" inquired Kritika. "Oh, I did not check for her name. Truth be told, I could not hear a single word after she walked in." "Dude, what are you talking about? Which woman? What happened?" Agni jumped, "That one, that one! 3 o'clock," as he saw her walking into the cafeteria. "Oh, that's Maya. She is in the leadership team. What about her?" Agni sighed, "She is divine. Isn't she?" He surveyed Maya's back as she walked unhurriedly towards an unoccupied table. She raised her velvet arms to her head, lifting her blouse by a bit on both sides, revealing her waist entirely. Then she opened her tresses as her slender fingers played with her hair to tame them back into a knot in a habitual sort of way. But she was with a man. "Who is that man?" Agni asked Kritika. "Will you eat something or not? I must go back to my workstation, Agni. He is Aniket. They are close friends. Or so I think," said Kritika, not too pleased. "You carry on Kritika. I will go bring my food. Will catch you later." Kritika left the table. Agni thought to himself, as he watched Maya and Aniket talk to each other with a comfort that made him strangely uncomfortable – do not listen to your heart. It cannot be in the right. Why else is it placed to the left of your body! Listen to your brain. That is always on top of everything.

In a few weeks, Agni got introduced to many more

people, some through Kritika and some directly, including Venu who worked with Aniket, who Agni had developed a contempt for. Simply because he had Maya's unhindered company. He made friends with Anu in HR and Abhinav in IT. A girl named Shirley within his team, he had grown quite fond of, she was Kritika's friend as well. Agni now moved around in a group of five and got to see Maya often. He crossed her in corridors, the cafeteria or shared the elevator space with her on a lucky day. Every time that happened, celestial music played inside his head. He even participated in the talent competition at the office party only so he could see her closely. He was smitten and joyful. Agni did think of Pari occasionally when something triggered her memory, but he was not sad anymore. It was Maya who occupied his mind most of the time.

    The room from where his team worked had a large window that overlooked the smoking zone. For most large organizations, smoking zones are somewhat like unofficial meeting places. Many decisions, sometimes significant ones, are taken there over the drags of cigarettes, and not in the conference rooms. Agni gathered that Maya was there occasionally. He observed that she never smoked, never held a cigarette in her hand. She came there with someone or the other for a dialog or to finish a conversation that could not be done in a formal setting of her cabin or a meeting room. He started to watch her silently. However long Maya stayed, Agni watched. This was easy because the windowpanes did not allow anyone to look in, owing to client confidentiality, whereas Agni could from the inside. He abhorred every man who spent time with Maya and concluded that all of

them wanted her. Some smart ones who recognized that they can never earn her, reconciled by being friends with her, just so they have some proximity than nothing. And the others tried to impress her at every opportunity. But a few of them, to Agni, were nothing more than an eyesore next to his Goddess. He wasn't sure if Maya knew all this and overlooked it or couldn't see it at all. While he watched Maya day after day, Shirley observed him.

Once, when Agni's manager announced an HR activity where some of the leadership members would be present and he named Maya, Agni's joy knew no bounds. Maya stood there right in front of him, and all Agni did was gawk at her unblinkingly with a silly smile. Once again, spoken words were alien to his ears. Everything was white noise. After a while, Shirley chucked a whiteboard marker at him, which barely missed his eye. Later she took Agni out to the coffee machine, "Sorry, you could have lost an eye today!" she chuckled. "But what's up with you Agni?" "I am crazy about her, Shirley. I know she is beyond my reach. It has been over a year now. I may never speak to her. I do not know how to explain this. But I cannot help looking at her." Shirley smiled, thinking of this as Agni's rebound. Although a strange rebound, for Maya did not even know he existed.

After Shirley found out, Agni became relaxed about discussing her with the group, which he did for the most part of the day. He began checking with Venu, who worked with Aniket, on when and where Aniket met Maya. Shirley elbowed him every time Maya was around. Except Kritika, everyone was now Agni's spy. At the annual party, his eyes searched only for Maya. After his team performance, when

Agni came back to the changing rooms, he found his friend Anu weeping. He heard her out, consoled her, cheered her up by clicking a few pictures of her and flattered her. She felt important and expressed gratitude to Agni. But "You could thank me by getting Maya to agree for a picture with me. Can you?" wisecracked Agni. "Bloody hell Agni! I work with HR. I do not run a matrimonial service," yelled an already disturbed Anu. Saying so, she went out in a huff and told Kritika about it. Agni joined the group at the bar. Shortly, Maya came to the bar and behind her was Aniket. Agni seethed with jealousy, his nails dug into his palms and his teeth into his lower lip. Kritika quipped, "They make a great couple, don't they?" and gave Agni a sidelong glance. Coming from a friend as close as Kritika, Agni could not stand this. Shirley saw it, "Agni, I know how you feel. We all do. But I hope you know that her full name is Maya-Abrol-Babbar. Having a little fun is something else, but can you not see she is married?" "I know everything about her, Shirley. She is married. She is older than me by a decade. She is much-much senior to me professionally. And that she is unachievable. Why else do you think I have never approached her? I will not. But like I said, I cannot help what I feel. Quite like I cannot help feeling inferior to all the people who have access to her. All these people in the leadership team who can walk up to her and talk to her anytime they wish to. Particularly Aniket, who is closest to her. But why can I not admire her? Love her? Is my love invalid, only because she doesn't know I exist?" After that day, Agni stopped talking to Kritika. He averted eating lunch with the group.

December that year, Kritika's sister, Ritika, who was more than a sister to Agni, invited him to her birthday party. "I know you and Kritika are not speaking to each other. But how can I celebrate without you Agni? Do come, it will be a nice garden party." Ritika's husband was an army officer who worked as an aide-de-camp to the Army Chief. She was wearing a mini-skirt, stockings with boots and a sharp trench coat. "Oh, how I wish Maya was here. Do you think she wears things like these, Kritika?" queried Agni. "Aargh! Stop chewing my brains and go to your Maya," retorted Kritika. "Talking about birthdays. You know I ordered a bouquet for Maya's birthday. Categorically told the florist to not put my name on it. But guess what, he did! I was petrified. Thankfully, I was in the office lobby and grabbed hold of him. I told him I was her PA and took it from him. With a heart as heavy as a mountain, I had to trash those 30 scarlet roses," Agni disclosed. Astounded and miffed, Kritika walked away, leaving Agni alone with his drink.

Agni had understood by now that Kritika had feelings for him. However, he was feigning innocence to discourage her. But then he decided to reduce Maya's mentions to her. A few weeks later, the group ordered pizzas to celebrate a client win. They all logged out to go to the cafeteria, but as they were leaving, Agni saw Maya walking up to the smoking zone. "Oh, I don't feel so good, you guys carry on!", announced Agni. "What happened? Never mind, you and I can eat here at your workstation. I will go bring a pizza here," Kritika said affectionately. "No, I do not think I will eat pizza. You should go with the group." Kritika felt slighted. She was anyway feeling overlooked by him for

a long time. But Shirley saw Maya through the window. The group went to the cafeteria and Agni stayed behind to watch Maya to his heart's fill. "Are you feeling any better, Agni," asked Kritika as she entered the room. "He is all good, Kritika, it is all Maya's maya," commented Shirley. Kritika looked at Agni to confirm if that was true. Agni smiled sheepishly. After that episode, Kritika distanced herself, and the group stopped checking with him for lunch or any other outings.

Agni began to fib. He told them that he had overcome his feelings and that there will be no more Maya-Maya-Maya insanity. However, the truth was far from it. One day, when he entered the office, Maya was walking right ahead of him. She was wearing an Indian outfit. Her voluptuous back hugged in a *kurti*. Hair tossed on one side. The mole on her nape. Her swaying waist. Her bare arms under her dupatta. Desire gripped Agni. She strode towards her cabin, but Agni's mind went into a tizzy. He could not think of anything other than Maya. That day, he had to submit a pilot project that everyone on the team coveted. As soon as he made his submission, his manager, who was ever so nice to him, called for him and told him that it was full of errors. Giant errors! He gave Agni one last opportunity to correct it, but the project was way too important for niceties. The manager told him plainly that if it was not done right the very same day, he could consider himself out of the project. Agni stayed back for the night. But Maya had him in her grip. He decided to fantasize about her for half an hour before focusing on the work single-mindedly. It soon became an hour, then two and then three. He never

got to fix the project.

The next morning, Agni took the stairs to evade Maya. Before he could reach his workstation, his Subject Matter Expert called him, "The manager does not want to see your face. Go to room no. 8 and do your routine work." Shortly he received mail that he was removed from his dream project because of underperformance. Agni wrote an apology mail, but it was too late. The insanity for over four years was making him pay dearly, but he still wanted Maya, hopelessly. He took two days off to recover from the loss and gather some courage to face his manager and his friends again.

The day Agni got back to work, Abhinav, his friend from IT, was waiting for him outside the building. He looked harrowed, "Agni, did you get to know?" "What?" asked Agni. "Maya has left the organization," declared Abhinav pensively. Agni rushed to Maya's cabin, where he had not had the nerve to go before and found it empty. His life of loveliness seemed to be crashing down. Agni went to the washroom and sobbed like a baby, not knowing what to do. He tried to get Maya's contact number from his sources, but either they didn't have it, or they couldn't give it because of company policies. He searched for her on social media but did not have the courage to send her a friend request. For the fear of rejection. Or worse, no response, because she did not even know who he was. Agni could not bear to spend the day at work when Maya was not in the same building. He canceled his drop by the office cab, took a rickshaw to the metro station and reached home. He found himself choking up every half hour. This was not a breakup,

for Maya was within Agni and nowhere else. Yet the despair was tremendous. It was silent. It was more private than before. It had no mourners. No sympathizers. No supporters. It was a lone excruciating internal battle. Agni could not have let history repeat itself. He bewailed the loss yet trusted that this was not the end. The next morning, he hauled himself out of his bed and went to work. Following few weeks, he was mostly confined to his room, his floor. Inaudible. Broken and dim.

Agni went and stood outside Maya's cabin every day, despite the cameras, imagining her inside it, till one day the cabin was occupied by Maya's successor. It was a lady again. He went in, introduced himself, and conversed with the new lady. Ended up discussing Maya even with her. But when he stepped out of the cabin, he appreciated his feeling more than ever. The lady he had just met was around the same age, the same level as Maya and pretty in her own way, but he felt no nervousness, no dire need to impress her, no desire. Like he did for Maya. He was not crazy after all. It was love. An illusion, a fantasy, a mirage, but love, nonetheless.

In some months, Kritika also left the organization. Perhaps she had finally given up on Agni. And a few months thereupon, Agni too resigned from his job at Welman. He started his own legal practice and got involved in politics, which was his chief interest before Maya. In a year or two, he gathered the poise to follow Maya on social media. His phone permanently carried a private gallery full of Maya's pictures, which he had collected from her stint at Welman, and the rest from her social media pages.

Years gave way to years, and it was now twelve years

since Agni had left Welman Brothers, but he felt the exact same way about Maya as he did on his first day inside the training room. While Agni thought of Maya many times a day, every day, for all seventeen years, Maya never found out. Time, distance, even the presence of other women had failed to dampen Agni's feelings for an unobtainable and heedless Maya. For years, he went to spiritual places to seek her. Met and confided in holy men and women to find the right path. Observed fasts, took holy dips, meditated, and did many a ritual to find peace, if not Maya. Yet his madness turned fiercer with every passing year, and he conceded that her place could never be filled in. In these twelve years of worshipping Maya's memories, and five years of deifying her at Welman, Agni was explicitly clear that no one or nothing can be enough to replace Maya's absence in his life. Even her absence had an attendance that was irreplaceable and non-negotiable. He abdicated. Submitted to it and gave up the strife.

He now referred to her absence as Noor, the light of his life. His life had no room for anyone else, for he had married Noor. He came home to her and shared all his meals with her. He went to bed with Noor and woke up with her. Agni argued with her and then reconciled with her. Noor had filled up every nook and corner of Agni's insides and outsides. She was journeying with him through his life.

At 36, Agni vowed complete celibacy and that he will take no woman in his lifetime. Physically or emotionally. Noor, the light of Maya's absence, was the goddess he worshipped and would do so for the rest of his life. He

would either find deliverance in the next life, or Moksha[1]. In Maya, he had found his Goddess of Salvation.

PS: Based on true events

Maya: The form of Mahadevi, the wealth of body, mind and soul which makes life worth living. She is wellness and she is power. Her presence can make the impossible possible. Her absence, on the other hand, can drive a person to insanity. Her unimpeded pursuit can lead a person to the blindness of the mind's eye and a never-ending chase. But her pursuance could also open the doorway to Vaikuntha, to liberation. The labyrinth to unravel is Maya.

---

[1] Moksha – Salvation

SATI
Love and Renunciation

Yaa Devi Sarva-Bhuteshu Vritti-Roopenna Samsthitaa |
To that Devi who in all beings abides as Vacillation,

Yaa Devi Sarva-Bhuteshu Smriti-Roopenna Samsthitaa |
To that Devi who in all beings abides as Memory,

Namas-Tasyai Namas-Tasyai Namas-Tasyai Namo Namah ||
Salutations to Her, Salutations to Her, Salutations to Her,
Salutations again and again.

SATI

CHAPTER 6

SATI
Love and Renunciation

Sati Sharma and her husband Ajah were holidaying in Mussoorie with Sati's sister, her husband, and their kids when they read about Operation Blue Star. Amritsar was their home and *Harmandir Sahab* was as sacred to them as was *Durgiana Temple*. Eighteen months before the operation a prominent political leader from Punjab had invited the leader of the rebellion to reside inside the Golden Temple in order to evade arrest by government authorities.

The decision to launch the operation was taken by the then Prime Minister of India, Indira Gandhi. It was a military operation carried out by Indian security forces in early June 1984 to drive out Damdami Taksal, Bhindrawale[1] and their followers from the Golden Temple complex. It was supposed to be a day-long operation that went out of control and hurt the sentiment of every Punjabi. *Harmandir Sahib* was revered by Sikhs and Hindus alike. But the

---

[1] Bhindrawale – leader of the Sikh organization Damdami Taksal

news was petrifying for Hindus in particular because this meant there will be more hostility for Hindus in an already perilous environment of Punjab, especially Amritsar, where this episode had taken place.

"Last year in October, they stopped a bus going to Jalandhar and killed six Hindu passengers. One of them was my friend's brother. This was just a few months after DIG Atwal was murdered inside Harmandir Sahib. Can you believe it? Inside the temple! Then something happened in Gobindgarh too. I do not know if we should live in Amritsar anymore. Communal riot is not something uncommon across the world. Promises of brotherhood become moth-eaten. Cities that were home heavens to numerous people turned into junkyards. However, what gets impacted the most is humanity. Any of us becoming bait to the rampage is not even the last thing I would wish for," expressed a distressed Sati to her husband. "Now-now do not think about it too much. Nothing will go wrong. I do not want this to trigger your epilepsy. You are here for a holiday. Enjoy your today," said her husband mildly. "How can I relax when Amritsar is burning? That is where we have everything. And now with this episode, something is bound to happen added Sati, overcome by anxiety. "We shall see, Sati! All our business is there. We cannot pick up the factories and leave. Can we? We have a responsibility towards our workers too. They are in Punjab because of their work. And most importantly, Punjab is as much ours as theirs, don't you think," explained Ajah. "So, what are we going to do? Last time you encountered them, you lost an eye, Ajah! Have you forgotten what happened when your

car simply overtook theirs? They stopped your car in the middle of a busy road and banged your head on the steering. No one could do a thing! I mean, you lost the vision in one eye. Is it not a loss big enough? I have nothing but gratitude that you came back safe to me that night. But merely the thought of what all could have happened makes me tremble with fear." Ajah held his wife by her shoulders, gave her a reassuring, wordless smile and asked her to come for dinner.

The fact that there was military action inside the Harmandir Sahab was criticized. World over it was seen as an attack on Sikhism. As a mark of protest, some Sikh soldiers in the army deserted their units, as did several others from government roles, and many returned the awards they had once received.

On the 31$^{st\,of}$ October 1984 came the news that Indira Gandhi was assassinated by her bodyguards Satwant Singh and Beant Singh. Her death, the revenge of rebellion leader's killing, the payback for Operation Blue Star was celebrated by some. Some said they were seen distributing sweets at traffic signals in Delhi and some other cities of India. This further led to a separate public uproar, especially by the supporters of the Indian National Congress, resulting in the 1984 anti-Sikh riots. Delhi was set on fire for several days. As for Punjab, it had been burning for years and continued to burn.

Four years later, Sati's kid sister, who lived in Jammu, delivered a baby boy. Sati received a telegram carrying the good news. Her parents' house was also in Jammu and her sister was living with them for a while. This was a joyful time for the entire family, and Sati wanted to join them.

Ajah suggested to her, "Why don't you go spend a month or so with them? You can be of help too." "I would love to, but you have not been keeping well these days. This off and on fever of yours!" said Sati. "Oh, it is a minor seasonal thing. You must go," dismissed Ajah. Sati spoke filled with anguish, "And I have not been able to get rid of the images in my head from the blast at *Shivala Bhaiyan*. Your mother and sister were barely home from the Shivala when we heard the explosion. This *Shivratri* will be recalled by so many families for the wrong reason." Ajah looking out of the window at the Laburnum tree, said softly, "Mere Guru Sahab ne keha si - Har bhagat Bhagautee tisai kee jo ranadheer dharei, teh ang sang tum lag rahu jo paachhe pag na dharei! (My Guru Sahab said, Bhagwati assists the devotee who remains composed in a battlefield. She is beside the warrior who never retreats.) They are terrorists Sati and their objective is to terrorize us. We cannot stop living. Because that is what they want. They want us to run for our lives like mice. Punjab is as much mine as theirs. I refuse to abandon my motherland" said an ever-composed Ajah. Few weeks later he booked Sati's tickets and sent her to Jammu.

On the evening of the 21st of June 1988, Ajah had to go to Ahluwalia Katra to meet his business partners. The militants not only wanted to terrorize the Hindus but also meant to cripple their economic standing. A bomb was deviously planted at Ahluwalia Katra, a bustling Amritsari market with constricted lanes and by lanes. This was where all cloth producers and merchants used to meet and that fateful evening, they were on target. The narrow lanes of the bazaar were dotted by numerous sweetshops that used to stock LPG cylinders. At about 7 in

the evening, a potent RDX blast shook the market to its roots. Scores of cylinders surrounding the blast area caught fire and were flung into the sky by the impact. One such cylinder came flying and hit Ajah on the back of his head. He dropped dead in the same moment. And so were all his business partners. Over a hundred people were dead in a minute and around a hundred more were seriously injured.

People from neighboring locations rushed to the spot. Once the smoke and fire were doused, all they saw was torn limbs, gore from human flesh and seared dead bodies everywhere. The electricity wires above their heads had human body parts dangling on them. The injured were crying for help. Some women who had probably come for shopping were lying charred and naked, for their clothes got burned. There were dead children and some alive, howling helplessly next to their dead mothers. Shopping bags, footwears, spectacles and burning vehicles of the dead and wounded littered the streets. A strange stench of roasted humans made the air thick.

When Sati's father got the terrible news in Jammu, he could not believe what he was told. He certainly did not have the courage to give Sati the worst news of her life. So, he lied. He told her that her husband was not feeling too well and that they both had to leave immediately to attend to him. "Yes, he was not feeling well when I left. Let me pack up quickly, Bauji[2], then we can leave." She was surprised to see that her mother was also joining them, but she did not pay too much attention to this detail as her

---

[2] Bauji – father

mind was thinking of what her husband must have eaten in her absence, or perhaps the heat got to him. She was confident that whatever it was, she will handle it devotedly, and he will be up and about in no time.

Sati chose to drape her husband's favorite sari, a tomato red chiffon. Then she wore a striking dot on her forehead and hurriedly stepped into the drawing room where her parents were waiting for her. Her father shuddered to see her and winced within to imagine what will become of her when she gets to know. As their car reached close to Sati's house in Katra Sher Singh, she saw an unusually large crowd outside the gate. Baffled, she looked at her father, whose eyes were now bloodshot, and his lips trembled. She now wondered why her father was wordless throughout the journey. Also, he refused to eat anything on the way. She then looked at her mother, who now had a stream of tears flowing through her eyes. Sati gathered why her mother kept kissing her head a bit too much since they left for Amritsar. She jumped out of the car, tore through the crowd, almost tumbled upon the bamboo frame in the courtyard waiting for her husband's dead body and passed out before she could enter the house.

Sati mutely went through the rituals of cremation and thereafter her world was a gigantic silence. But there were millions of thoughts playing in her head. What if she did not leave him alone? What if she did not go to her parents' place at all? Would that have stopped him from going to the market? May be not. Had she known he was to go so soon, she would have spent every moment of her married life with him. How would she ever know who killed him? Who planted that bomb? What did that person look like?

Do these people look like normal humans? Would they know how they have brought everything down to ashes for her in a day? Would they know what all plans they had as a couple? Would they know with him was the only life she knew? Why couldn't he leave Punjab? Did he love his land more than her? More than a life with her? More than his own life? What did this bravado bring him? Bring her? She collapsed in her bed with no answers and more questions.

When she woke up, it was morning. The sun was rising from the east and the sky was orange. She looked at the sky and screamed, "Ki karan aiho jahe savere da, mera teh hanera ho gaya." (What good is this morning when my life is but an endless darkness). Young and devastated Sati knew little about her husband's business. Nor was she left with the life energy to learn and make a new beginning. Despondent, she would sit day long in her room, gazing at her late husband's clothes and other belongings. She ran her fingers over things remembering his face, his smile, his words. His bedroom slippers were kept the way he had left them. Only she had covered them with a piece of silk. She would take the cloth off, slip her feet in them to feel his presence for a while, step out and cover them back again. His used towel in the washroom was still in its place. It smelled of him. His extra pair of spectacles were kept just the way he had left them on that catastrophic day. She had decided to keep everything just the way it was. Forever. Looking through his wardrobe she would sniff his favorite clothes and cry bitterly. She held his shirt for the most part of her day and wept now and then. Unable to sleep a wink, she would stray to Ajah's home office. Pulling out a ledger

from the pile, she would leaf through some random pages. Seeing the cryptic numbers, she would crash on the floor howling and helpless. She would peep out of the window, wanting to see him walk in from somewhere. Watch his favorite tree drop leaves and wonder if he was watching it too. More importantly, was he watching her too? Could he see how distraught she was without him?

On a similar afternoon, when she was lying lifeless, soaking her pillow with her tears, she heard the family servant shouting fretfully for her from the verandah of the house, "Bibaji[3]…bibaji…bibaji, where are you bibaji?" Sati collected herself with all her might and went out of the room to see his pale face. He said "Bibiji, the militants are inside the plastics factory. They want us to shut the machines and stop the work." Terrified, he added, "They said they will kill you too, Bibaji."

Sati did not say a word. She went back into her room with the vigor that seemed to have left her. She opened her wardrobe, pulled out her husband's Mauser from the drawer, and asked the servant "Shera, tu gaddi kadh. Mainu factory jaana aa. (Shera, you take the Jeep out and drive me to the factory)." The servant opened his mouth to say something but fell silent taking in Sati's fierce face. He looked awestruck at her as if he had seen a lioness. Then he retreated a few steps without turning his back at her as she adjusted the holster on her waist, picked up her dupatta from the chair next to her and wrapped it around her

---

[3] Bibaji – an address for young women in Punjabi

shoulders. Shera sprinted towards the garage as Sati paced after him.

Sati reached the factory and dashed straight into her husband's office to find those militants. Dozens of her workers were already outside the room. With her chin up, face enflamed and composure of a lioness before an attack, she strode into the office with one hand on the holster by her side. She looked around the room, her workers began to make way for her as she peered at the tall and hefty men wielding firearms. Sati calmly took her husband's seat. She put both her hands on the table, looked directly at the armed men and spoke the lines her husband once spoke to her, "Har bhagat Bhagautee tisai kee jo ranadheer dharei, teh ang sang tum lag rahu jo paachhe pag na dharei!" Then Sati wore a death stare and spoke in Punjabi, "Main sunya tussi mainu vi maarna chahnde ho. Meri vi badi iccha si tuhanu vekhan di. Factoryan teh challan giyan. Main chalawan gi. Jad tak meriyan sahaan chaldiya ne, factoryan chalan giyan. Tussi mere husband nu nahi, mere khauf nu maar ditta. Hun koi darr he nahi mainu. Main apna kum karan gi, tussi apna karo" (I heard you want to kill me. Truth is, I too hoped to see you. I will run my husband's factories. The work will not stop until I stop breathing. You haven't killed my husband; you have killed my fear. I have nothing more to lose. I will do what I choose, and you can do what you like).

Sati drowned herself in work and ran the factories thereafter. Every single day. Even during the curfews, when everyone else's business was shut, her factories used to run like a normal day. Many times, it seemed like she was on a mission to invite their attention, their fury towards her. But they had understood that once a person's fear is dead, they become unconquerable. They never bothered her again!

PS: Based on true events

Sati: She is unbridled love that almost always demands renunciation. The form of Mahadevi, the absolute power that can inspire both Vairagya (Dispassion) and Maya (Passion). The galvanizer, the spawner, of Bhog (Worldly Desires), Shakti (Influence) and Darshan (Philosophy of Life).

BHAGWATI
Feminine Prowess and Justice

Yaa Devi Sarva-Bhuteshu Shakti-Roopenna Samsthitaa |
To that Devi who in all beings abides as Power,

Namas-Tasyai Namas-Tasyai Namas-Tasyai Namo Namah ||
Salutations to Her, Salutations to Her, Salutations to Her,
Salutations again and again.

BHAGWATI

CHAPTER 7

BHAGWATI
Feminine Prowess and Justice

"The number of reports of girls missing in Sundarbans seem to be at par with Mumbai. And you are right, the modus operandi is quite similar. Yes, Mahisha seems to be the kingpin!" said SP Bhagwati Roy to her batch mate Brahma Kar on a phone call as she entered home after her morning run. "You leave things with me, Brahma. I have a meeting scheduled with Srikant sir today. Of course, I will come to your wedding. I have applied for a leave already. You focus on getting married bro. Do not push your luck! Sandhya has not yet married you," laughed Bhagwati, teasing her friend and kept the phone down.

"I will have an early breakfast today, Ganga Didi!" said Bhagwati, hollering towards the kitchen in a hurry, but there was no response. Her house help Jaya walked up to her, "Ganga hasn't come to work today. Her daughter has gone missing!" "What do you mean has gone missing? The girl I had met that day. The one who said she wanted to be a cop!" Bhagwati asked concernedly. "Yes, you have been quite an inspiration to her. But Ganga tells me she looked disturbed in the last few days. Her father wanted to get rid of her. He had found a boy to marry her off, while she wanted to help her mother and work to be independent. Oh, she never liked her father. She never liked any man, in fact. Stupid girl! Her mother is half dead now. Whenever she comes back home, that is if she does, her life will be a living hell. No boy will marry her. Everyone will think she had eloped with someone," explained Jaya and left the room, cursing the situation, walking towards the kitchen. Bhagwati followed and intonated, "She was looking for ways to make money, Jaya Didi! Earn respect for herself and her mother. Please go to Ganga Didi at once and report it to their local police station if they have not yet. I will investigate it."

Bhagwati worked with the Mumbai Crime Branch. She was an IPS Officer, a trained commando, raised by a grandfather who was a freedom fighter and would choose nation over anything at any given point in time. She had been following Mahisha for a few years now. He was a dreaded criminal who ran many illicit businesses, including drugs and human trafficking. He trafficked young girls from Nepal and parts of India. In the last one year, it had blown out of control and there were reports of girls missing in the states of Jharkhand, West Bengal, Bihar, and Maharashtra, mainly Mumbai. Most of these girls were lured from their parents' houses on a false pretext of better job prospects. Mahisha ran a whole organization with deep roots in the system, including the police force, law, and politics.

"Sir, the last time when we were about to nab him,

he slipped away, as if he had some premonition. You know how our leads took a one-eighty and witnesses changed their statements overnight, and some of them just vanished. I have not found any trace of them since. It wasted two years of my research and hard work. I had to redevelop informers and the whole network. Threw me back by a few years. Not to mention the small and big encounters, that attack on Sher Singh and the fact my cover was completely exposed," Bhagwati recounted to Srikant Manjrekar. Srikant interrupted her, "Yes, allow someone else to take over, may be!" "No sir! This is my case. I know the risks, both for the force and me. I want to run this independently in my own way. One last time, sir," insisted Bhagwati. "Your cover was exposed, and the pressure is too much, officer. You will have to play offensive this time. Outdo them at their game of deception. Handpick your people, make a Task Force and report directly to me," instructed the IG of Police to Bhagwati. "And listen to me SP Bhagwati. Do not ask me why at this point, but if there is anyone who can put an end to this, it is only you. Just pick the right weapons!" This case had carried on long enough for Bhagwati to be haunted by the faces of the trafficked girls, their mothers wailing at police stations, and most of all, the face of failure. "Jai Hind Sir!" smiled Bhagwati vacantly with her chin up.

"Meet me at my residence in an hour, Shera," she said to Sher Singh waiting for her outside the IG's office and got into her car. "Yes, Sahab!" nodded the Inspector.

Bhagwati reached the main door of her house by 8 in the evening and saw it was ajar. That was very unlike

Jaya, who was a paranoid person by nature. Bhagwati instinctively reached for her sidearm, removed the safety catch and entered the house. She was barely two steps inside when someone jumped at her, throwing her off her balance and flinging the gun from her hand. She sprang back to her feet, but before she knew, she was garroted with a wire. From the corner of her eye, she could see Jaya's lifeless body lying on the floor in a pool of blood. "I could have slaughtered you in a moment, but king wants you to see yourself dying. Bit by bit. Oh, this silken neck. See how delicate you are, SP Bhagwati Roy. Now watch, I will slowly choke you to death," the man hissed, sucking his teeth, like a serpent close to Bhagwati's ear. Struggling to breathe, she could still estimate the man's height from his voice. She raised her arms, grabbed his face, and with the coldness of a lioness, she tunneled her thumbs into both his eyes. The man yowled in pain and loosened his grip. Bhagwati turned around swiftly, wiped the gore off her hands on his shirt, seized him by his shoulders and knocked her right knee straight into his crotch. "Tamra! That is what your name is. Right?" she roared at him as he grabbed his groin with bleeding eye hollows. Tamra dropped on his knees, reeling in pain. Bhagwati checked on Jaya. She was not breathing anymore. That was when she heard two gunshots outside her house. It was Chika, an accomplice of Tamra, who must have been outside all along, and had seen Sher Singh entering Bhagwati's premises. One of the bullets had hit Sher Singh on his shoulder from close range, making him drop against a wall. Now Chika started to run towards Bhagwati's house, but Sher Singh dived and grabbed his

leg. Chika fell on his face and his gun slipped out of his grip. Sher Singh tackled Chika, but owing to the injured shoulder, Chika prevailed over him. However, then at some point, Sher Singh kicked Chika's gun away into the bushes.

Meanwhile, Bhagwati turned back to Tamra, dug her knee on his right shoulder and heaved his arm out of its socket. Then she sat on his chest and warped his left arm from the elbow. Tamra, now maimed, bellowed in pain. Chika outside heard Tamra's yelps. He seized Sher Singh into a chokehold. Neighbors were now peeping through their windows to see what was playing out, but no one stepped out. Bhagwati reached for her service gun fallen on the ground and ran out to the western annex of the building. She aimed at Chika's temple, while he was still clutching Sher Singh and yelled, "Now Shera!" Sher Singh stopped the scuffle, stomped on Chika's foot with all his strength, and fell to the ground. Bhagwati had a clear shot; in a second, she fired the bullet which drilled a hole in Chika' big head, spilling his brain matter to the other side.

Then Bhagwati came back inside and kicked Tamra writhing in pain, "Begin singing Tamra. Chika is dead. Where is Mahisha? Do you now wish for an easy death or want more of this?" she thundered. "No one knows where king is. We only have a phone number," bawled Tamra. Sher Singh walked into the room. He had already called reinforcements. He took the number from Tamra and then Tamra was sent to the hospital. Bhagwati now allowed herself to be overtaken by the grief of losing Jaya. She sat on her knees next to Jaya's dead body and apologized to her. "Only if I reached home a little earlier!" "So, we still

have a mole inside the team, SP Sahab, and why did you leave Tamra alive?" asked Shera, Bhagwati's most reliable man in the forces. "Blinded and crippled, he is of no use to Mahisha. You get to a hospital Shera, you are shot. I will see you later," said Bhagwati, still looking at Jaya's dead face with regret.

Bhagwati moved to another house. Started to carry Kalashnikov in the boot of her car and used a more robust security detail. She and Srikant switched to a secure line for their communication. The phone number Tamra gave them was put on electronic tracking. It turned out to be a woman's, named Mansha. A few months later, combing through various reports and electronic surveillance, Bhagwati finally got intel that Mahisha frequented a farmhouse in Delhi, where he met a woman called Mansha. Now Mansha was not on any social media for obvious reasons. She had no existence anywhere. But Bhagwati's team could finally find out one or two old pictures of her from her modeling days. People around the farmhouse, who were befriended and enquired by cops in plain clothes, confirmed that Mansha lived there when in Delhi. And that she was seen with the same man always. Rarely, but surely. A liquor storekeeper, a chemist, watchmen and housekeeping staff at the colony, they all told similar things to different cops. Sketches could be made from all that information and the Task Force now knew what Mahisha, the shape shifter may look like in his various shapes and forms.

The Task Force moved to Delhi in a safe house. On a winter midnight, Bhagwati received a message: "Lady Buffalo is home. 7 people inside the house." She gathered

her team, kept the Delhi Police on standby and moved towards the farmhouse. And then, the second message came in at 5 a.m.: "A black SUV arrived. Lady Buffalo receives the Buffalo king." Bhagwati instructed the Delhi Police in plain clothes to cordon off the farmhouse and wait on the wireless set. Today was her chance to catch him alive. By 6 a.m., an announcement was made on the PA system, "This is Mumbai Police. You are surrounded Mahisha. Lay down your arms, step out and surrender." In a few minutes, Bhagwati's phone rang, and it flashed Mansha'a name. Bhagwati moved aside and Shera shadowed her. She picked the call and put it on speaker, "I am Mansha, SP Bhagwati. Why have you come all the way to Delhi? A smart woman like you should not be wasting her youth like this. You did not need that seven-degree black belt or Military Martial Arts, when your beauty is so lethal. Oh, it is such a shame", Mansha sniggered devilishly. Sher Singh got visibly agitated upon hearing this, but Bhagwati gestured him to stay calm. "I am listening. Go on Mansha!" said Bhagwati softly. "Just because you got lucky that night and killed Tamra and Chika, you think you will arrest Mahisha today; the Police force will reward you; you will become a star and live happily ever after?", continued Mansha.

"Wake up, you idealistic fool! That maid servant of yours, Jaya, who Tamra neutralized that night, worked for me. She was becoming a cost, so we finished her. Mahisha is the king of the underworld. Have you completely forgotten the last humiliation! No one will dare speak against him in the court anyway. Such a shame that you are here to ruin your insignificant little life. Find a way to work out

something for your sake and your family back at home. Think about your younger sister. Do you know about her boyfriend? No? Well-well, you should have done your checks. We know him. Your mother is dead already. Is she not your responsibility now?", Bhagwati who was listening uninterrupted was reminded of her trainer at the academy, Mahadev Sir. He drilled into her mind the principles of *Jeet Kune Do*[1], not just in combat situations, but as life skills. The form of no form, freedom of choosing your style, adapting your attack to your enemy's weakness. She was also reminded of what IG Srikant Manjrekar had said to her, "Pick the right weapons!"

"I see Mansha, you don't mind sharing Mahisha with me!" said Bhagwati seductively, as Sher Singh gawked at her face, "But Mahisha seems too shy to show his face to me! Let me come inside and meet you both. I will carry no weapons. Now do not ask me to leave the weapon of my beauty outside your house. Would you? Goes without saying, my team will hold fire while I am inside. Would that be okay with you and Mahisha?"

Bhagwati finished the call, took off her holster and handed the pistol to Sher Singh, "If I do not come out in twenty minutes, begin the fire. Not before that, that is my order. Close quarter battle is my specialization, Shera. Hand to weapon. Keep an eye on your watch!" instructed Bhagwati. In the next moment, she set an alarm for 20 minutes on her wristwatch and walked inside the house. Mansha came out, told the two guards to step back, frisked

---

[1] Jeet Kune Do – an expression of martial arts developed by Bruce Lee

Bhagwati and walked her in. "I am glad that you are thinking straight now," she said. Bhagwati nodded, counted three inside her mind and kept walking with Mansha. They entered a room where she introduced her to a man sitting on a couch sporting a wry smile, saying, "This is my king." His face somewhat matched the sketches, but his overall appearance was nowhere close to Bhagwati's imagination. He did not look his age and could pass for any family man on the street. Mahisha got up, came close to Bhagwati, and stroked her cheek. Bhagwati got a taste of Mahisha's derision for the police force and absolute belief in his own power, even when his house was surrounded. "My cook here in this house was earlier a police officer. He makes more money now," he said smugly as Mansha giggled. He was about to say something more when Bhagwati reached for the metal stick stuck in her hair bun and dug it into Mahisha's left eye. She pulled it out swiftly and then drove it neatly into his neck. Then she yanked him by his arm, hurled him up in the air, and threw him on the marble floor with a loud thud. In barely few moments Bhagwati's foot was on Mahisha's chest. He had spouts of blood bursting from his eye and throat, grimacing in agony and cursing Bhagwati, he shouted, "Kill this woman!" He could not reach his pocket, which probably had a gun, because Bhagwati now had her shoe crushing his right wrist and the bones in his back were possibly broken. Everything happened exceptionally fast. With her unleashed hair hanging behind her like a cloak, she turned around to see Mansha, who had pulled out her gun and taken a shot at Bhagwati. Bhagwati dodged it with the speed of a cheetah and glided on the floor to knock

Mansha down. Mansha's gun was tossed away, and she was tangled in her own sari. Bhagwati grabbed the gun and shot at Mahisha's wrists. Outside, in the hush of a cold Delhi night, Sher Singh had heard three gunshots. He aimed at the guard on the terrace, shot him in the head, and made his way inside the house. The other guard on the terrace was firing back at the police force, which had now swung into action. One of the guards outside the house, who too had heard the gunshot, sprinted in where Bhagwati now had Mansha's gun in her hand. And the other guard was shot by someone in the force outside the house.

Mahisha probably had a few of his ribs broken, blood flowing through his eye and neck, and visibly limp wrists, but he dragged himself on the floor and managed to hold the gun in Bhagwati's direction. Bhagwati aimed at Mahisha lying on the floor to incapacitate him further, but Mansha threw herself between Mahisha and Bhagwati. She was shot in the abdomen. "Good, now I am certain that this is Mahisha," murmured Bhagwati. The guard was now inside and behind him was Sher Singh, who shot him in the back of his head. Bhagwati counted three again when she was dragging Mahisha out by his leg, but a man entered the room with a butcher's knife in his hand. He was wearing an apron. He attacked Bhagwati to stop her and slashed her uniform at the waist. Sher Singh shot him in his chest and that is when his alarm for twenty minutes started to tweet. The knife dropped with a clang. "Birds Shera. Really!" chuckled Bhagwati. She whipped out her belt, tied it around Mahisha's neck, dragged him by that and counted four. Sher Singh said, "Seven! All seven down SP Sahab."

It was broad daylight now, somehow the sunlight was unusually bright that winter morning. Mahisha was unconscious. "Put him in the police van," said Bhagwati. Mansha was alive too; she was put in another ambulance. Bhagwati checked on her team, quickly thanked them and jumped into the van that carried Mahisha. She sat next to the driver's seat. Sher Singh fired up the engine. Now that this was done, she began picturing what would happen next. It took her not more than a few minutes to measure things up nicely and vividly. What Mansha said was not entirely untrue. If Mahisha was allowed to get better, he would go scot-free. With his political connections and deep pockets, he will slither away.

Bhagwati turned to Sher Singh, "Shera, let the other van take this route. We will take another one." "Sahab, the other route is longer. This beast is bleeding profusely. He may die." Bhagwati answered, looking straight at the road, adjusting her aviators, "I know."

Mansha's bullet injury was not fatal. She survived and eventually informed the police about all of Mahisha's businesses and locations. Barring a few girls, who could not make it because of the overdose of drugs or abuse, most of them got back home.

Bhagwati: The warrior form of Mahadevi symbolizes the transformation of an enabler into a doer. She represents a modest, unassuming force who reveals herself to establish her supremacy. She symbolizes feminine prowess, which is visibly different from the masculine, but far more visceral.

UMA
Penance and Marital Permanence

Yaa Devi Sarva- Bhuteshu Kshudhaa-Roopenna Samsthitaa |
To that Devi who in all beings abides as Desire,

Yaa Devi Sarva-Bhuteshu Trshnnaa-Roopenna Samsthitaa |
To that Devi who in all beings abides as Thirst,

Yaa Devi Sarva-Bhuteshu Lajjaa-Roopenna Samsthitaa |
To that Devi who in all beings abides as Modesty,

Namas-Tasyai Namas-Tasyai Namas-Tasyai Namo Namah ||
Salutations to Her, Salutations to Her, Salutations to Her, Salutations again and again.

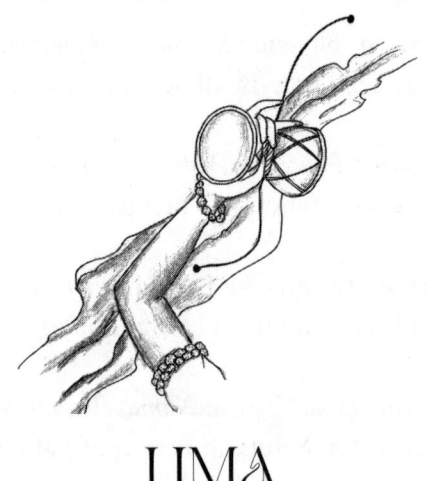

UMA

CHAPTER 8

UMA

Penance and Marital Permanence

Uma woke up at 7 in the morning, languidly picked up her phone and clicked on a Facebook notification saying – Ugra Saxena has made a new post. It was a cozy picture of him with a woman captioned – "How on earth can someone be so pretty!" This was the very line he had been using for Uma for the past few months. The woman in the post was the one she suspected Ugra had been dating, but Uma never asked. It was not her business. There was nothing between them apart from a friendship, yet for some odd reason, something inside her had shifted.

"Look Uma, I have the pictures from the wedding. Oh, you look so beautiful!" said a cheery Shekhar, sitting next to her in the bed. He grabbed Uma by her waist and kissed her cheek. He was referring to the recent wedding they went to Jaipur for. Uma scrolled through the pictures, smiled at Shekhar, held his face, and gave him a kiss, "Yes, these are quite nice! But I must get to work, should head for a shower now." Later in the day, Uma and Ugra had a fleeting chat about the FB post. Ugra declared that he

was seeing the woman in the picture, albeit not in too many words, but enough for Uma to visualize the scenario. Though she could not comprehend as to why did she have to find it on FB when he spoke to her so often. She did not get any reasonable declarations from Ugra, and her pride didn't allow her to prod more.

Ugra had connected with Uma six months before this episode. He had begun the conversation as a business associate from the past, but after a few weeks into their dialogs, a day before the Dussehra holiday, he professed his fondness for her. "I have always liked you. No, the truth is, I have always desired you from afar. Been a few years now," Ugra heard Uma's altered cadence of breath on the other side of the call. So, he hurriedly added, "Hey don't keep the phone down, please. I have desired you as a whole person - mind, body and soul. I call it desire because frankly, I do not know how to separate these three elements from one another. Do not keep the phone down before hearing me out entirely, I request you. This is important to me please!" Ugra paused for a moment and then continued when he sensed that Uma was still breathing on the other end, "Not long ago, I gathered that you have been married for years. I did not know this earlier. Actually, I learned this when I read your first email, two weeks back. Your signature carried another surname with your maiden name, and I do not want to describe how I felt. We had met socially before that and for some odd reason, I never ever got to see your business card or know your full name. Since that email Uma, I have saved your name as "Temptation" in my phone book. I mean no insolence; it is just to remind myself that even a

Sita can be a temptation if there is a Ravana around. But hell, I am no Ravana!", said Ugra, sucking his teeth. He exhaled, then added, "You know that I have been married once and divorced. I do not believe in the institution of marriage anymore. But I must believe in what I am feeling these days. I wish no trouble, but a question hovers over my mind. Would it be too forward of me to ask if yours is a happy marriage? If it is, I promise, I will step back. But if it is not, then we may have a future together." Uma inhaled deeply, somewhat shakingly, and said, "Ugra, I do not know what you went through in your marriage and why. But then, every marriage has its journey. Some more trying than the others. Through my ride, I chose my husband, and I will time and again. So, to answer your question – I do not know your definition of happiness. It is different for different people. But I think I married well, and would like to keep it going strong," Uma responded gently. Ugra's voice dipped, "I heard you! I will work on my feelings, for it is my problem, not yours. But it will be a shame if, after years of my quest to know you, after this dialogue I ultimately lose a friend in you. Honestly, I would like you to stay in my life, please. Can we continue to be friends?" asked Ugra. "Of course, we can, like we have been so far," Uma comforted Ugra, but she said it merely out of politeness.

Over the next few months, Ugra dated several women. And he told Uma about each one of them. "I am trying to digress my mind away from you. But I do not know why I think of you so much more when I am with other women." "Perhaps you should stop connecting with me for a while and focus on piecing your own life?" Uma suggested

concernedly. "If you do not wish to talk to me, I cannot implore you, Uma, you aren't mine. But I think I am not ready to let go off you yet. These sporadic chats keep me going," intonated Ugra as humbly as he could. Ugra talked to Uma about his life, family, his fortunes and misfortunes, his career, his fears, the women, and his past relationships, and most importantly the debacles and pains. It was mainly Ugra speaking and Uma hearing him out. He did not ask much about Uma's life. Or simply put, he steered clear from the parts of her life which did not include him, "Your life stories would unavoidably include the people you chose over me, or people fortunate enough to be in your proximity when the time was right. I will feature nowhere, so best not to tread that sorrowful path." In every single conversation, Ugra simply bared his heart and laid it open in front of Uma, incessantly and relentlessly for months. It was quite like an open invitation for Uma to do with it, what she pleased. She could either trample it or attempt to salvage some parts. Ugra opened himself with such belief in Uma that she started to guard his defenselessness.

By now she had known enough to deduce that he was damaged goods. Perhaps he could not be put together, but someone had to make a genuine attempt to save what was left of him. Uma had heard Ugra's side of life story, the other characters in it were merely sketches in her head, so she stayed away from drawing any opinions. At the same time, she consciously kept away from any judgments about him either. She never tried to find more than what she was told. No names, locations or any details were ever asked. She saw no need for that. Ugra had many friends, but Uma

became his sanctuary. Someone he could confide in, speak about his vulnerabilities, show his darkness, keep his pride aside and seek support from. Possibly because he recognized she will not abandon him for being human. At some point, she turned into a wall that stood between him and the rest of the world. All unknowingly. Inadvertently. Organically. But love, by definition, is complicated. More so when one loves someone unattainable.

Earlier, on her trip to the wedding at Jaipur, Uma had received from Ugra a text with a picture that her husband had posted minutes back on FB. The message read – "Is he with you?" Uma knew Ugra meant to ask about her husband. He could never get himself to name him. He said saying the word Shekhar pronounced his great significance in Uma's life. Uma responded– "Yes, he is. We are here for a wedding." Something got galvanized inside Ugra that day – "How can you be with him all the time? Why do you give so much affection to me if he is the only one for you? Why are you toying with my emotions?" Uma was astounded. She fell silent. The same eerie silence was prevailing loud and wide between the two of them for months until the day Uma saw Ugra's picture with his lady on FB.

A month or so after Ugra's post, he connected with Uma and requested her to meet him. "I did not see any Awws from you on the picture with my girlfriend. Or at least a love for a reaction?" Ugra tried to instigate Uma, but she unheeded it. They talked about their common friends and work life before Ugra repeated himself, "But why no reaction on my post, Uma? Seriously!" Uma picked up her phone and pressed a love reaction on Ugra's post. Ugra was dumbfounded.

He promptly checked his phone, "Wow, you left a heart! I cannot get myself to press a love on any of your pictures with your husband, even if you goaded me. That, right there is the difference between you and me. The stark difference in our feelings for each other. Right there!" said a dismayed Ugra. "What would you have me do Ugra? I care for you so much, can you not see," asked Uma. "But you aren't in love with me," jibed Ugra. "I think what I have for you, is a form of love! Clearly the form you do not appreciate," replied Uma. "Phew, I do not want that kind of love. Oh, that stench of sympathy!" rumbled Ugra with moist eyes. Uma stayed quiet. By now, he had downed quite a few drinks on an empty stomach. He got up to leave in a huff, or perhaps to hide his tears, but lost his balance. Uma grabbed him and made him settle back in his seat. He continued, "My girlfriend is waiting for me, but here I am sitting with you revealing my soul to you once again. She is there for me in every way, every day, while you are but a virtual presence in my life. I get to lay my eyes on you once in a few months for a few hours. I do not get to feel your warmth, which I daydream about every ludicrous day of my life. The bigger problem is that when I am not in your company, I still am in your company. You live in my freaking head. I thought I was some stud, that I would love a married woman, be friends with her, and keep a dispassionate relationship going. When I go away from you, my heart aches like hell, yet when I am near you, it hurts in a whole different way. Since my ex-wife left, I have been a free man, maybe a rogue, but after being with you, or should I say, after knowing that I cannot be with you, I feel like a homeless wanderer. You have ruined me, Uma! Not intentionally. But

your absence has ruined me," Ugra narrated his agony with eyes welled up and glistening in the tinted lights of a busy club. When he looked at Uma, he saw tears streaming down her face. "It is what it is, Ugra. But I ask again, what would you have me do?" she asked delicately. "Nothing! You can do nothing. This is my destiny. Only do not leave me yet, I may die. This is not a threat. This is an appeal from a man who is at his weakest," said Ugra leaving cash on the table and making his way to the exit of the club with wobbling feet. "Wait, why are you dating that woman then? Don't you think it is wrong?" asked Uma following Ugra to the car park. "Remember your picture on FB, the one your husband posted from Jaipur? This woman was my retort to you. Do not question me for my wrongs and rights. This is love, not intellect, and certainly not a lesson in morality. Did I not say I am ruined? What more am I supposed to say," said a distraught Ugra and left.

Uma distanced herself. Not entirely though. She checked on him every now and then but kept space enough for Ugra to try and find stability in his life. As and when Ugra needed her attention, she made herself available. On rare occasions when she couldn't, Ugra told himself aloud for Uma to hear, "You see!" and Uma didn't contend. Six months later, Uma received a text - "I and my girlfriend broke up." Uma and Ugra spoke a few times, but she still kept her distance. She had understood that whether there is a woman in Ugra's life or not, she is the key cause of his recent despair. A month later, she found out that Ugra's ex-girlfriend had slapped a case on him, for sexual intercourse based on a false promise to marry. Now Ugra was in greater

trouble than before. A large part of his life was consumed by interrogating cops, lawyers, and a perpetual hanging sword of an arrest. This situation could be seriously damaging for his professional life and was already affecting his parents' health. Uma had earlier thought that her decision to stay away would help him find his feet. But then this new pile of mess along with his existing mental muddle, partly because of her and partly carried forward from his past, was enough to drown him in an abyss of depression. Not many knew of his latest trauma anyway. If they did, chances were there would be moral verdicts and no real support. Uma knew it could have been Ugra's own doing. He may have promised marriage in a weak moment, but had it not been for her absence, or her virtual presence, this may not have happened.

"Ugra, is my existence somewhat responsible for this chaos?" Uma asked directly. "No! Only I manufactured this chaos for myself. You should not allow yourself to think like this. You have been my greatest support. That is all you have been," assured Ugra. Uma began to check on him regularly. Sometimes more than once a day. Her typical text to him would be, "Alive?" And his response would be, "Yes so far!" He had stopped getting any sleep, could not eat and threw up whatever little he did, convulsed with worry and nervousness. "Are you awake? I am scared. Will I be arrested?" was his standard message every other night. "Can you ask someone? Do I have jail time in my astrological charts?" Ugra's bank accounts were draining fast and soon emptied. He was living month on month. He had already taken an aid from his father and needed another five lakhs. Uma offered help, but Ugra politely declined.

"I am aware that I do not do many things for you, but this one little thing I can," she declared one day to him when she gathered that he was denied by many. "Thanks Uma. I have applied for a loan. But I will ask you if I cannot manage," he responded, but had to come back reluctantly. That evening, Uma spoke to her husband, "I will have to help Ugra with some money. Hope that is okay with you." "Yes, I know your friend, Ugra. The same person you went to a cancer hospital with, to discuss someone's reports. His ex-father-in-law's, if my mind serves me correctly. I remember you said he was petrified. The one whose car broke down that day, right? And how is his father recovering? Last I heard he was hospitalized with a fever. There is a lot going on in his life. But you did show his charts to our family astrologer. I was quite amazed frankly, knowing that you do not like the warps of astrology. Clearly, you have been worried for him," Shekhar went on. "So, you are okay if I give him about 5 lacs? He is a good man from a good family," asked Uma. "You do not need to convince me. I am okay if you are okay," responded Shekhar in an instant.

"The closest of friends look away when it comes to money, Uma. Dark times reveal a lot of things which even light fails to do. Especially about the people in your circle. You have stood with me. And I will never forget this," said Ugra and returned her money in a week's time. Thereafter, whensoever Ugra was hard pressed, sorrowful, or anxious, he never went anywhere else. His assured and anonymous reserve, Uma, was only a ping away.

Months gave way to months. The case ultimately got

shelved, and Ugra breathed easy. He also moved jobs. But their bond devoid of physical intimacy, obligation or a title had grown thicker under the clouds of rough times. Yet on Uma's birthday when Ugra said, "You are 24-carat gold," she did not know how to take it. If it was her value or her price in Ugra's life. Now Ugra was getting calmer. His loans were getting paid off, his work was flowing smoothly, and he did not need Uma as much. His objective was to build a morally and legally accurate life and make his parents feel safe. When he contacted Uma after a break, she sensed a strange disquiet from Ugra's end. "This is the kind of hush I felt when you were seeing your last girlfriend. Have you found someone nice, Ugra?" she asked straight. Uma had been waiting for a sign to know when to walk away from Ugra's life. She knew the clock was ticking. She also knew it would not be pleasant. She may not even get the chance to say a proper goodbye. That is how most departures are regrettably. But Ugra had detected Uma's plans. He knew this time around she will walk away the moment she finds out, "Are you crazy! There is no one," Ugra responded swiftly. "Okay, what is this quiet about then?" enquired Uma. "My divorce proceedings are going on and it is not quite agreeable," he said plainly. "Divorce! Aren't you divorced already? What am I missing here!" Uma was taken aback with a thunder within, but she played cool. "No, I was not. I was separated for seven years, so now I am going for it legally," he explained quite plainly, again. "I think you used the word 'divorced' to me, and not separated. But what is driving this decision now after so many years?" she sought the complete truth. "She is troubling my parents

behind my back, asking for her share in the property," he was now a little uneasy. "And you could get married to a nice girl, finally?" Uma added. "Huh! And who would marry me?" Ugra said sneeringly, pointing towards himself. Uma cracked a few lame jokes to placate the situation, but inside she was shaken up from her roots.

Uma believed Ugra did not tell her about the pending divorce on purpose. Not that the truth would have changed anything. Or perhaps it would have stopped Uma from befriending him. But then, he did not owe her anything. Just as she did not owe him anything. Except truth! So why did he lie? Why? The question haunted her. It took merely a month, and she started to see signs on social media that made her think there was more than what met her eyes. And one day, accidentally the truth spilled out. He was indeed dating a new woman, this time to marry, and Uma was excluded from his social media posts. On one of the platforms, she was removed as a follower on a false pretext that the platform was hacked. All along, Ugra had been in touch with Uma on the phone, talking about every other thing except his new woman and marriage plans. The whole world knew about it except Uma. The anonymous, silent reserve of unconditional support Uma was still there but neatly cleaved off from some vital facts of Ugra's life. When confronted, Ugra said, "I did not lie to you, Uma. She and I have just begun. Truth is, I have gotten weary of the storms. This endless battle. The wandering. I drink all night, all alone, wallowing in the shadows of your absence. I am exhausted. I want someone completely and wholly mine, someone physically with me and mine. Someone to keep me

warm at nights, to celebrate Diwali with, go to movies with, see the world with, someone to go back home to. I want a person who can be called home. I want to feel normal." Yet he added, "But listen Uma. I cannot lose you. Please. Why should you leave only because I may get married? You have been married, and I have been here. What changes? You have seen me like no one else has. Utterly vulnerable and broken. No one can find me in my darkness except you. I need you, I always will, Uma. I cannot lose you," were his last few sentences, she reflected.

After the quake passed and noises in Uma's head muted, she realized what had transpired. Ugra's need to keep Uma in his life, his sanctuary, in case things did not fall in place, had birthed an abject liar in him. He wanted to fix his wrecked life, which had started showing holes only since Uma's arrival. He had grappled to plug the holes with whatever he found. Alcohol, work, fitness routines, social media, or women. And this time, he was plugging a large hole of rootlessness and homelessness. Hence, a wedlock was the resolution. Only if Ugra could see that Uma's presence by itself may never allow his life to appear whole. As for the deception and fabrications, it was nothing but his fear. Fear of losing Uma. Very often when love does not work out, it is replaced by fear, which is an equally controlling but an inverse force. And fear manifests in eccentric ways. The man who was bold enough to be defenseless in love, had erected defenses to somehow keep Uma in his life.

Uma asked herself, "What was my purpose to be in his life when there was no conventional reason to be there? Why did I stick around? To be his light, his strength? Or to be his darkness, his weakness?" Ugra's circumstances had made him inept to see how this deception was affecting the person he was so frightened to lose. And more importantly, how his choices were affecting his own personality. "I am not his light anymore. I am his weakness," said Uma to herself. "Is this the Kintsugi[1] I had wished on this beautifully broken man? Surely fear cannot be the gold we can paste together a broken person with. If I am his fear, it should be killed before it is too late for him."

Against her character, Uma blocked Ugra everywhere. Ugra loathed her. Uma loathed herself even more. But her role in Ugra's life was over. Had he not found a virtual home in Uma, he would have been ready to launch himself entirely and fearlessly in his new life. The season named Uma had to come to an end for the new season to begin. The new green shoots of hope and companionship deserved fresh air and open, unafraid skies.

PS: Based on true events

Uma: She is the definition of strong-minded devotion. She is the form of Mahadevi who brought Rudra away from remoteness, detachment, and his rogue ways into creative participations of the world. She is the force that rouses extreme penance within herself that leads to love, marital permanence and ofttimes both.

---

[1] Kintsugi – Japanese art of repairing broken pottery

AMBIKA
The Warrior

Yaa Devi Sarva-Bhuteshu Dayaa-Roopenna Samsthitaa |
To that Devi who in all beings abides as Compassion,

Yaa Devi Sarva-Bhuteshu Maatri-Roopenna Samsthitaa | To that Devi who in all beings abides as Mother,

Namas-Tasyai Namas-Tasyai Namas-Tasyai Namo Namah ||
Salutations to Her, Salutations to Her, Salutations to Her, Salutations again and again.

AMBIKA

CHAPTER 9

AMBIKA
The Warrior

Ambika, an oncology researcher, had been working on the code to contain fast-moving cancer cells. Every time she got close to cracking it, the cell mutated and presented a new challenge. She was running against time, for her battle with malignant cells had become personal when her baby sister, her closest friend, her mirror soul Bhoomi, was diagnosed with Leukemia. Bhoomi was not just a sibling but the ground beneath Ambika's feet, the gravity, without which her small world could just fly away. Bhoomi was the earth and its force, which is not seeable but detected only if one values a sense of balance. Whose presence did not ask for recognition but caused all life around her. Bhoomi, the girl without whom nothing made sense to Ambika. Without whom her life would be hollow and gravity-less.

As for their parents, they had aged faster in the last decade, watching Bhoomi slip away bit by bit. A brilliant doctor with a super specialization in Oncology, Ambika studied and researched day and night, spoke and met

with other researchers, scientists, and doctors in medical oncology, all to find a protocol to slow down Bhoomi's prognosis. She did absolutely nothing other than thinking and working on AML. She had no personal life, no love life, no life whatsoever. She did not go out for anything which could remotely be called entertainment. If she did on some occasion, she would be constantly checking her phone for any missed calls or double checking that it was not kept on silent. She would hear Bhoomi's voice in her head, as if she was calling out for her and be endlessly anxious and swallowed by guilt for leaving her baby sister at home. Almost always, Ambika would just dash back home to sit next to Bhoomi, talk to her about their childhood, or read her something. If her work required travel, she would hardly sleep at night and rush back as fast as she could. Ambika had put her whole life on a halt, including the part Shivankar so eagerly wanted to play.

Ambika's singular purpose in life was to add some quality years to her beloved sister's lifespan. Deep down, Ambika knew she was trying for the insurmountable, and all by herself. The reality was, her sister had lived with the disease for ten years now, which was indeed a few years more than what was predicted. But she had decided to give it all that she had. There was no point in being an oncologist if she could not save her own sister.

Ambika was 9 when her mother had brought home her little sister. It was before noon when her father, Sushant, walked in hurriedly through the main door. Following him was her mother with a swaddled baby in her arms. Her father went straight to her parents' bedroom to leave the

bags he had brought from the hospital, looked at his mother waiting in the living room momentarily, and left for his work immediately. Ambika's grandmother, who was home with her while her parents were away, mumbled, "This one is not even fair. A girl and a dark one. Bhagwati-Bhagwati!!!" She was visibly gloomy.

Ambika, dressed in her new sky colored frilly frock which looked perfect on her pearly skin, hurried after her mother and grabbed her sari's *pallu* like she always did, "I want to see my dolly, Ma." Her mother, Gauri, holding the baby in her left arm, stroked Ambika's head with her right hand, "Yes Mumma is going to make the baby comfortable on the bed first, and then you can play with her as much as you like." Ambika quickly jumped to the other side of the bed, "Awww Ma, she is so beautiful! She is even prettier than Shuchi's sister Ma. Can I hold her? Do you think I can take her out to Shuchi's house, Ma? Oh, her eyes shine like stars…," a wonderstruck Ambika touched the baby's caramel cheeks and posed a dozen other questions. She looked proud and thrilled in equal measures, as if the baby was a reward. Gauri responded as much as she could before she dozed off with exhaustion.

"She is so beautiful, aunty, like she has been sent with eye makeup on. Her hair is so black, her fingers so slender and her eyes sparkle. You have to see to believe how lovely my sister is," said one of Gauri's friends, perkily referring to what Ambika has been telling the entire neighborhood. "Yes, she seems to be the only person truly happy about this girl's birth," said Gauri, looking adoringly at her baby's face. "Did you think of a name?" asked the friend. "No one seems to be concerned and that's why I think I am going to name her Bhoomi. As persevering and resolute as Bhoomi."

Four months later, Gauri, with both her daughters and husband, went to her parent's place in Bareilly. One day, her elder brother, who had two boys and always wanted a daughter, pleaded, "Your home needs a boy and mine needs a girl. Why don't you give Bhoomi to me? I assure you, I and your Bhabhi will love her as much as we loved our dear Ambika or my own sons, if not more." "I have no reservations, bhaiya. You and Bhabhi have loved Ambika like your own daughter," responded Gauri feebly. "We will always be indebted to you Gauri. Bhoomi will be the living Goddess in our humble abode, her light will illuminate this house and my home will become a shrine. She will always be a piece of my heart," Ashok sat at his younger sister's feet with folded hands begging for Bhoomi, briefly turned his face towards Sushant imploringly, as his wife watched them all with expectant eyes. Gauri fleetingly looked towards her husband, who was quietly listening to this conversation, "She is your daughter, bhaiya. Tomorrow before I leave here, I will unpack her things and give them to Bhabhi", Gauri conceded. Everyone rejoiced and embraced whereas Ambika wordlessly gaped at her mother, then at her father and then again at her mother. She slept close to her sister that night with her one hand grabbing the baby's little arm.

The next morning, Ashok's family and parents were preparing for Gauri's family's departure. They were unthinkingly talking about their plans for Bhoomi and how they would visit Gauri's house with Bhoomi in a few months. Ambika was unnerved and helpless. So was Gauri, but she had frozen her heart to numb her fragility. As they

picked up the luggage and everyone moved towards the main gate, Ambika rushed to her baby sister and picked her up in her small arms, "I am not scared of any of you. She is my sister and she is coming with me!" she declared, and charged out. "Stop Ambika!" shouted a distraught Gauri, as she took the baby from her and slapped Ambika across her face. Ambika broke into tears, growled in fury and scratched her mother's arms out of frustration. That was when Sushant appeared from nowhere, grabbed the baby from Gauri and sprinted out. Ambika, who was weeping, dried her tears, followed her father, didn't look back and stomped straight into the taxi waiting for them outside. She was now chuffed but did not let it show. Gauri's husband did not meet his eyes with anyone, did not say any goodbyes, got into the taxi and kept the baby close to his chest. The whole family watched this rather amused and stunned at the same time. Ambika did not talk to her mother after that episode, until she apologized for her weak decision. But something got stamped in Ambika's heart which will stay forever.

The girls grew up to be the best of friends. Despite the age difference, they ate together, played together, slept together, and did not need any friends. When it was time for Bhoomi to go to school, Ambika tried with all her might, but Bhoomi could not be admitted in the same school as her. Years went by, Ambika started to ride to school, so they stopped taking the bus. She would first drop Bhoomi and then go to her own school. She would watch her walk into the school, let out a sigh, both girls would wave at each other and then Ambika would leave for her own school. After school, she would pick her up and then head home.

Now Ambika was 17 years old, and she was preparing for her entrance to medical school and Bhoomi was 8. "Didi, have you learned all the spellings," asked Bhoomi when Ambika was leaving for her exam. Everyone in the room had a good laugh. Gauri grabbed Bhoomi's little shoulders and said, "Didi is going to be a doctor, she knows her spellings. You too will know all the spellings and do some great things in life, Bhoomi." Bhoomi smiled ear to ear and gave a kiss to her elder sister. Ambika went to the All-India Institute of Medical Sciences and studied medicine when Bhoomi was in class 3. About five years later, when Bhoomi turned 13, Ambika was back home preparing for her MS. This was the time Bhoomi had her first period. "Bhoomi, you are bleeding. See, you have left a dot everywhere you sat," Ambika told her sister softly, "Come, I will tell you what to do." "No Didi, I am fine. I have told Mumma already. I am quite fine," said Bhoomi sheepishly, while Gauri was listening to her daughters, hiding behind the agape door. "It is okay. All of us women go through this. Me, Mumma… it is something natural. If you ask me, it is a blessing, and do not let anyone tell you otherwise. Do you trust me?" explained Ambika, putting Bhoomi's hair behind her ear. "I always trust you!" smiled Bhoomi. "Do not worry, I will take care of those stains. It is not your fault!" said Ambika, holding her baby sister in her arms and kissing her head.

A few months later, Ambika went to Madras for her MS (master's in science). Bhoomi once went to visit her sister. "You still sleeping? Why are you sleeping so much Bhoomi? Did I not tell you to be ready before I am back? We have to go out," yelled Ambika as she walked into the flat. "I am

on my period, Didi," answered a pale Bhoomi. "So?" asked Ambika, checking her forehead. "Today is the fifteenth day. I cannot get up," explained Bhoomi. "Fifteenth? Why did you not tell me?" said a harrowed Ambika. That day was the beginning of a catastrophic journey the family was to tread on. Ambika took Bhoomi through all the tests to rule out any platelet disorder or clotting factors. But eventually, to their horror, it turned out to be Acute Myeloid Leukemia. What ensued thereafter changed the lives of the entire family. Cancer is not just a disease of the body; it plunders the psychology of the patient and the caregivers'. It plays havoc with the family's day-to-day functioning, finances, aspirations, dreams and so much more which cannot even be measured in units. As for Ambika, she had shape-shifted from a tender-hearted doctor into a ferocious warrior tackling the demon of cancer, and a powder keg for anyone who stood in her way.

Ambika was at the Washington airport, in the middle of the night, waiting for her flight back to India when the dreaded text flashed on her phone: "Beta, Bhoomi has left us." She was in the US to attend a conference on Haemato-Oncology. Before leaving home, Ambika had promised her sister to take the next flight back, to be at her side. Doctors were trying a new aggressive protocol and Bhoomi's body was not taking it too well. They were not really left with any other option, so Ambika had reluctantly agreed. She was now angry with the whole world, mad about the way it worked and the futility of life. Ambika believed she was failed by time and felt completely wasted. Alone, she wailed for hours, peered into oblivion with empty eyes on her tear

smudged face and then cried more. Inside the flight, she lost her cool on the attendant who simply asked her for her choice of meal.

Ambika and her sister Bhoomi, Ambika's gravity, had lost the battle and grief was now swallowing her. Grief, which is not merely an emotion. But a location, thrown in a different dimension of time, light years away from the world where everyone else lives. It feels close to sort of a black hole with its own tremendous gravity, made only worse by its dense air and a quick sinking earth, which drags everything down to an unspeakable lull inward and outwards. Squelching through that lull too, all Ambika did was look for the code.

Today, six years later, she had, at last, cracked the code to delay the prognosis. Every inch of her cabin was filled with flowers. The phone was ringing incessantly. Though no one received those calls. Yet again, she sat all alone, barefoot, colorless, curled up on the couch next to her desk, holding the picture of her sister, not knowing what to tell her. With a crumpled sweatshirt on, disheveled wild hair unwashed for days, eyes puffed up by lack of sleep and too much caffeine, she looked stoned. The world had found hope; it was a moment of triumph for the medicine and pharmaceutical industries, yet Ambika felt a great void. The war she had fought for the last 16 years was all she had known. All she knew was Bhoomi, and her disease. After Bhoomi's departure, the battle with malignancy that took her away was Ambika's sole reason for existence. Now what was she to do with her lifetime?

Shivankar heard the news. A fellow researcher and an

equally dedicated medicine man, he was akin to a home for Ambika. A home she stayed away from. The home she chose not to live in for fear that the warmth inside it may slow her down. Or the gentle spring breezes through its windows may douse her fire. What if she became too content to pursue her war? What if she fails to remember her objective? What if she forgets her sister's face, her desolation, and the promise she had made to her dying melancholic eyes? Three years ago, Shivankar was told by an angst-ridden Ambika to leave her alone. But today was no ordinary day. He snuck to the door of her cabin. The sound of his footsteps made Ambika look up. She found Shivankar resting his head on the jamb of the door, looking at her timidly. Tears started to flow down her cheeks as their eyes met. Ambika sat upright on the couch and dropped her feet to the ground, Bhoomi's picture still hanging loosely in one of her hands. Then she looked down and cried bitterly. Her arms hanging by her sides lifelessly, she rained tears on her own feet.

Shivankar walked up to her and sat on the floor close to her soundlessly. He grabbed her feet and wiped them with his sleeves. Ambika looked at Shivankar with soaked eyes that had not slept well in years. He kept his hands on her fatigued knees, rubbed them reverently, and said, "This battle is over, Ambika! It may not feel like a victory to you personally, but it certainly is for many other Bhoomis and Ambikas around the world." Shivankar wiped Ambika's face, planted a kiss on her forehead and said, "Let us go for coffee. I long awaited this day."

Ambika: The warrior form of Mahadevi symbolizes the fatalities and struggles to purge malevolence. She liberated the world from the malignancy called Raktabeej, the asura whose every drop of blood fallen on the ground birthed another Raktabeej. Kalika, her darker form forfeited herself by downing Raktbeej's malicious blood so no more Raktabeejs could be born before Ambika neutralized the original one.

GLOSSARY II

A

Abbu- used as an address to father in Muslim families

B

Bhaagwan- the holder of Bhagya, destiny. Typically used by husbands to address their wives in Punjabi

Baithak- drawing room

Baltis- an ethnic group of Tibetan descent who are native to the Pakistani-administered territory of Gilgit–Baltistan

Batashas- a sugar cake served as a holy offering in temples

Beta ji- a respectful denotation to address a kid or someone younger in Punjabi

Bailkhana- cowshed

Bibaji – an address for young women in Punjabi

Bibiji – an address for older women in Punjabi

Bhai- brother

Bhindrawale- leader of the Sikh organization Damdami Taksal

Bauji- father

C

Chacha - uncle

D

Dupatta – a long Indian scarf worn with salwar suit by Indian women

J

Jutties - a type of footwear common in North India

Jeet Kune Do- an expression of martial arts developed by Bruce Lee

K

Kintsugi- Japanese art of repairing broken pottery

Khabdan – Ladakhi carpet

Khambir – a traditional Ladakhi bread

Kurta- traditional Indian men's wear

M

Matchon – address for aunt from mother's side in Ladakhi

Moksha – Salvation

P

Pagri – turban for Indian men

Pandit ji – a Hindu scholar. Generally used as an address for Brahmins

Parathas- an Indian flatbread fried in a pan

Pitaji- father in Hindi

Puttar- son in Punjabi. Many times, used for daughters too

Q

Qafirs- the ones who reject or disbelieve in God as per Islam

S

Sahab- sir

Salwar suits- an Indian traditional dress for females

Sanyasa- a form of asceticism marked by renunciation of material desires

Sari- a long piece of cloth traditionally worn by Indian women by draping around the body

V
Verandah- porch

Z
Zaildar – landowner, in charge of a Zail, an administrative unit for a group of villages during the British Indian Empire